"You tricked me."

"You tricked yourself," Nora said mildly. "You jumped to a conclusion."

"A logical one," Zeb sai

"A biased one."

"You knew I'd think you

"You're right." She wrinkled her nose like a little girl. "I apologize."

She looked downright cute. Zeb wanted to kiss her. The thought made him crazy. What was he thinking? She was an uppity know-it-all woman. She had too much education and too much ambition. The next woman he kissed would be his future wife, whoever annoyed him the least. Dr. Mitchell annoyed him the most.

"You're hired for one month. Make it work or get out."

AFTER THE STORM:
THE FOUNDING YEARS
A tornado can't tear apart the fabric of faith and love in a frontier Kansas town

High Plains Bride—
Valerie Hansen, January 2010
Heartland Wedding—
Renee Ryan, February 2010
Kansas Courtship—
Victoria Bylin, March 2010

Books by Victoria Bylin

Love Inspired Historical

The Bounty Hunter's Bride
The Maverick Preacher
Kansas Courtship

VICTORIA BYLIN

fell in love with God and her husband at the same time. It started with a ride on a big red motorcycle and a date to see a *Star Trek* movie. A recent graduate of UC Berkeley, Victoria had been seeking that elusive "something more" when Michael rode into her life. Neither knew it, but they were each reading the Bible.

Five months later they got married and the blessings began. They have two sons and have lived in California and Virginia. Michael's career allowed Victoria to be both a stay-at-home mom and a writer. She's living a dream that started when she read her first book and thought, "I want to tell stories." For that gift, she will be forever grateful.

Feel free to drop Victoria an e-mail at VictoriaBylin@aol.com or visit her Web site at www.victoriabylin.com.

VICTORIA BYLIN
Kansas Courtship

Steeple
Hill®

Published by Steeple Hill Books™

Special thanks and acknowledgment
to Victoria Bylin for her contribution to the
AFTER THE STORM: THE FOUNDING YEARS
miniseries.

STEEPLE HILL BOOKS

Steeple
Hill®

Recycling programs
for this product may
not exist in your area.

ISBN-13: 978-0-373-82831-9

KANSAS COURTSHIP

www.SteepleHill.com

Printed in U.S.A.

Thanks be to God who always leads us in triumph in Christ, and manifests through us the sweet aroma of the knowledge of him in every place.

—II *Corinthians* 2:14

For my grandmothers,
Ethel Kennedy Bylin and Cecille Jewel Vickers

Nana Bylin bought me books
And Grandma Vickers gave me a love of writing
Eternal love to you both!

Prologue

Zeb Garrison didn't think much of church or preachers. Still, he had to give Reverend Preston credit for striking a chord that hadn't stopped echoing since Sunday morning. Zeb had been sitting in the back pew, alone because he'd overslept and his sister, Cassandra, had left without him. He'd been half asleep when the reverend jarred him awake with a single statement.

If you died tomorrow, what would you leave behind?

The reverend hadn't shouted the words. He hadn't even raised his voice. He'd made a statement, but the question had stayed in Zeb's mind for five solid days as he went about the business of running Garrison Mill. It hung there now, dangling like a ripe apple ready to drop.

Positioned at the standing desk in his mill's office, a custom piece of furniture built to match his height, Zeb dragged his hand through his dark hair. He needed a haircut, badly. As always, he'd put it off to the point of rebellion. A glance at the wall clock told him the town barber would be open, but a look out the window confirmed what he'd noticed earlier. Bad weather was coming. Fast. Through the window, he saw clouds racing across the grasslands, picking up speed like a runaway horse.

He had no desire to get stuck at the mill in a storm. His workers had finished early and he'd sent them home to their wives and families. Zeb had no such obligations, beyond his responsibility to his sister. It was better that way. Females, he'd learned, were treacherous. Frannie, his former fiancée, had taught him that painful lesson.

Instead, he'd poured his soul into building Garrison Mill. Along with his friend Will Logan, Zeb had founded High Plains eighteen months ago. Someday the town would be a hub for farms and businesses. Once the wheat crops became plentiful, he'd turn the sawmill into a gristmill. Eventually he'd be shipping flour all over America.

The thought humbled him. Who'd have thought a poor kid from Bellville would ever own a mill? Zeb owed everything to Jon Gridley, a renowned Boston millwright. Pleased to have a protégé, Gridley had filled Zeb's head with the mechanics of gears and water power. When the old man died, he'd left everything to Zeb, making him a rich man in spite of his humble beginnings. With wealth came a burden Zeb hadn't expected. If Garrison Mill succeeded, High Plains would prosper. If it failed, the town could turn to dust. Not an hour passed that he didn't feel responsible for the families he and Will had brought west.

Zeb walked to the window and studied the sky. If he hurried, he could get home before the storm struck. Frowning, he lifted his broad-brimmed hat from a wooden peg, locked the door behind him and stepped into the yard. What he saw sucked the air from his lungs. Funnel clouds were reaching down from the sky like bony fingers. Twisting. Turning. White and gray, they looked like a hand ready to snatch innocent victims from the earth. Zeb froze in amazement. He'd heard about twisters, but he'd never seen one.

In a blink, the storm turned and picked up speed. The fingers were coming for *him*. Blood rushed to his brain and he ran back to the mill for cover.

Will had cautioned him to build a cellar for such an event, but Zeb had been arrogant. He had only one place to hide, his office, and he'd locked the door. Fumbling for the key, he heard a roar unlike anything he'd ever heard. The wind grabbed at his coat. Twenty feet away, a stack of shingles exploded into a flock of birds.

Fumbling, he found the key and turned the knob. As the door opened, the wind ripped it from its hinges and shoved him to his belly. He couldn't breathe. He could only lay sprawled on the floor, twisting to put his back against the wall as he watched the chaos of the wind.

One thought came to him, only one. If he died today, who would care? What would he leave behind? A pile of rubble, that's what. Loneliness whipped through his soul with the force of the wind. Cassandra would miss him, but someday she'd marry.

And he himself? He'd have sawdust and splinters. A black wind hurled debris past the open door. No sons or daughters. A wagon somersaulted and broke apart. More shingles flew by, a hundred of them. Hail pounded the roof, and the window blew out. The mill groaned as it fought to stand. He heard the waterwheel going berserk and the clatter of gears.

As suddenly as the tornado struck, the wind stilled. In the silence, he heard the soft echo of Reverend Preston's question and thought of that dangling apple. The storm had knocked the ripe fruit to the ground, forcing Zeb to admit to a need. If he died tomorrow, he wanted to leave behind more than splinters. He wanted a son to carry on the Garrison name. If it meant putting up with a wife, so be it.

Chapter One

August 1860
High Plains, Kansas

"Look over yonder, missy," said the old man driving the freight wagon. "That's where the twister snatched up those children."

Dr. Nora Mitchell turned on the high seat. With the dusty bonnet shielding her eyes, she looked past Mr. Crandall's gray beard to a lush meadow. A breeze stirred the grass and she smelled loamy earth. With the scent came a whiff of the mules pulling the three freight wagons the last miles to High Plains. In her black medical bag she had the precious letter from Zebulun Garrison inviting her to interview for her first position as a paid physician.

If, that is, he'd overlook that she'd signed her letter to him as "Dr. N. Mitchell." Her gender made no difference when it came to practicing medicine, but it mattered terribly to men with old-fashioned ideas.

She'd lived with that prejudice since the day she'd entered Geneva Medical College, the alma mater of Elizabeth Blackwell, the first female doctor in America. The prejudice had become even more challenging once she graduated. She'd interviewed for fourteen positions in the past year and received fourteen rejections, all because of her gender.

You're female, Dr. Mitchell. That makes you unqualified. Women shouldn't be subjected to the vulgarities of medicine. Perhaps you can find work as a midwife. That would suit you as a woman.

She'd been close to despair, when a cousin wrote to her about an advertisement in the Kansas Gazette.

Wanted: a licensed physician for a new Kansas town. Compensation dependent on experience. Contact Zebulun Garrison, High Plains, Kansas.

She'd posted a letter to Mr. Garrison immediately. Not only had he offered "Dr. N. Mitchell" an interview, he'd sounded enthusiastic. "Our current doctor is retiring," he'd written back. "We are a growing community in need of a skilled practitioner with an adventurous spirit."

Nora had pictured bustling shops and a busy church. She'd imagined delivering babies, setting broken bones and treating croup and sore throats. Those expectations had changed as she'd traveled with the Crandalls. She'd split the riding time between Mr. Crandall and his wife, a buxom woman who'd birthed nine children and never stopped talking. As they'd traveled from Saint Joseph to Topeka, south to Fort Riley and on to High Plains, the woman had told horrific tales about Kansas weather. Two months ago, a tornado wiped out half of High Plains and devastated a wagon train. Most frightening of all, it had snatched away a set of eight-year-old orphan twins, traveling with one of the families on the wagon train. According to Mr. Crandall, the last person to see the twins, a young girl named Bess Carter who now lived in High Plains, had been so horrified by what had occurred that she hadn't spoken since.

Nora knew how it felt to have someone taken without warning. When she was ten years old, her younger brother died of asthma. Grief-stricken, she'd looked at the stars and told God she wanted to be a doctor. When a meteorite shot across the sky, she'd taken it as a sign of His blessing.

She still felt blessed, but the road to this moment had been harrowing. At Geneva Medical College, she'd endured pranks ranging from crass to cruel. She'd tolerated ridicule from professors and mockery from fellow students. She'd also lost friends. Women with whom she'd grown up called her unladylike and turned their backs. Hardest of all, she'd lost some of her father's affection.

Is it worth it, daughter? You should be attending dances and teasing young men. You should be seeking a husband.

She had, but the search for a spouse had been as futile as her hunt for a position as a doctor.

Nora wanted a husband and family as much as any woman, but the men who courted her hadn't respected her career. To her father's chagrin, she'd turned down two proposals including one from his business partner, a man named Albert Bowers, when the men had insisted she stop practicing medicine after she was wed. Mr. Garrison's letter had arrived two days after Nora refused Albert's offer. She'd danced around the room, waving the letter under her father's nose while her mother wrung her hands with worry. With her life in pieces, much like the devastated wagon train, Nora had written back immediately to confirm the interview.

Now here she was…perched on a splintery wagon seat next to Mr. Crandall, facing the aftermath of a tornado. No physician in the world could have stopped the suffering. The Lord alone gave life and took it away. Whatever gift Nora had for healing, she never lost sight of the one true Healer.

Mr. Crandall shouted "whoa" and reined the mules to a halt. As the wagons rattled to silence, he removed his hat and held it over his heart. "Ladies and gentlemen," he bellowed to the other wagons. "Let us pray."

As Nora bowed her head, Mr. Crandall spoke to the sky. "Father God, we pray for mercy for the injured and the lost, especially those two children, Mikey and Missy. We pray they would be found. We pray for Your hand on their tender lives. Amen."

"Amen," she whispered.

A chorus of "amens" echoed from Mrs. Crandall and the four children she had with her. As Nora looked again at the empty meadow, Mr. Crandall jammed his hat on his balding head, gave the reins a shake and shouted at the mules. The wagons rolled forward, creaking as they stumbled in ruts. Awed by the vastness of the land, Nora contemplated the next step in her journey.

Within the hour, she'd meet Mr. Garrison. The tone of his letter had been terse, his penmanship bold. As she'd traveled from New York, enduring grime and crowded trains, she'd imagined their meeting. Judging by his responsibilities, she pictured him as a man in his middle years, perhaps portly with a balding head like Mr. Crandall. Her belly churned as she contemplated their first encounter. If necessary, she'd fight for her right to be a doctor, but the battle would take a toll.

She'd had little experience with Westerners until meeting the Crandalls. They were decent folk but unschooled. She figured Mr. Garrison came from the same hardworking stock. He could read and write, but she doubted he'd appreciate the book of poetry in her satchel, or the oil painting she'd brought to remind her of home.

"There's Garrison Mill," Mr. Crandall called in a booming voice. "That's the start of High Plains."

Nora sat higher in the seat. Straining her neck, she saw a two-story building on the river. Half the shingles were new, a sign of the tornado's damage. On the river side, she saw a waterwheel turning with the lazy summer current. Mr. Garrison may be unschooled, but he clearly had a keen intelligence to build a mill. It also took money, a sign he was older, as she'd imagined.

As the wagons rolled closer to town, she saw more signs of devastation. Along the river, families were living in tents and wagons. A few had constructed shacks from storm-damaged boards of different colors. Down the road she saw a whitewashed school, miraculously untouched. Farther in the distance, she saw a steeple pointing to the bright blue sky.

At the edge of town, a rough sign identified a dirt road as Main Street. Back east, main streets were cobbled and alive with business. This one looked haggard, but she sensed pride in the sign. Soon she'd meet the people she'd come to serve. Would they accept her? Not at first, but she could win their hearts. She felt sure of it.

First, though, she had to win over Mr. Garrison. She wanted to look professional, so this morning she'd put on her New York best. Under the duster she'd bought for the wagon ride, she wore a bottle-green jacket with pagoda sleeves, a white shirtwaist and a narrower-than-usual skirt. She'd gladly left her crinolines in New York, along with the navy suits she'd worn in medical college. In her satchel she had a porkpie hat with a feather. When Mr. Crandall stopped the wagon, she'd whip off the bonnet, slip out of the duster and pin the hat to her red hair. Then, with her medical bag in hand, she'd go in search of Mr. Garrison.

When they reached a mercantile, Mr. Crandall reined in the mules. As the wagon lurched to a halt, Nora lifted her hands to unbutton the duster. She'd worked the first button, when she spotted a tall man with dark hair striding in her direction. Dressed in black trousers, a white shirt and a brocade vest, she judged him to be a local businessman. As he neared the wagon, he looked at her, not once but twice.

She didn't believe in love at first sight, but she believed God had someone special for her. Looking at the tall stranger, she felt a hitch in her belly and wondered… Could he be the one? When the man slowed his steps, she wondered if he'd offer to hand her out of the wagon. She imagined her gloves growing warm at his touch, the strength of his hand as he'd guide her to the street. She'd never been shy, but neither did she want to be considered brazen. Her father's words rang in her head.

Mind your tongue, Nora. You're too outspoken for a lady.

Maybe, but some things had to be said. Some risks had to be taken.

As the man neared the wagon, she smiled.

He tipped his hat in reply. "Good afternoon, miss."

"Good afternoon," she answered.

Mr. Crandall greeted the man with a nod. "Howdy there, sir. How's it going for ya?"

"Excellent. I trust you had a good trip?"

"The finest," Mr. Crandall replied. "If you'll excuse me, I've a wagon to unload."

The freighter, more concerned with his delivery than social graces, hopped off the seat without introducing her.

The man in the vest propped an arm on the edge of the wagon and planted a boot on the wheel. His green eyes held a mix of mirth and intensity.

Nora's cheeks flushed pink.

He smiled at her. "You're new in town."

"I am." She wanted to know this man, but she didn't want to introduce herself to anyone—especially not as Dr. Nora Mitchell—until she met Mr. Garrison. She hoped to see this man again, but she needed to be on her way. She indicated the step down from the wagon. "If you'll excuse me—"

"Allow me." With a roguish smile, he offered his hand.

Nora saw a spark of fun in his eyes. The pale green reminded her of waving grass, but the rugged line of his jaw testified to his boldness. So did the strength of his hand when she gripped his fingers.

"Thank you, sir."

As she dropped to the street, the duster caught on her medical bag and she stumbled. He caught her waist with both hands, steadied her and stepped back. Rugged or not, he had the air of a gentleman.

"Welcome to High Plains," he said. "I'm—"

"There you are!"

They both turned to the mercantile where a petite blonde was coming through the door. Clad in a royal-blue gown with snow-white piping, the woman wore a porkpie hat that matched the one in Nora's satchel. She couldn't have been lovelier…or more feminine. In the duster and bonnet, Nora felt drab.

Her gaze drifted back to the man. In his eyes she saw an aloofness that reminded her of her professors in college.

"Hello, Abigail," he said.

"Oh—Oh no!" The blonde swayed on her feet. Her eyes fluttered shut, and her knees buckled in the start of a swoon. Nora rushed forward to catch her. So did the man. He reached her first and caught her in his arms. As he lowered her to the planking, Nora grabbed her medical bag and charged to her side, whipping off her bonnet when it impeded her vision.

She checked the woman's pulse and found it to be normal. She looked for perspiration and saw only a summer sheen. Next she glanced at the bodice of the blue dress. In New York she'd seen women faint because of too-tight corsets. Nora loathed fashion that harmed a woman's health. She suspected this woman had submitted to such an indignity, but a quick run of her fingers along the woman's rib cage revealed no such encumbrance.

The blonde had swooned for no apparent reason…or had she? Nora looked at the man crouched next to her. His dark hair brushed the rim of his collarless shirt, a linen garment that clung to broad shoulders and well-muscled arms. Black boots, scuffed but made of fine leather, tightened on his calves as he crouched. Gone was the charming stranger. In his place was a man with a smirk, a look she associated with arrogant men…handsome men. Had the woman swooned to get his attention? It wouldn't have surprised her.

The blonde stirred, blinking as if she couldn't focus until she found the man's face.

"Zeb?" she murmured. "Is that you?"

Nora gasped. How many *Zebs* could there be in High Plains? *Please, Lord. Don't let this man be the one.* Knowing she couldn't hide from the truth, she lifted her chin. "Are you Mr. Zebulun Garrison?"

His eyes traveled to her medical bag, and back. He frowned. "I am."

"I'm—"

"You're Dr. *N.* Mitchell," he said coldly. "And you're a liar."

"I am not!" She wanted to settle the matter now, but the blonde needed her attention. Nora turned to her patient. "I'm Dr. Nora Mitchell."

"Get away from me!" the woman declared.

"I'm a doctor."

"You're a woman," she complained. "You *can't* be a doctor."

"I'm fully trained, Miss—?"

"Miss Johnson," she said coldly. "Abigail Johnson."

Nora gripped the woman's wrist, retook her pulse and detected no change. "Did you eat breakfast today?"

"Of course."

Nora surmised the woman to be single. She wouldn't ask about pregnancy directly, but it had to be considered. "Have you been ill, perhaps nauseous on occasion?"

The blonde glared at her as she sat up. "That's a rude question to ask. Zeb, would you help me? I want to go inside."

"Of course." He sounded gentle, even sweet.

Nora surmised they were close and wondered if they were courting. She also recalled the way he'd looked at her. Zebulun Garrison was either weak willed or a womanizer. Either way, she didn't like him.

As he stood, so did she. Their gazes slammed together at an angle, reminding her of his height. In addition to wide shoulders, he had a strong jaw and sharp cheekbones. Her professional eye told her his nose had never been broken. Her female eyes noticed he hadn't shaved in a few days. He was not middle-aged, portly or balding.

His frank gaze reminded her of her own lackluster appearance, and she became acutely aware of what he was seeing…a woman with red hair in a dirty coat. She didn't appreciate his critical stare, especially after the way his eyes had initially sparked with male interest. As dusty as a prairie dog, she stared back to remind him of his manners.

His gaze narrowed with disgust. As he lowered his chin to speak, Abigail waved for attention. "Zeb?" she murmured.

Looking irked, he gripped the blonde's gloved fingers and lifted her, steadying her as she swayed. Abigail Johnson didn't fool Nora for a minute. The woman had faked a swoon to gain Mr. Garrison's attention. Judging by his demeanor, he knew this as well.

After steadying the blonde, he turned back to Nora. His lips thinned to a line. "The interview's over, Miss Mitchell. You'll be leaving with the Crandalls."

"No, sir," she answered. "I will *not* be leaving. You promised me an interview. I expect a chance to prove myself."

"You just did, Dr. *N.* Mitchell."

"I never said I was male. You assumed—"

"You didn't say you weren't."

"When you sign a letter, do *you* tell people you're a man?"

"Of course not."

Nora fought to stay calm. "Do you sign your letters, 'Zebulun Garrison, Member of the Human Race, Male'?"

His stare could have boiled water.

The blonde tugged on his sleeve. "Zeb, please! I want to go inside."

"Wait here," he snapped at Nora.

She hadn't taken orders since medical college, not even from her father. She wanted the respect of her title, but she did *not* want a public scene when they discussed the terms of her employment. Neither did she want to have that talk wearing the duster, with dirt on her face.

"I'll be at the boardinghouse as we arranged," she said to him. "I'll expect you this afternoon. Is two o'clock acceptable?"

He stared at her for five long seconds. "You've got a lot of nerve."

"I have as much *nerve* as you."

His mouth curved into a bitter smile. "I doubt that, *Miss* Mitchell. I'll be at the boardinghouse at one o'clock. I have work to do."

He'd changed the time to make a point. She'd have to hurry to get ready, but she'd manage. "Fine," she said.

"Fine," he replied.

The blonde gave Nora a nasty look, then gripped Mr. Garrison's arm and steered him into the mercantile. As they passed through the door, Mr. Crandall came out. "How ya doing, missy?"

"Just fine," she answered. "I thought I'd walk to the boardinghouse. Would you deliver my trunk when you're done here?"

"Sure thing, girl." He held out his big hand. "It's been a pleasure hauling ya."

Nora clasped it in both of hers. "The pleasure was mine. And remember, if you or the missus need a doctor, I'm here."

His gray eyes turned serious. "I will, miss. But I'm worried about ya. Mr. Garrison's a mite bent out of shape. If you need a ride back to Saint Joseph, just holler. The wife and I leave in the morning."

"I'll be fine."

"I hope so." He shook his head. "That man doesn't think much of females. Might be different if he had himself a wife like mine."

Nora had enjoyed the older couple, bickering and all. "You and Mrs. Crandall were very kind to me."

He tipped his hat. "Good day, miss. I'll see to that trunk of yours."

As he turned to leave, Nora realized she needed directions. She called back to Mr. Crandall. "Would you point me to the boardinghouse?"

"Go that way." He jerked his thumb down the dusty street. "Turn right at the end and you'll see it. Mrs. Jennings runs the place. She's on the crabby side, but you'll like her cook, Rebecca. She makes the best meals in Kansas."

"Thank you."

Gripping her medical bag, Nora paced down the street, avoiding the broken boardwalk as she took in buildings with boarded-up windows. Some of the structures were brand new. Others were a mix of wood weathered by time and fresh lumber. At the end of the street she saw a whitewashed church with glass windows and a perfect roof. A cross topped a bell tower and pointed at the sky. The sight of it gave Nora hope. She refused to be shaken by anything—not tornadoes and not Zebulun Garrison. Before she left New York, she'd prayed for God's will to be done in her life. Surely the Lord wouldn't let her down.

As for Mr. Garrison, he'd met his match. When he arrived at the boardinghouse, she wouldn't be wearing a duster. She'd look her best and be armed with her medical degree, a quick wit and her good intentions. She'd been asked to come for an interview, and she intended to hold him to his word. If he thought he could disrespect her, she'd be glad to set him straight.

Chapter Two

Zeb handed Abigail off to her mother, who ran the mercantile along with Abigail's father, and left the store. Ever since he'd let it slip that he wanted a wife, he'd felt like a rabbit in a hunt. Abigail had been the most obvious, but he'd received supper invitations from half a dozen families with daughters, including Winnie Morrow and her mother. Either Winnie or Abigail would do for a wife. He just had to choose one over the other.

As he crossed the street, he saw Mr. Crandall driving to the boardinghouse. In the wagon sat a trunk that had to belong to Dr. Nora Mitchell. A woman! Of all the fool things... If Doc Dempsey hadn't died last week, Zeb wouldn't even speak to her. As things stood, the town desperately needed a physician. At Doc's funeral, Zeb had taken comfort in knowing Dr. Mitchell was on his way.

Her way, he corrected himself.

Stifling an oath, he headed for the livery to tell Pete Benjamin the news. Of all the people in High Plains, the blacksmith surely understood the need for a physician most personally. A year ago, Pete's first wife, Sarah, had died in childbirth, and the baby had been lost with her. Dr. Dempsey, a gentleman in his eighties, had done his best, but his methods were old-fashioned at best and lethal at worst.

At the funeral, the first in High Plains, Zeb had set his mind on finding a skilled physician. He'd received a dozen letters and had interviewed four men. He didn't think the choices could get any worse, but he'd been wrong. No way would he hire a woman. Zeb dreaded giving the bad news to Pete. The livery owner had remarried and found happiness with Rebecca Gunderson, the boardinghouse cook. One of these days he'd be a father again.

Pete knew the need for a good physician most personally, but Zeb had strong feelings, too. As long as he lived, he'd be haunted by the aftermath of the tornado. How many people had suffered because Doc Dempsey couldn't keep up? Some had died instantly. Others had lingered for days with festering wounds. Doc had done his best, but he'd lacked the skill and stamina to treat all the injured. On that horrible day, Zeb had renewed his vow to find a skilled physician for High Plains.

As he neared the livery, he gritted his teeth against a flare of temper. Not only had Dr. Mitchell lied about her gender, she'd left him with egg on his face. Just last week, he'd bragged to Will Logan that he'd found the perfect man for the job. Dr. Mitchell had impeccable credentials, including a letter of reference from Dr. Gunter Zeiss, a name Zeb recognized from his cavalier days in Boston. Dr. Zeiss, a famous German neurologist, had praised Dr. Mitchell as a skilled diagnostician and a brilliant clinician. He'd described his "colleague" as talented, dedicated and a true humanitarian.

In Zeb's opinion, Dr. Zeiss had more brains than common sense. No way could a woman handle the rigors of doctoring.

As he neared the livery stable, he backhanded the sweat off his brow. The day, already warm, turned insufferable as he neared the forge. Heat spilled in waves off the brick table where Pete was pounding a glowing piece of iron. Between caring for horses and making everything from plow blades to door latches, the blacksmith was the busiest man in town.

The men had known each other for years. Zeb saw no need for small talk as he peered into the gloom. "I've got bad news."

Pete kept hammering. "What happened?"

"Dr. Mitchell arrived."

"You don't sound happy about it."

"I'm not."

The blacksmith grunted. "Another dud?" He looked as glum as Zeb felt about the situation.

"Remember when that letter arrived? You said nothing could be worse than the last fellow, and I said you were wrong. It *could* be worse."

"I asked how, and you said the new doctor could be a woman."

"That's right."

Pete kept hammering. "Are you telling me—"

"I sure am," Zeb said with disgust. "Dr. N. Mitchell isn't Norman or Ned. Her name's Nora."

"Well, I'll be," Pete murmured.

"I'm sending her back. She can leave with the Crandalls."

Pete's hammer pinged in a steady rhythm. "I'm not so sure that's a good idea."

"It's the only answer." Zeb took a handkerchief from his pocket and mopped the sweat off his neck.

The blacksmith kept working. "With Doc's passing, maybe you should give the woman a chance. You said yourself she's qualified."

"I said *he* was qualified. This isn't a job for a woman and you know it."

Pete held up the piece of metal, inspected it with a sharp eye then put it back in the fire. "Seems to me a female doctor's better than no doctor at all."

Not in Zeb's opinion. "You know as well as I do she won't last. Either she'll get fed up and go back to New York, or she'll get married and quit the medicine business. No woman is cut out for that kind of work."

"I don't know," Pete said. "Rebecca's talking about opening an inn. I'd be a fool to try and stop her."

"That's different." Zeb frowned at the object in Pete's hand. "She'll be cooking and cleaning like she always does. It's woman's work."

Pete huffed at him. "I wouldn't say *woman's work* with that tone if you want to keep enjoying my wife's good cooking. Rebecca works as hard as I do."

"I'm sure she does," Zeb drawled. "But it's not the same as what you do."

"Maybe." Pete sounded wry. "She'll also be keeping the books, ordering supplies, hiring folks and bossing everyone around."

"So?"

"Isn't that what *you* do?" Pete argued. "Especially the 'bossing' part?"

Zeb faked a scowl. "Are you picking a fight?"

"No." Pete's voice lost its humor. "I'm asking you to give the lady doctor a chance. Aside from being female, how does she seem?"

Beautiful. Kind. Brave.

Before he'd seen the medical bag, he'd felt like a love-struck adolescent. Her blue eyes, wide and innocent, had a spark of daring he admired. When she'd lifted her lips in a smile, he'd thought of kissing her and wondered if his search for a wife had come to an end. Then Abigail had faked another swoon and the woman had grabbed that heavy case.

"Zeb?"

"What?"

"You didn't answer the question." Pete's lips turned up. "What is she like?"

"Normal, I guess." Except for that hair. He'd never seen anything like it.

Pete pulled the metal from the fire, inspected it and went back to hammering. "*Normal* is more than I can say for that last fellow."

Zeb had to agree. Not one of the four men he'd interviewed had met his standards. They'd nicknamed the last one "Dr. Gruesome" when he'd talked about exhuming graves for his "research." No way could Zeb see him birthing babies.

He could see Dr. Mitchell at a birthing, but did she have the grit to cut off a man's leg? Of course not. Zeb had seen mill accidents in Bellville, including a mistake that had cut off Timmy Cooper's hand. A woman wouldn't have the stomach for such things. Most men didn't, either. *He* didn't, though he'd witnessed his share of injuries.

Pete held up the piece of iron and looked again at the color. The orange had cooled to red, so he put aside the hammer, lifted a chisel and began to shape the edge of a hoe blade. His eyes twinkled with mischief.

"So," he said. "Just how *normal* does the lady doctor look? Is she pretty?"

Zeb scowled. "She's pretty enough, not that it matters to you. You've got Rebecca."

"And no woman's lovelier," Pete replied. "I was thinking about you."

"Don't."

Pete chuckled. "The whole town's in on it, you know."

Last month Zeb had let it slip to Pete he was *considering*

marriage. Abigail's mother, Matilda Johnson, had overheard and started pushing Abigail in his path. The Ladies Aid Society had started buzzing and Zeb had received six supper invitations in two days. The attention irked him. "I wish I'd kept my mouth shut," he said to Pete.

With his arms crossed over his chest, he told his friend about Abigail faking another swoon, how the lady doctor had jumped to her rescue and how Abigail had taken her down a peg.

Pete's brows snapped together. "I don't like the Johnsons. I never will."

"I don't blame you." Zeb knew the history. After the tornado, Mrs. Johnson had accused Pete and Rebecca of immoral behavior in the storm cellar where they'd taken shelter together. She'd said hateful things about Rebecca until Pete proposed marriage to stop the talk. Still grieving Sarah and their child, the blacksmith had taken the high road when he'd done nothing wrong. Zeb admired his friend's integrity and wanted to match it by providing a real doctor. Unfortunately, the only doctor within a hundred miles was female.

The blacksmith looked Zeb in the eye. "If the lady doctor stood up to Abigail, she's got my vote for staying."

"I don't know, Pete."

"What's the harm in giving her a chance?"

Zeb shook his head. "What if she kills someone with her incompetence?"

"She just might be a good doctor," Pete replied. "Besides, Doc did that already."

Zeb looked beyond Pete through the open door and flashed back to the day of the tornado. Doc did his best, but people had died because he couldn't move fast enough. Zeb's gaze narrowed to the backside of Dr. Dempsey's former office. The tornado had damaged the roof, so Doc had used a closet at the church as an infirmary. Zeb had a place for the new physician, but his plan wouldn't work with a female.

"You got any ideas?" he said to Pete.

"Hire her for a month," the blacksmith replied. "See how she does."

The idea had merit. Zeb could place another ad in the *Kansas Gazette*. While he waited for replies, the lady doctor could treat sore throats and hangnails. "It would buy time," he said. But where could he *put* her for that time? No, his first instinct was right—the best solution would be for her to leave in the morning with the Crandalls.

"Who knows?" Pete replied. "She might work out just fine."

Zeb doubted it. Thanks to Frannie, he knew all about women like Dr. Nora Mitchell. She was ambitious. She'd do anything— even twist the truth—to get her way.

With sweat beading his brow, he recalled the day Frannie left him standing on the church steps, engagement ring in hand. Plain and simple, she'd jilted him for her career. Losing the love of his life had changed him the way Pete's pounding had shaped the hoe. Like the iron, Zeb's heart had been red-hot and pliable. He'd have done anything for Frannie. After being jilted, his heart had cooled to black.

So had his soul. In Zeb's opinion, the Almighty was either lazy or cruel. Zeb had no love for a God who ignored tornadoes and let children be snatched away. He feared Him, though. Who wouldn't?

He wondered what Dr. Mitchell would say about such matters, then decided he didn't care. Aside from telling Pete about the lady doctor, he had other business with the blacksmith. With the need for lumber, Zeb was running the mill eighteen hours a day. Long hours meant more stress on men and equipment, but he had no choice. A half-dozen buildings needed major repairs before winter, and he'd vowed to finish the town hall in time for a summer jubilee. He had a month to go and needed the sawmill at full power. But with the long hours, there were equipment breakdowns at least twice a week.

"A blade lost a few teeth yesterday," he said to Pete. "Can you fix it?"

"Bring it tomorrow."

Pete inspected the hoe, set it down and whipped off his heavy gloves. "How's the town hall coming along?"

"It's framed," Zeb answered. "I've got a crew working on the roof."

The men slipped into an easy conversation about wood and welding, things they understood. Women weren't on that list. Zeb opened his pocket watch, a gift he treasured from Mr. Gridley, and saw he had two minutes to get to the boarding-house. "I've got to go see that lady doctor."

The blacksmith put his gloves back on. "Maybe she'll surprise you."

Zeb doubted it, but for his friend's sake he'd give her a chance. For *her* sake, he intended to spell out what she'd be facing. Once she saw the tornado damage, particularly Doc's old office, she'd be crazy to stay in High Plains.

Considering she'd been crazy to become a doctor, the thought gave him no comfort.

With her medical bag in hand, Nora knocked on the front door of the boardinghouse. No answer. She knocked again, more boldly this time.

A middle-aged woman with a tight bun flung it open. "What is it, miss?"

"I'm Dr. Mitchell. I believe you have a room for me?"

"You're not Dr. Mitchell," she said. "You're a woman."

"I'm both." Nora tried to disarm her with a smile, but she had no expectations. In her experience, older women were as resistant to a female doctor as men, even more so.

The woman appeared honestly confused. "Does Zeb know about this?"

"Yes." Nora spoke through tight lips. "You must be Mrs. Jennings."

"That's right." She buried her hands in her apron. "The room I've got is plain at best. You're not going to like it, miss."

"All I need is a bed and a dresser." Nora had had fine things in New York. She'd enjoyed them, but she didn't need high-class furniture to be comfortable. She indicated the duster. "I'm meeting Mr. Garrison, and I'm eager to freshen up. Could you show me to my room?"

The woman hesitated, then heaved a sigh. "I guess. You'll need to sleep somewhere."

Nora followed her into the entry hall. To the left she saw a parlor with an upholstered divan, side chairs and tables decorated with lace doilies. The room could have been in a Boston town house except for the smell of Kansas dust.

Mrs. Jennings indicated a row of hooks by the door. "Put your duster there."

Nora set down her medical bag, slipped out of the filthy garment and hung it up. Later she'd shake out the dust. Satisfied, she picked up her medical bag and followed the landlady up the stairs.

Mrs. Jennings ran her hand along the railing. "I've got to warn you, miss. This town's not expecting a lady doctor."

"I understand."

"Zeb must have had a fit when he saw you." The woman looked over her shoulder, as if she still couldn't believe her eyes. "I don't know if you heard, but Dr. Dempsey died last week."

The doctor's passing meant High Plains needed her more than ever, but Nora's heart sank. One thing she'd discovered—male doctors didn't like or trust her, but they never compromised their patients. Dr. Dempsey would have helped her, even if he'd had to hold his nose while doing it.

"I'm sorry," she murmured.

"He was a fine man." The woman's voice softened. "If you ask me, he worked himself to death after the tornado."

"It must have been awful." Nora thought of the missing twins. How many people had been injured? How many lives had been lost? And the damage to homes and businesses… Repairs had been going on for weeks, yet she'd been staggered by the extent of the work still required.

"At least the church is still standing," Mrs. Jennings said. "It didn't get a scratch. I can't say the same about the town hall. There wasn't a speck left except the foundation."

At the top of the stairs, the woman turned down a long hall. Nora saw four doors on each side of the corridor and a single row of wall sconces. A window at the end of the hall shot a beam of light to the carpet. Dust motes floated like fireflies.

Mrs. Jennings opened the second door on the right. "Here's your room, miss."

"Please," Nora said, sounding friendly. "Call me Dr. Nora."

Mrs. Jennings looked over her shoulder and frowned. "That doesn't seem right."

Nora knew she was objecting to the title and not the use of her first name, but she deliberately misunderstood to make a point. If she didn't ask for respect, she'd never get it. "Nora's my name, but if you'd prefer to call me Dr. Mitchell, that's fine, too."

"Whatever you want, miss."

Nora held in a sigh. If Zeb Garrison and Mrs. Jennings

were typical of the folks in High Plains, she had a long road ahead of her.

Mrs. Jennings unlocked the door. As Nora stepped inside, she saw a narrow bed, a rough-hewn wardrobe and a vanity with a metal pitcher and washbowl. A red-and-blue quilt decorated the bed, and a window let in fresh air. The room struck her as plain, functional and the loveliest place she'd ever lived because it belonged to her alone.

She set the medical bag on the floor, then smiled at Mrs. Jennings. "This is perfect."

The landlady huffed. "It is what it is. With the storm, I've got guests in every nook and cranny. Six families are living up here, along with an orphan boy from the wagon train. Don't expect too much quiet."

"I won't." Nora loved children, especially boys who couldn't hold still.

Mrs. Jennings looked grim. "You're going to have a hard time, miss."

"How so?"

"The Ladies Aid Society has certain ideas, especially Matilda Johnson at the mercantile."

"I met Abigail—"

"Matilda is her mother." Mrs. Jennings tsked her tongue. "Matilda thinks High Plains should be the next Chicago. She won't like having a lady doctor."

"I'll have to change her mind."

"It'd be easier to stop another storm."

Nora said nothing, but her stomach rumbled. She hadn't eaten in hours. Mrs. Jennings acknowledged the growling with a nod. "Supper's not until six, but you can ask Rebecca for a bite to eat."

Nora recalled Mr. Crandall's praise. "She's the cook, isn't she?"

"That's right. Head to the kitchen and she'll fix you something."

"I will. But first I have a meeting with Mr. Garrison. If we could use the parlor—"

"That's what it's for." Mrs. Jennings looked her up and down, taking in the green dress with its fancy sleeves. Nora had worn her best gown to impress Mr. Garrison with her professionalism. Under Mrs. Jennings's scrutiny, she worried that it made her look snooty.

Nora indicated the skirt with a sweep of her hand. "I'm dressed for a job interview."

"You're a pretty thing," said the landlady. "What do you need a job for?"

I love my work. It's who I am. Nora wouldn't change Mrs. Jennings's attitude with an argument, so she bit her tongue.

The woman's face softened into a smile. "Judging by your looks, you won't be a 'miss' for long. Just so you know, I've got rules. Supper's at six. No muddy boots past the entry. And no gentleman callers after eight o'clock. There will be no improper behavior under *my* roof."

"Certainly not," Nora agreed, though she had little experience with men and courtship. Growing up, she'd been intent on becoming a doctor. She'd attended social events at her mother's urging, but she'd never mastered the art of flirting. As her father said, she was too outspoken, too bold. Even too smart. Maybe, but she still wanted a husband. Not just any man, but the man God made just for her, assuming He intended to bestow such a gift.

As Mrs. Jennings turned to leave, two boys ran down the hall. One of them had golden-brown hair and reminded Nora of her brother. She guessed him to be eight years old.

Mrs. Jennings called after them. "Alex! Jonah! Stop it! You'll bother Miss Mitchell!"

"Oh, no!" Nora protested. "I love children."

"Good, because with the families, I've got ten of 'em here." She crossed her arms over her bosom. "Zeb's a good man. He gave me a dairy cow so all these children can have milk."

"Mr. Garrison did that?"

"He sure did."

Surely a man who took care of orphans wouldn't leave High Plains without a doctor. Nora regretted Dr. Dempsey's death, but his passing helped her position with Mr. Garrison. The town had a need, and she could fill it.

Heavy steps broke into her thoughts. She looked at the doorway and saw Mr. Crandall with her trunk on his wide shoulder. Grunting, he set it at the foot of the bed. "There you go, missy."

Nora appreciated his friendly tone. "Thank you, Mr. Crandall."

Mrs. Jennings gave the room a final glance, then put her hands on her hips. "If you need something, ask."

"I will. Thank you."

"That's it, Miss Nora."

She'd hadn't been called "Doctor," but she counted "Miss Nora" as progress. "I'm sure I'll be fine."

Mrs. Jennings followed Mr. Crandall out of the room and closed the door. Alone for the first time in weeks, Nora opened her trunk and unpacked. She hung up her clothes, then filled the basin and washed her face thoroughly with her mother's lavender soap. The scent took her back to New York and what she'd left behind.

She loved her father and he loved her, but he'd spoken stern words the day she'd left. *This is your last chance, Nora. If you come home, I'll expect you to put aside that medical nonsense and marry Albert Bowers.*

Her father's business partner was thoughtful, hardworking

and generous. He was also fifty-nine years old and as modern as a powdered wig. She didn't love him and never would. She *had* to succeed in High Plains. That meant impressing Zebulun Garrison with her abilities. As she washed her face, she prayed God would soften the mill owner's heart, and that she'd find favor in the eyes of the town.

"Be with me, Lord," she said out loud. "I belong here. I *know* it. Amen."

Strengthened, she hung the flour-sack towel on the windowsill to dry. The opening had no glass, only two shutters spread wide to let in the light. To the right she saw the backs of the buildings on Main Street. Below her, she saw Mr. Crandall driving his empty wagon to the livery stable. As he rattled past her window, he tipped his hat to a man coming out of a low building with a new roof.

Squinting against the sun, Nora recognized Zeb Garrison and his flashy vest. The man acknowledged Mr. Crandall with a stern wave, then removed his hat and wiped his brow with his sleeve, not stopping for a moment. From the vantage point of the window, she saw the crown of his head. No bald spot there…just thick hair that needed trimming. Everything about this man, even his hair, was bold, strong and defiant.

A smile played across her lips. She had the same traits. She also had an unshakable faith in God. As long as she stuck to her principles, she'd be safe from prejudice and cruel words. She'd treat Mr. Garrison the way she wanted to be treated. The Bible said to do unto others as you would have it done to you. That's what she'd do now.

When Mr. Garrison threw stones, she'd duck.

When he criticized her, she'd smile.

When he mocked her, she'd turn the other cheek.

Nora knew all about loving her enemies. She also knew

some enemies were more challenging than others. Mr. Garrison, she feared, would be the most challenging of all. With a prayer on her lips, she lifted the porkpie hat from her medical bag, pinned it in place and went to meet him in the parlor.

Chapter Three

Zeb caught a whiff of lavender. He hated lavender. It reminded him of Frannie.

He'd been staring out the parlor window, thinking about all the work he had to do, when the scent reached his nose. Turning, he saw Dr. Mitchell in the doorway. Instead of the duster that made her look like a farm girl, she wore a green dress with fancy sleeves and a hat with a silly feather. He dipped his chin. "Good afternoon, *Dr.* Mitchell."

"Good afternoon, *Mr.* Garrison." Striding forward, she offered her hand. "It's a pleasure to meet you, again."

"Once was enough for me."

She kept her hand extended. "I'm hoping we can start fresh."

Zeb smirked. "You can't unring a bell, Dr. Mitchell."

"No," she countered. "But you can ring it again if it strikes the wrong note."

She stood with her hand loose and ready, wearing a look that dared him to be civil. The moment called for formal manners, the ones he'd learned in Boston, except Zeb didn't want to be civil. He wanted to fan the air to get rid of her feminine scent. He answered her by indicating a chair. "Please, sit down."

Without a hint of defeat, she lowered her hand and sat on the sofa. Zeb dropped into a chair across from her, draped a boot over his knee and steepled his fingers. Her chin went up a notch. His went down.

If she wanted an interview, he'd give her one. "Tell me, Dr. Mitchell. Why do you want to practice medicine in High Plains?"

She smiled, but Zeb refused to be disarmed. Never mind her red hair and a dress that showed off her curves. She was female and not fit to practice medicine. She also smelled like Frannie. The scent brought back a rush of memories that gave him a headache.

Dr. Mitchell laced her gloved fingers in her lap. "Thank you for using my title. Most people—"

"You're a doctor, aren't you?"

"Of course."

"Then that's what I'll call you."

He expected her to bristle at his tone. Instead, her eyes met his with a patience beyond her years. "Shall we skip the pleasantries and get down to business?"

"Absolutely."

"In the past year, I've applied for fourteen positions and been turned down fourteen times because of my gender. I've come to High Plains for a chance to prove myself. Will you give it to me, Mr. Garrison?"

Coming from a woman, the directness surprised him. "Why should I?"

"Because Dr. Dempsey is deceased, and I have the skills to replace him."

Again, she'd been blunt. Zeb liked her style, but nothing could change her unsuitability. Whether she wanted to admit it or not, being female caused problems—including one he was about to introduce.

"Suppose I give you this chance." He tapped his index fingers together. "What will you do for an office?"

"I'll use Dr. Dempsey's."

"I don't think so, Miss—Dr. Mitchell."

"Why not?"

"Doc's office was damaged in the tornado. After the storm he used a room in the church."

She folded her hands in her lap. "A room at the church would do nicely."

"It wasn't exactly a room," Zeb said dryly. "It was more of a closet. Besides, a family took it over the day Doc died. We're that short of space."

"I see." Her eyes dimmed, but nothing else betrayed her surprise. "You must have had plans for the new physician. Whatever you arranged will be fine."

"I don't think so, Dr. Mitchell." Zeb didn't bother to hide a smirk. "I had planned to invite the new doctor to use part of my house for his practice. The offer was to include room and board in my home."

Zeb expected a gasp at the news, maybe hysterics or a fluttering hankie. Dr. Mitchell said nothing for a solid minute, then she stood up. "We obviously need an alternative. I'd like to see Dr. Dempsey's office."

Zeb stayed seated. "Forget it. I wouldn't let a dog live there."

"I'm not a helpless pet," she countered. "I'm a capable woman who can adapt to harsh conditions. If the building has four walls and a roof, I'll manage."

"It has four walls," he said, pushing to his feet, "but I can't promise you a roof."

Doubt flickered across her face. He'd won a small victory, but he didn't feel good about it. Zeb knew the pain of a dying dream. That's what he saw on the lady doctor's face.

In spite of worry in her eyes, she squared her shoulders. "I'd like to see it for myself."

"We'll go now, but I warn you. It's been damaged."

When she stepped into the entry hall, he passed her with the intention of holding the door. If she'd been a man, he wouldn't have bothered. Dr. Mitchell didn't want to admit it, but her gender mattered. Zeb didn't view women as less intelligent than men. His mother had been as sharp as a whipsaw. Cassandra could play him like a fiddle. As for Frannie, she'd owned his every thought. He'd have died for her, but she'd gone to Paris alone to prove a point.

Zeb wondered if Dr. Mitchell was one of those self-righteous women crowing about equality. What did equal mean anyway? Men and women were different. Any fool could see that…especially a fool looking at Dr. Mitchell in her green dress.

As she passed through the door, the feather on her hat swished by his nose. He found himself taking long strides to keep up with her, watching as she looked across the road to the church. With the sun high and bright, the siding glistened white and the windows turned to silver.

"It's a lovely church," she said. "It's a miracle it survived."

"Blind luck is more like it."

She tipped her face up to his. "You don't believe in miracles, Mr. Garrison?"

"No, I don't."

"Neither do I," she countered. "Not exactly."

He wanted to know what she meant, but refused to ask. If the survival of the church counted as a miracle, what would she call the tragedy of the missing children? Zeb called it cruel. He'd prayed as a boy, but he didn't believe in God like Will did. Will's faith gave him confidence in bleak times, even joy. Zeb had no such foundation.

The dust stirred as they approached Doc's office. Zeb stopped in front of it, pausing to let her take in the boarded-up windows and chinks in the siding from flying debris. The roof had a hole the size of a wagon, but he expected the walls to hold. The door, half off its hinges, hung like a broken arm.

He indicated the entrance with his chin. "There it is."

"My goodness." Her voice wobbled.

Good, he thought. Maybe she'd leave with the Crandalls. Leaving *him* back where he'd started with his doctor search. What would he do if someone broke an arm? And Bess Carter…the girl hadn't said a word since the storm. Zeb recalled the tornado and how Will had rescued Emmeline Carter and her family, including her fifteen-year-old sister who'd been struck mute after losing the twins. No one knew why Bess couldn't talk, and Doc Dempsey hadn't been able to help her.

"May I go inside?" Dr. Mitchell asked.

"Be my guest." Zeb shoved the door wide and waited for her to pass. Along with lavender, he smelled rot from the building. The fan of light revealed stains on the floor from rain coming through the window, and no one had swept up the broken apothecary jars. The shards, a mix of green, brown and gold, caught the light and glittered like fallen leaves.

Dr. Mitchell surveyed every corner with a keen eye. "It's a mess."

"That's a fact."

She looked at the empty shelves, then peered into the back rooms. "I don't see anything that can't be fixed with a mop and a scrub bucket."

"You haven't seen the roof."

She looked up the stairs. "How bad is it?"

"Bad enough."

"I'd like to see it."

"Suit yourself, but I've wasted enough time for today. I won't hire you."

Zeb felt bad, but the townspeople would have to understand. No way could he have a female doctor working in his parlor. As for finding another place, he'd already tried and found nothing suitable. He shook his head. "Give up, Miss Mitchell. This isn't going to work."

Her eyes filled with cool disdain. "It's Dr. Mitchell, and I never give up."

"There's always a first time."

"This isn't it," she replied. "I have an offer for you. Will you listen?"

"Sure."

"Hire me for one month. I'll find an office, but I expect the town to pay for it. As far as room and board, I'll stay at the board-inghouse. I'd like the cost to be included in our agreement."

Pete had suggested the same thing. "Sure, why not?" Zeb said generously. She'd never find an office in High Plains. With those terms, she'd be gone in a week, and he could truthfully tell Pete she hadn't worked out. Tonight he'd write another ad for the *Kansas Gazette*. The Crandalls could take it with the letters waiting at the mercantile.

Suspicion clouded her eyes. "That was too easy."

"I'm giving you that chance you wanted." He planted his boots wide and crossed his arms. If she wanted to act like a man, he'd treat her like one. "Name your price."

"Twelve dollars a week," she said boldly. "Plus room and board."

She'd named a high price, expecting to negotiate. Zeb was glad to oblige. "I'll pay you five. That *includes* room and board."

"That's insulting."

"Yep."

He wanted to rile her, but she didn't blink. "This town needs a doctor, Mr. Garrison. You can't afford to turn me down. Make it ten dollars a week, including room and board, and you have a deal."

She had a point about the town's need. Dr. Dempsey's passing left him with a bad choice—a woman doctor or no doctor at all. For a few weeks, he'd have to tolerate her. "Fine, Dr. Mitchell. Ten dollars a week, it is."

"Then it's settled." She came forward with her hand outstretched to shake on the deal. Again she met his gaze, demanding his respect and daring him to deny it.

Looking down at the beige glove, he saw the lace covering her fingers and the silky ribbon tied at her wrist. This wasn't a man-to-man agreement. If he shook her hand, he'd notice the shape of her fingers, the warmth of her palm inside the lace. He didn't want to touch her, but she'd win if he didn't accept the gesture.

Annoyed, he gripped her fingers, but didn't squeeze the way he would have shaken a man's hand. Her bones felt too delicate for a show of strength. Neither could he ignore the scent of lavender.

Dr. Mitchell had no qualms about squeezing *his* hand. Those delicate bones had been deceptive. The woman had an iron grip.

She smiled at him. "You won't be sorry, Mr. Garrison."

He already was, but he kept the thought to himself.

Her eyes sparked with determination. "It won't be easy. I'm well aware of the prejudice I'll encounter."

"Is that so?"

"Absolutely." Her gaze hardened into blue glass. "You're not the first man to ruffle my skirts."

He couldn't stop himself from looking her up and down. Pretty. Proud. And as stubborn as winter. He'd heard enough of her smart talk. "Let me be frank, Dr. Mitchell. I wouldn't hire you if I had a choice. In the past year, four men interviewed for the position. Not one of them worked out."

She raised one brow. "Let me guess. Patent medicines for sale?"

"Maybe." He didn't appreciate her tone.

"Did anyone bring leeches?"

He shuddered.

"I'm not surprised." Her voice leveled into friendly banter. "Medicine is changing fast. Twenty years from now, *my* skills will be considered primitive, but right now I'm among the most highly trained physicians in America."

"You're also female."

"That's irrelevant."

"Maybe to you. Not to me." He put his hands on his hips and stared hard.

The lady doctor stared back, reminding him of the woman in the duster. She'd been all female when she'd smiled a greeting, and he'd liked what he'd seen. He liked her now, too. If it wasn't for her medical degree, he'd have invited her to supper, maybe taken her on a buggy ride along the river.

She tipped her head to the side. "Tell me, Mr. Garrison. What worries you the most about hiring a female physician?"

"Everything."

"That's not an answer."

"All right." He thought for a second. "Women are tender-hearted. If a man gets his hand cut off at the mill, you'll faint."

"No, I won't," she said with a casual wave. "I've performed autopsies. They're gruesome but necessary."

Zeb's stomach recoiled. He took another approach. "You're from back East, a big city with streets and shops. Life is harsh in High Plains. I don't think you can handle it."

"I did fine with the Crandalls."

He snorted. "It didn't even rain. What about winter? A blizzard can last a week. The snow's so deep—"

"I'm from New York," she said impatiently. "I know what snow looks like."

She had no cause to be irritated. He was trying to warn her, to prepare her for hardships unique to Kansas. "Then tell me, Dr. Mitchell. Have you ever seen a tornado?"

Memories came at him in a roar. Knowing she'd see the upset in his eyes, he strode to the broken window and looked at the sky. He relived the wind buffeting the mill, and hail beating on the roof. He recalled running to town and seeing the wreckage. He'd almost died that day. Others *had* died. He pictured the missing children and felt wretched. He thought of Bess Carter all tongue-tied from what she'd seen.

He heard footsteps on the floor, the swish of skirts. An instant later, Dr. Mitchell laid a gentle hand on his bicep. The touch took his breath as the tornado had done. His muscles clenched beneath her long fingers. Whether from anger or awareness, he couldn't say.

She spoke in a hush. "I want you to know, Mr. Garrison, I'm sorry for what you've lost. The Crandalls told me about Mikey and Missy. They showed me the spot and we prayed—"

"A waste of time."

"I disagree." She lowered her hand, but her words hung between them. "God brought me here to serve this town. You can growl all you want—"

"I don't growl."

"Fine," she argued with a smile. "You can grumble, then. But there's nothing you can do to chase me back to New York."

"Is that a dare, Miss—" He cocked one brow. "I mean, *Dr.* Mitchell?"

"No," she said. "It's a fact. I've been tested by male arrogance every day for three years. Compared to some of the men I've dealt with, you've been a tea party."

Zeb had been called a lot of names in his life, but *tea party* wasn't one of them. He didn't care for the comparison, either. He'd been harsh because he wanted her to leave. "Life here isn't a party, Doc. If Dr. Dempsey hadn't passed on, you'd be leaving with the Crandalls."

"But I'm not, am I?"

"You should be." His voice rose with irritation. "You tricked me by using your initial instead of your real name."

"You tricked yourself," she said mildly. "You jumped to a conclusion."

"A logical one."

"A biased one," she countered.

"You *knew* I'd think you were male."

"You're right." She wrinkled her nose like a little girl. "I apologize."

She looked downright cute. Zeb wanted to kiss her. The thought made him crazy. What was he thinking? She was an uppity know-it-all woman like Frannie. She had too much education and too much ambition. The next woman he kissed would be his future wife, either Winnie or Abigail, whichever one annoyed him the least. Dr. Mitchell annoyed him the most. "You're hired for one month. Make it work or get out."

"I'll make it work." She meant it. He heard the fight in her voice.

Zeb headed for the door. He couldn't get back to the mill quick enough.

"Mr. Garrison!"

He stopped and faced her. "What is it?"

She looked into his eyes, staring hard as if she expected him to read her thoughts. Oddly, he could. She'd traveled a thousand miles and had arrived to a disaster. He hadn't offered her a meal, even a cup of water. He'd been a jerk and they both knew it.

She spoke in a gentle tone that shamed him more than sarcasm. "Tell me, Mr. Garrison. Are you *always* this mean?"

"You bet I am." Determined to have the last word, he walked out the door, leaving Dr. Mitchell adrift in the sea of broken glass.

Chapter Four

Nora hugged her waist and shivered, but not from a chill.

She shouldn't have touched Zeb Garrison's arm, but she'd seen the trauma in his eyes when he'd spoken of the tornado. When he turned to the window, she'd felt compelled to comfort him. She didn't know about tornadoes, but she understood suffering. She wanted to dislike Mr. Garrison for his arrogance, but that moment had peeled back his bitter facade and revealed a genuine concern for High Plains.

"Not that genuine," she said out loud.

She hadn't been fooled by his acceptance of her offer. He'd agreed to the one-month trial out of desperation, and because he didn't think she could find a suitable office. Like most men, he'd underestimated her.

So far, she hadn't seen anything that couldn't be fixed. The cracked windows could be tolerated, and she could scrub away the dirt. The broken apothecary jars could be swept into a bin, and she could wax the floor herself. Nora glanced at the ceiling. He'd told her the roof had a hole, but he hadn't said how big it was. Considering his eagerness to get rid of her, he'd probably exaggerated the damage. If necessary, she'd put on pants, climb a ladder and cover it with a tarp until she could hire someone to replace the shingles.

When that would be, she didn't know. She had just enough money to get back to New York and didn't want to use her emergency fund. Even if she found a different office, she couldn't afford the rent. The salary she'd negotiated would pay her living expenses, but money would be tight until she had patients. Everything depended on the condition of the roof.

Something rattled on the second floor. She looked up and saw a huge watermark. Her heart sank, but she refused to give up hope. The size of the stain didn't have to match the size of the hole. Rainwater could have puddled and spread. She had to make this office work. If she didn't succeed in High Plains, she'd end up back in New York married to Albert Bowers.

She walked to the stairs and started to climb. As the risers creaked, she heard the chirp of birds. The twittering reminded her of a truth she'd almost forgotten. The Lord had His eye on the sparrow. He knew every hair on her head. Surely He'd provide for her.

Hope welled in her chest, but so did fear. Had she been crazy to think the Lord had led her to this place? Had she been too prideful to listen to her father? Fear dragged her down the road that started with her brother's death. She'd been so sure God had called her to heal. She'd fought to go to medical college. She'd prayed. She'd worked. Most of all, she'd trusted.

Alone in this dirty building, she felt her faith withering like a drought-stricken vine.

The chirping intensified into a symphony of sorts. Nora whispered a prayer. "I need Your help, Lord."

Peering up the stairs, she made a decision. If she could cover the hole with a tarpaulin, she'd stay. If it was beyond repair, she'd consider going back with the Crandalls.

She climbed the stairs slowly, gripping the railing because she didn't trust the steps. She reached the first landing and looked up into darkness. A good sign, she decided. If the roof had been gaping, there'd be light. She climbed the second flight. It ended at a closed door that explained the darkness.

With a prayer on her lips, she opened the door and saw a shaft of light. A hundred birds took flight, funneling upward through a hole the size of a bathtub. The fluttering wings stole her breath, her dreams, and she burst into tears. She couldn't do it. She could scrub and clean, but she couldn't fix the roof.

She slid to her knees and wept. Zeb Garrison had won. Unless something happened, she'd be leaving High Plains with the Crandalls. With her face buried in her hands, she cried out in groans beyond words.

Why, Lord? Why did you bring me here?

Something birdlike touched her shoulder. Startled, she looked up and saw a girl with white-blond hair. She guessed her to be fifteen years old, a girl on the cusp of womanhood. The child didn't speak, but her blue eyes shimmered with intelligence. In that silent exchange, Nora received more compassion than she'd experienced in months. Her tears didn't shame her. This child understood and wanted to help her. Then the danger of their situation struck home, and Nora gasped. There were on the upper level of a storm-damaged building, standing on a floor that had been compromised further by water from a leaky roof. They needed to leave straightaway before one—or both—of them fell right through the floor. Nora took a deep breath and reminded herself to stay calm and not spook the girl.

Nora wiped her eyes. "Hi. I'm Dr. Nora."

The girl nodded but didn't speak. Perhaps she was deaf.

Nora's feet were tingling from a lack of blood, so she slid to a sitting position. "What's your name?"

The girl didn't answer.

"Can you hear me, or do you read lips?" Nora tried again.

The girl opened her mouth, then clamped it shut. She looked down at the floor then looked up at the sound of a bird chirping on the roof. Well, that answered *that* question.

"That's good," Nora said, encouraging her. "You can hear pretty sounds, like music and birds."

The girl smiled at that, then tipped her head, as if to ask a question. *Why are you here?*

Instead of answering, Nora did a cursory assessment. The girl could hear, and seemed to want to speak. If she'd been born mute, the instinct to open her mouth to reply to a question wouldn't be there. Her neck showed no sign of injury, an indication her vocal cords hadn't been damaged. Without an apparent physical cause, Nora suspected her muteness had hysterical origins, perhaps related to the tornado. The pieces clicked into place. This was the girl the Crandalls had told her about.

"You're Bess," Nora said. "Bess Carter." The girl—Bess—nodded.

"Are you in town with your sister?" The Crandalls had said that Bess's sister Emmeline had married town cofounder Will Logan, and that they all lived on the Circle-L ranch, outside of town.

"I'd like to meet her."

The girl shrugged as if to say okay, then pushed to her feet. Nora stood, too. "I'll follow you." And do her best to make sure Bess wasn't injured on her way out of the rickety building.

As the girl led the way down the stairs, Nora took in her appearance. She was so slight the risers didn't creak. Blonde and pale, she had a serenity that reminded Nora of a painting she'd seen at medical college. The artist had depicted angels guarding a surgery from above. Bess had the same expression.

The realization blasted through her like Gideon's trumpet. God had sent a child—a damaged child—to keep her in High Plains. Bess needed help. No way could Nora leave. She couldn't work in this building, but surely the Lord would provide a place for her. As she followed Bess to the first floor, Nora nearly danced with joy. She belonged here. She had a purpose.

A woman's voice drifted in from the street. "Bess! Where are you?"

The girl scampered outside. As Nora came down the last step, Bess dragged a dark-haired woman through the door.

"Bess!" the woman scolded. "You shouldn't be in there. It's dangerous!"

"I agree," Nora called from the stairs. "Let's talk outside."

The woman peered into the gloom. When she saw Nora, her eyes widened with curiosity. "I don't believe we've met."

"I'm Dr. Nora Mitchell. I just arrived, and you're right. This building isn't fit for pigs." As she crossed the room, Nora brushed the dust from her skirt. "You must be Bess's sister."

"I am."

"It's nice to meet you." Nora smiled, but Emmeline didn't see it. She'd turned to her sister and was tipping up Bess's chin with her index finger, forcing the girl to look into her eyes, as if she couldn't understand any other way. "You scared me, Bess. Don't run off, okay?"

The girl pulled back and turned to Nora. Her eyes told a story, but Nora couldn't read it. She only knew Bess had something buried in her psyche. Nora had never been shy, particularly when it came to children.

"What were you doing in there, anyway?" Emmeline asked Bess, though she clearly didn't expect an answer.

"That would be my fault," Nora replied. "I went upstairs to check the roof. She followed me."

The woman looked at Nora as if seeing her for the first time. "You're the new doctor, the one Zeb's been bragging about."

"He's not bragging anymore." Nora indicated her dress. "He wasn't expecting a woman."

Emmeline laughed. "I wish I could have seen his face! I like Zeb. He's my husband's best friend, but he's got some wrong ideas, especially about women."

Nora wanted to hug Emmeline Logan. For the first time, she felt welcome in High Plains. "It's a pleasure to meet you, Mrs. Logan."

"Call me Emmeline."

"Then I'm Nora."

The brunette patted her sister's arm. "I want to talk to Dr. Mitchell. Go find Will, all right?"

Bess turned to go, then looked back at Nora as if they had a secret. Nora supposed they did. Bess had seen her at her weakest point since leaving New York. That moment made them friends. Nora waggled her fingers. "Bye, Bess. I'll see you later."

After waving back, the girl scurried through the door. Emmeline followed her with her eyes, then turned back to Nora. Her eyes glistened with the desperation Nora saw every time she tended an ailing child.

"Please, Dr. Mitchell," she said quietly. "Will you help my sister?"

Nora's doubts about staying had already burned to cinders. Emmeline's plea blew away the ash. "I'll do my best. How long has she been mute?"

"Just since the storm."

"Was she injured?"

"Not exactly," Emmeline replied. "Doc Dempsey examined

her, but he didn't find anything wrong. I keep wondering if it's in her head, or if she's hurt and can't tell us. Maybe she—"

Nora interrupted. "Can she cough?"

"Yes." Emmeline's brows collided. "What does that mean?"

"Coughing indicates functional vocal cords. I suspect Bess's problem is psychological, and that it's related to the trauma of the tornado."

Emmeline bit her lip, then spoke in a low, frightened tone. "Do you think she's gone crazy?"

"Far from it." Nora had seen the girl's intelligence, her compassion. "In some ways, her reaction is logical. Not speaking keeps the memories of the tornado from surfacing. Do you know what happened to Bess during the storm?"

Emmeline bit her lip. "I can barely talk about it myself."

Nora hated to push, but she needed Emmeline's help. So did Bess. "I know about the twins."

"Mikey and Missy have been missing for weeks now." Emmeline turned to the open door. Sunlight silhouetted her upswept hair and the slope of her shoulders. She spoke to the sky to keep from looking at the damage still evident on the street. "The twins are orphans. My parents took them in for the trip to Oregon. We think Bess saw the twins get snatched."

Nora pictured flying bodies and shivered. "I see."

"We were headed to Oregon with a wagon train, but we'd separated from the rest of the group when they stopped to wait out the storm while we pushed on ahead. When the storm flipped our wagon, my father was crushed under an ox. After that, we saw Kansa warriors—" She bent her neck. "I just want to forget."

"So does Bess," Nora said gently. "But she won't recover until she lets herself remember."

Emmeline shuddered.

Nora stepped to her side. "I have a colleague in New York who's an expert in problems like Bess's. With your permission, I'd like to write to Dr. Zeiss about your sister."

Tears welled in Emmeline's eyes. "I'd be grateful if you would, but I'm afraid to hope."

"I'm not." Nora thought of her little brother. "What scares *me* is doing nothing."

Emmeline turned back to the inside of the building. Instead of focusing on Nora, she scanned the glass on the floor and the dirty walls. "Zeb doesn't expect you to practice here, does he?"

Nora looked at the mess with Emmeline. "He doesn't expect me to practice anywhere. If he has his way, I'll leave tomorrow with the Crandalls."

"He refused to hire you?" Emmeline's brows shot up. "That's just plain stupid! I don't care if you're a woman. This town needs a doctor. And Bess—"

Nora held up her hand. "I'm not leaving. He agreed to a one-month trial, but there's a catch. I have to find my own office."

"Maybe Will can help." Her cheeks turned a pretty pink. "He's my husband."

"I'd appreciate anything he could do."

"I'll speak to him," Emmeline said. "But there's something else I have to say."

"Of course." Nora appreciated frank talk.

Emmeline paused to measure her words. "Zeb's not a bad person. He's just…troubled."

"I'd have said prejudiced."

"Maybe," Emmeline replied. "Mostly he blames himself for what happened after the storm. Doc did his best, but he couldn't keep up and people died. If Zeb had found a new doctor sooner, lives might have been saved."

Nora understood guilt. She felt responsible every time she lost a patient until she remembered only God had the power to give and take life. She thought of Zeb Garrison's eyes, the same color as the broken glass on the floor, and she wondered if his bitterness ran deeper. "Did he lose someone special in the tornado?"

"No," Emmeline said. "But he lost someone in Boston."

A wife? Was he a widower? Nora's heart clenched for him. "Please, give him my condolences."

"Oh, no!" Emmeline corrected herself. "It's nothing like that."

Then what is it? Nora wanted to know more, but she couldn't ask without being guilty of gossip.

The brunette shook her head. "I'm talking too much. It's just that I like Zeb. He can be difficult, but deep down he's a good man."

Nora gave a wry smile. "Considering the deal we negotiated, I'd say he's a bit of a scoundrel."

Emmeline grinned. "He is, but in a good way."

A good scoundrel? Nora had seen the two sides of the man for herself. His prejudice toward women annoyed her, but he cared deeply about High Plains. Beneath his arrogant gaze, she'd seen suffering. Instead of disliking him, she found herself worrying about him. Not wise, she told herself. She had a practice to build and people who needed her, including a girl who couldn't speak. She didn't have time to worry about a man who was determined to dislike her. She decided to change the subject.

"I'll write to Dr. Zeiss tonight," she said to Emmeline.

"I'd be grateful. We'll pay you, of course."

As much as Nora needed patients, she couldn't charge the Logans. She had an interest in psychiatry, but she didn't have the expertise to consider Bess a patient. Helping the girl was an act of friendship. "Bess's situation is unique," she said. "There's no charge."

"But—"

"I insist." Nora never took money from her friends. "When can I visit with her?"

"Anytime," Emmeline answered. "She helps Rebecca at the boardinghouse. You're staying there, aren't you?"

Nora recalled Mr. Garrison's original plan for room and board. "It's my new home."

"Then you'll see a lot of her. I'm glad you're here, Dr. Mitchell." Emmeline held out her hand. "Welcome to High Plains."

Nora gripped Emmeline's hand in both of hers. "I'm Nora, remember?"

"How about Dr. Nora? I like how that sounds."

"So do I." She beamed a smile.

As the brunette headed for the door, Nora followed her outside to the boardwalk. The ping of hammers pulled her attention to the half-finished building across the street. Judging by the size and location, she was looking at the new town hall, a building Mr. Crandall had described during the trip.

Two men stood on scaffolding about six feet apart, each holding the end of a board and nailing it in place. A third man stood below them, shouting instructions over the racket. She recognized Zeb Garrison and felt the low beat of anger in her pulse. She could tolerate his rudeness. It came with being a woman in a man's world. But how could he justify running her out of town? High Plains desperately needed a doctor. With the construction, men were sure to have accidents. Emmeline Logan had recently married. God willing, she and her husband would start a family of their own. And Bess…who would help her speak again?

The more Nora thought about Bess and Emmeline, the hotter her blood ran. Instead of treating her like a quack, Zeb

Garrison should have been helping her find a suitable office. He deserved an earful, but she couldn't escape the memory of her father's voice.

Before you speak your mind, daughter, count to ten. If that doesn't settle you down, count to a hundred.

The harder she tried to calm herself, the angrier she became. Emmeline saw the good in him, but Nora saw the arrogance. "Help me, Lord," she murmured. "I don't want to turn the other cheek. I want to tell that arrogant, self-righteous *scoundrel* what I think of him." She wanted to fight. She wanted—

Before she could finish the thought, he turned and caught her staring. He smirked. Furious, Nora started to count. "Ten, nine… Forget it!"

With her temper flaring, she headed across the street to give Zeb Garrison a piece of her mind.

Chapter Five

Zeb saw Dr. Mitchell coming straight at him and felt the uncomfortable urge to run away. He enjoyed a good fight as much as any man, but he didn't want to argue with *her*. A few moments ago, Will had taken him to task.

You showed her Doc's place? Are you stupid?

No, just hopping mad. She'd tricked him by using her initial, then she'd had the audacity to be poised and pretty about it. Why couldn't she have had warts on her chin…warts with hairs growing out of them? Warts so ugly he wouldn't keep smelling lavender and recalling her hand on his arm and the kindness in her blue eyes.

He'd argued with Will for two minutes and ended up feeling like an oaf.

We need a doctor, Zeb. I don't care if he—she—whatever—is wearing skirts. I've got a family now. So does Pete.

Where am I supposed to put her? She can't work in my parlor!

So find someplace else. We help each other in High Plains. Have you forgotten that? It's called Christian charity.

Will was right. The town needed Dr. Mitchell until he could

find a replacement. And whether he liked it or not, he owed her amends for his surliness.

Tom Briggs, his foreman, called down from the scaffolding. "More lumber tomorrow, boss?"

"Plan on it."

"Good." Tom's hammer pinged on a nail. "We're about out."

The demand for lumber kept Garrison Mill running from dawn to dusk and Zeb looking at ledgers well past midnight. Folks chipped in what money they could spare, but Zeb cheerfully absorbed most of the costs. He could afford it and others couldn't. With good weather and a little luck, the town hall would be finished and High Plains would celebrate a full recovery with a summer jubilee. If he had to work like a mule to make it happen, so be it. He didn't have time to eat or sleep, much less deal with Dr. Mitchell, but she was coming at him like a summer storm.

"Mr. Garrison!" she called. "I need a word with you."

He did *not* want to have this conversation in front of a work crew, but he couldn't avoid her without looking cowardly. "Get back to work," he said to the man. The hammering resumed, but in a slower cadence.

As she hurried in his direction, he heard the rustle of her skirts and the scuff of her shoes, sounds that should have been drowned out by hammering, but Tom and the other man had stopped working. Zeb felt their eyes on his back, turned to glare at them and realized he'd been wrong. The men weren't looking at *him*. They were gawking at Dr. Mitchell.

Briggs, a married man, went back to work. The other fellow looked like a starving man at Sunday supper.

"What do you want?" he demanded.

"Thank you for speaking with me." Panting for breath, she put her hand on her chest in an Abigail-like gesture.

He hadn't judged her as prone to vapors. "Are you all right?"

"I'll be fine," she said. "I came to thank you for setting me straight."

Zeb liked this kind of talk. "About what?"

"What it's *really* like in High Plains. How *hard* my life would be here." She bit her lip, then blinked as if fighting tears. Her eyes had a shine and he wondered if he'd made her cry. He hoped not, but the sheen revealed a simple fact. If Doc's office could drive her to tears, she didn't belong in High Plains.

He crossed his arms over his vest. "It's tough here. That's a fact."

"It's such a warm day! Too hot for a woman to be hurrying, don't you think?" She took a hankie from her pocket and dabbed at her forehead. "I thought I could hire someone to fix the roof, but the hole's too big."

"I know."

"I went upstairs to check for myself. There were *birds* everywhere." She indicated the smudges on her skirt. "I ruined my *best frock!*"

Well, what do you know? Dr. Mitchell had just proven him right about women. Knowing she wouldn't stay longer than necessary, he could afford to be magnanimous. "I'll pay for the laundering."

"That's kind of you, but I'm not worried about the dress."

"Then what is it?"

The simpering female vanished in a blink. "I came to tell you that you're a fool, Mr. Garrison. I am *not* the shallow woman you've assumed me to be. Being who you are—a town leader, someone who's responsible and intelligent—you *know* High Plains needs a doctor. You should be helping me, not running me out of town! It's reckless. It's selfish. It's—"

"Stop it, Doc." Belatedly, he saw through her act. The woman was playing him. "You've made your point."

"I don't think so, Mr. Garrison."

"I do."

"You owe me an apology." She stood tall, her head high and her eyes burning with outrage.

Zeb said nothing.

After twenty seconds, she gave up. "Don't think you've won. At the very least, I deserve courtesy. As for your respect, I intend to earn it. When the time comes for you to eat crow, I'll expect that apology."

"You won't get it."

"It's not for *my* benefit," she said. "It's for yours. I'm assuming you *do* have a conscience?"

Zeb had a conscience, all right. It prickled every time someone in High Plains caught a cold. It twitched when he thought of his men working double shifts and ignoring their own families. It burned like fire when he thought of the tornado and how it had stripped High Plains bare. *He'd* picked this spot to settle. The death and destruction were on *his* hands. So was rebuilding. How dare this woman judge him? "You don't belong here, Doc. Go back to New York."

"I can't."

"Sure you can."

"Absolutely not! I care about people. I care about this town."

"You think I don't? I saw people *die* in the tornado, Miss Mitchell. What happens if you kill someone with your incompetence?"

"I'm not incompetent! I'm a highly trained physician."

"You're a *woman!*"

When the hammering stopped for the second time, Zeb realized he'd shouted at her. By tomorrow, the whole town would know he'd done battle with Dr. Mitchell. No way could he let her win.

She must have felt the same way, because she spoke in a voice loud enough for the work crew to hear. "You're very observant, Mr. Garrison. I am, in fact, *female*. I'm also a doctor, and I will *not* leave High Plains."

Zeb dropped his voice to a hush. "You'll break your word, Dr. Mitchell. Mark my words."

"Not a chance."

Like Frannie, she made promises too easily. "We'll see, won't we?"

When she stepped closer, he smelled her fancy lavender soap, reminding him of Frannie. Women were all alike—two-faced Jezebels with heady ambitions and flapping tongues.

Dr. Mitchell took another step, crowding him because he refused to budge as she lectured him. "You, Mr. Garrison, have misjudged me. I don't care about smudges on a dress. I don't mind scrubbing floors. But I will *not* be disrespected."

Zeb knew the feeling. The need for respect had driven him to build a mill instead of working for wages. Her breathing deepened and slowed as she fought for control. When she clenched her jaw, he imagined her counting to ten. The trick wouldn't work. Zeb knew, because he used it himself.

He flashed a grin. "Cat got your tongue, Doc?"

She raked his face with those fiery blue eyes. "You need to know what happened after you left."

"I don't care." He'd lied. He cared about everything in High Plains.

The redhead kept yammering at him. "You *should* care, Mr. Garrison. A girl came into the building. Bess Carter."

"She can't speak."

"That's right." Dr. Mitchell spoke in a rush. "I'm a grown woman. I'm accustomed to adolescent pranks from silly little boys—"

"Wait just a minute!"

"No, sir." She clipped the words. "I will *not* wait. That building should be boarded up. What if the roof had collapsed on her? You endangered a child today, a girl who couldn't call for help. You should be ashamed of yourself."

He was, but he'd never admit it. "Anything else, *Dr.* Mitchell?"

"Yes," she said. "With or without your help, I intend to find a place to practice."

"Good luck." He smirked at her.

"I won't quit," she repeated.

Zeb stared at her with a mix of disbelief and envy. Where had that faith come from? Didn't she know life took dangerous turns? He flung up his hand to indicate the framework of the town hall. "Are you blind, Doc? A tornado blew this town to pieces. There's not an inch of space that's not being used except *my* parlor."

"I don't need your parlor," she countered.

"Good, because you can't have it."

She stood ramrod straight. Zeb had a good six inches on her, but he felt no advantage. This woman had courage, the kind that made a small dog chase a bigger one. Of all the aggravating things, she reminded him of someone he used to know…not Frannie, but a young man who'd called on the foremost millwright in America.

I want to be your apprentice, Mr. Gridley.

So do a lot of men, Mr. Garrison. Why should I pick you?

Because I want it, sir.

Zeb had been full of faith that day, faith in God and faith in his dreams. Gridley had seen that confidence and taken him under his wing. A month later, the man arranged a dinner party to introduce his protégé to his upper-crust friends. Zeb had escorted Cassandra, but that night he'd fallen in love with Frannie.

Hammering pulled him back to the present. High Plains needed a doctor, not a debutante from New York. He couldn't stand the sight of Dr. Mitchell and her red hair. As for her skills, he'd trust her to paint sore throats but nothing else.

She waved her hand to get his attention. "Mr. Garrison? Did you hear me?"

He'd been caught off guard and didn't like it. "What?"

"I said, when I have a parlor of my own, I expect you to apologize."

"Sure," he said, mocking her. "Why not?"

"I'm serious."

"So am I." He'd never been more sure in his life. "You don't have a prayer of finding an office, Dr. Mitchell. No one here wants a lady doctor." Except Pete and Rebecca, Cassandra and Emmeline and Will and anyone with kids.

"I'll have to change their minds, won't I?" With a dip of her chin, she headed back to the street.

Her skirts swayed with lady-like grace, but Zeb saw past the poise. He'd just kicked a hornet's nest. He felt the sting of it now. Even more confusing, instead of running *away* from the hornet named Nora Mitchell, he wanted to chase after her. He wanted to see the sparks in her blue eyes and the waves of her red hair. That desire couldn't be tolerated.

"Dr. Mitchell!" he called.

She stopped and turned. "Yes, Mr. Garrison?"

"The Crandalls leave tomorrow. If you're smart, you'll go with them."

She turned fully, giving him a good look at the high-and-mighty dress and the feather that had tickled his nose. "I assure you, sir, the Crandalls will be leaving without me. You may not like my gender. You might not trust my abilities. But I'm a good doctor. I also have a conscience. The people in this town need me."

Yes, they do.

Pride sealed his lips, but he didn't turn away. Neither did she. They glared at each other until she gave a ladylike dip of her chin, followed by a smile and a sly wink.

Completely disarmed, Zeb couldn't think of a thing to say. The redheaded doctor had thrown down the gauntlet. They'd gone to war and he wanted to win. He also imagined kissing that smirk right off her pretty face. He had no right to such a thought, but he couldn't help it. Dr. Mitchell had gotten to him. For that reason alone, she needed to go back to New York.

Nora kept her chin high as she crossed the street, but her insides were churning. Winking at Zeb Garrison bordered on shameless. What had she been thinking? Even more frightening, what was *he* thinking? The wink had been a trick she'd learned from male students who'd harassed her. Whenever a man made that presumptuous gesture, she felt flustered. She doubted a wink would fluster Zebulun Garrison, but she hoped so.

"Oh, dear," she mumbled as she avoided the broken boardwalk. What if he misread the wink as flirting? They'd been alone in Dr. Dempsey's office when she touched his arm. She'd acted out of concern, but she'd felt something stronger, a connection that made her notice his green eyes, the stubble on his jaw. Winking at Zeb Garrison had been a mistake. Either she'd insulted her new boss, or he'd take it as a brazen invitation. At the thought of seeing him again, she stifled a groan. In a town the size of High Plains, their paths would cross no matter how hard she tried to avoid him.

Eager to escape the prickle of his gaze on her back, she rounded the corner and headed for the boardinghouse. There she climbed the steps, walked into the foyer and smelled fresh bread. The aroma reminded her of her empty stomach, so she went to the kitchen where she saw a tall blonde, presumably Rebecca, stirring a pot of soup. She hoped the cook would be pleasant. Even more than food, Nora needed a friend.

She tapped on the door frame. "Hi, are you Rebecca?"

Recognition lit the woman's eyes. "You must be Dr. Mitchell!"

Judging by her accent, the cook had recently come from Scandinavia. "That's right," Nora replied.

Rebecca indicated a small table by a window overlooking a meadow. "Please, sit down. Mrs. Jennings told me to expect you."

"I don't want to be a bother."

"You're not," the cook replied. "I'm eager to speak with you. Pete, my husband, was just here. There's already talk about you and plenty of it!"

Nora forced a smile. "I'm afraid Mr. Garrison wasn't expecting a woman."

"That's the truth!"

Unsure of the cook's opinion, Nora measured her words. "I'm a good doctor. I may be female, but—"

"Glory! You don't have to explain to me. My grandmother was a healer in Norway." The cook pointed at the chair. "Sit. You must be hungry."

"Starved is more like it," Nora admitted.

"We'll eat together, and I'll tell you about High Plains."

As the cook ladled soup into bowls and sliced bread, she told Nora how the town had been founded on Christmas Day almost two years ago. Will Logan and Zeb Garrison, boyhood friends, had come West to pursue their dreams. They'd picked the spot on the High Plains River and contracted with the New England Emigrant Aid Society for funding. When spring arrived, dozens of folks from Bellville, their hometown near Boston, followed the men to the Kansas Territory.

"My Pete is a blacksmith," Rebecca explained. "Will and

Zeb especially wanted him to come West." In between spoonfuls of soup, Rebecca told Nora how Pete's first wife had died in childbirth. When the cook finished the story, she looked at Nora with a gleam in her eyes. "I don't care what people think, Dr. Mitchell. Pete and I want you here. You won't have an easy time. I know, because I didn't either. More than once, I've been called a dirty immigrant."

Nora's family had sailed with the Pilgrims, but she and Rebecca had something in common. "We're both outsiders, aren't we?"

"Very much." Rebecca fetched the teakettle and refilled their cups. "That's why I want to talk to you about the Ladies Aid Society. Matilda Johnson is president. She and her husband own the mercantile."

"I already met Abigail."

Rebecca sat down. "She and her mother are very much alike, if you know what I mean."

"I think I do."

The cook's brows hitched into a scowl. "I'm not fond of Mrs. Johnson and she's not fond of me."

"If you don't mind my asking, what happened?"

"Pete and I were alone in a cellar during the tornado. She accused me of immoral behavior and spread rumors. I couldn't walk down the street without getting ugly looks."

Nora knew the feeling. "I got plenty of stares in medical college."

"But we survived, didn't we?" A smile lit up Rebecca's face. "Pete married me to stop the talk. We didn't know it, but God had plans for us. What Mrs. Johnson meant for harm turned into the greatest blessing of my life."

Envy stabbed through Nora. She loved being a doctor, but she wanted a husband and children of her own. "Pete sounds like a good man."

"He is." Pride rang in her voice. "Most of the folks here are decent, but a few cause trouble."

"Like Mrs. Johnson?"

"I'm afraid so." Rebecca's eyes glinted with anger. "She's telling folks you asked Abigail an indecent question."

"Illness is indecent," Nora countered. When a woman fainted, all possibilities—even indelicate ones—had to be considered.

Rebecca's eyes twinkled. "*I* know why Abigail swooned. She's set her cap for Zeb, that's why."

"I thought so," Nora said casually.

The blonde studied Nora from across the table. Both women stirred their tea until their lips tipped up in unison. When Rebecca gave in to a grin, so did Nora. The cook spoke first. "Are we thinking the same thing?"

"I don't know," Nora answered. "What are you thinking?"

Her blue eyes twinkled. "I'm thinking Abigail Johnson has some competition, and I'm glad for it. If Zeb didn't notice that pretty hair of yours, he's blind."

Nora's cheeks turned pink. Zeb Garrison, for all his faults, had excellent vision. When he'd looked her up and down in the office, he'd noticed her hair and the dress, too.

"It doesn't matter what he sees," Nora insisted. "My gender has nothing to do with my medical skills."

Rebecca grinned. "True, but you're still a woman and I'm sure he noticed."

Nora felt herself blush, but she shrugged off Rebecca's comment. "Abigail doesn't need to worry about competition from *me*. I want a husband and family as much as any woman, but I'm here to be a doctor."

Rebecca's hand went to her belly in the way of expecting women, or women with that hope. "We need you, Dr. Nora."

"And I need an office," she replied. "Do you think Mrs. Jennings would let me use a room here?"

"We're full to the rafters."

"Is there space at the church?"

"I don't think so," Rebecca replied. "Why don't you do what my grandmother did. People didn't come to her. She went to them."

The idea had merit. She'd see where people lived and get to know their families. Her patients wouldn't have privacy, but the plan would give her a start.

"I'll do it," she declared. "I'll visit every person in High Plains." Everyone *except* Zeb Garrison.

Rebecca raised her cup in a toast. "To you, Dr. Mitchell. May God bless your efforts."

"Please, call me Nora." She lifted her teacup in a salute to the future. She'd knock on every door. She'd call on every family. She wouldn't skip anyone. Like Joshua circling Jericho, she'd walk circles around High Plains, seven times if that's what it took to win the town's trust. Zeb Garrison wouldn't run her out of High Plains. She wouldn't allow it.

"To success!" she said.

As the women toasted with their cups, Nora felt blessed. Surely the Lord would guide her steps.

Chapter Six

"Cassandra, don't."

"You can't tell me what to do," his sister replied. "If I want to see Percival, I will."

Zeb pushed back from the breakfast table. Thanks to his sister, he had indigestion in spite of Mrs. Wright's perfectly fried bacon. The woman had been with the wagon train, traveling West with her husband and grown son. The men had died in the storm, leaving her as alone as a woman could be. Zeb hired her to cook and clean. With Cassandra busy getting ready for the school year, he needed the help.

What he didn't need was his sister's interest in Percival Walker. An attorney by trade, Percy had been hired by the New England Emigrant Aid Society to keep an eye on their investment. The man came from Boston money and it showed. Zeb disliked him, not because he had money but because of the way he threw his weight around.

The way you did with Dr. Mitchell.

He stifled a groan. Why wouldn't his conscience shut up? Four days had passed since her arrival, and he'd awoken each morning with a sense of guilt. He'd been a brute. He knew it.

He owed her an apology, but he wasn't about to seek out the woman who kept winking at him in his dreams. What had she meant by that wink? He didn't know and he refused to care. Right now, he had to deal with Cassandra, who'd just announced she'd be "lunching" with Percy. People in Boston "lunched." People in High Plains broke bread. Zeb preferred breaking bread.

He looked down at his sister, still seated and defiantly sipping tea from a porcelain cup. Cassandra set the cup down with a plink, then looked up at him. "I don't understand. Why don't you like Percy?"

"He's a dandy."

"He's a businessman," she insisted. "Like you."

"He's nothing like me." Zeb paced to the window. Turning his back, he rubbed his eye to stop it from twitching. He'd downed four cups of coffee, but the hot brew couldn't replace a good night's sleep. He'd been awake long past midnight, working on plans for the mill. As soon as High Plains was strong again, he planned to change the saw blades into millstones.

He didn't have time to waste arguing with his sister, especially when his opinion didn't matter. If it had, she'd have already married Clint Fuller. Zeb liked the cowboy. The man worked hard on Will's ranch, then came to town to help at the mill. Zeb knew he had his eyes on Cassandra because the cowboy had asked for permission to court her as soon as he had some money saved. Percy hadn't shown that courtesy. Just like a Boston bigwig, he'd presumed his attentions would be welcome. Unfortunately, from Cassandra's perspective, he'd been right.

Zeb turned away from the window. "I have to get to the mill."

His sister pouted. "Suit yourself."

Her tone irked him. "Do you think I *like* working sixteen hours a day?"

"No, but—"

"It's necessary, Cassandra. Winter's not far away. People need houses. I said the town hall would be done by the jubilee and I meant it."

"I know, Zeb. It's just that I'm so confused. Dr. Mitchell says—"

"What?"

"She came to the schoolhouse yesterday. We talked about Clint and Percy. She's smart and she has such *lovely* clothes. She says—"

"Hold on," Zeb ordered. Why was Nora Mitchell visiting his sister? And what kind of nonsense was she spouting? He got impatient with Cassandra, but he loved her and wanted her to have a good life. They just disagreed on what counted as "good." Considering Dr. Mitchell's background, he felt certain she'd side with Cassandra.

He crossed his arms. "Why were you talking to her?"

"Haven't you heard?"

"Heard what?"

"She's visiting everyone in town and introducing herself. I figured you knew."

Zeb only knew she'd winked at him, and in his dreams he winked back. "I don't know what she's up to. I thought she'd leave by now."

"Why would she do that?"

He said nothing.

"Zeb!" Cassandra scolded. "What did you do?"

"I didn't do anything." Now *he* sounded pouty. Annoyed, he lowered his arms and struck a more casual pose. "She needs a place to practice. Doc's office is a wreck, and she can't work in our parlor. I told her she's on her own. I can't help her."

"You mean you *won't* help her."

"I'm busy."

His sister shrugged. "It's all right. She doesn't need your help. I told her I'd ask Percy to find an office for her."

That figured. The Easterners were ganging up on him. "What's he going to do?" Zeb sneered. "Give her his office?"

"I don't know," Cassandra replied. "But he'll be polite about it, which is more than I can say for you. The whole town knows you yelled at her."

"Did the *whole town* tell you she yelled back?"

Cassandra's eyes twinkled. "I hear she put you in your place."

Zeb said nothing.

"You deserved it," she added. "Why would you show her Doc's place? It's a mess."

He'd hoped to run her out of town, but he couldn't admit that foolishness to Cassandra. She had him cornered. He couldn't lie and the truth condemned him again, so he took a side road. "She deserves to know what she's up against. Another tornado could hit. Indians could strike. You know the risks."

Her eyes misted. "You're thinking about the twins."

Those lost children were never far from his mind. Everyone in High Plains had helped with the search, to no avail.

Cassandra stood and lifted their plates. "I think about them a lot. Tornadoes don't hit in Boston. Sometimes I want to go home so badly—"

"I know, Cassie." He used the pet name she'd asked him to forget. "Just don't do it with Percy, okay?"

"I don't know what to think." She scrunched her face as if she were five years old again. "Percival treats me like a lady. He likes music and sometimes he quotes Shakespeare. But then there's Clint… He doesn't know about any of those things. He's gruff and tough and barely talks."

"A man doesn't need words to show what he means."

Cassandra looked at him as if he were crazy, but Zeb knew what he meant. He understood Clint just fine. The man loved Cassandra. He was working extra jobs to be able to marry her. That said "love" to Zeb. He knew because he'd loved Frannie with the same intensity. He'd never love like that again. He rubbed his jaw and felt bristles. Shaving took time he didn't have. So did speaking with Cassandra, but he wanted to know more about the lady doctor. "What else did Dr. Mitchell say?"

"About Percy and Clint?"

"About everything."

"Mostly we talked about clothes." Cassandra sounded dreamy. "She has wonderful gowns."

"I didn't notice," he said in a mocking tone. Of course he'd noticed. When he blinked, he saw green silk.

Cassandra ignored him. "I asked if she'd met Percy and she said yes, that he seemed like a gentleman."

"A fellow snob is more like it."

Cassandra sighed. "You don't know him at all."

"I know enough," Zeb argued. "The man hasn't done a day's work in his life. Now, take Clint—"

"Clint thinks he knows everything. Percival doesn't tell me what to do."

Zeb had to grit his teeth. "Clint's just trying to keep you safe. And so am I. I can't stop you from seeing Percy, Cassandra. Just be careful." He hated the thought of his little sister getting her heart broken by someone like Frannie.

Cassandra stood with the dirty dishes in hand, a reminder they hadn't always had servants in spite of her snooty tone. "If you don't mind, Zeb. I'll take Dr. Mitchell's advice instead."

His jaw tensed. "What did she tell you?"

"I won't say." Cassandra put her nose in the air. "You'd just get mad."

"I'm mad already." He raked his hand through his hair. "I want to know… *What did she tell you?*"

Cassandra had him by the scruff and she knew it. Chuckling, she headed for the door to the kitchen. "If you want to know what she's saying to people, ask her yourself."

Zeb didn't think folks would take her side, but he *had* been rotten to her.

Cassandra watched him thoughtfully. Then, as if she knew something Zeb didn't, as if that brazen redhead had enlisted his little sister in her army of pushy women, Cassandra winked at him. "See you later, big brother."

She swished through the doorway, leaving Zeb mad enough to hunt up Dr. Mitchell himself. Not right away. He had work to do. But later…after he'd counted to ten a dozen times and figured out what he wanted to do besides kiss her. He had to find a replacement so she could go back to New York. If she didn't leave soon, the town would go crazy and so would he.

"Everyone means everyone," Nora said out loud as she left the boardinghouse.

She'd finished a late breakfast and was headed to Garrison Mill. Its owner would doubtlessly bite her head off, but she had to take that chance. In the past few days, she'd visited everyone in High Plains except the man who'd hired her. Pete and Rebecca had been kind and she'd had a good visit with the Logan clan at the Circle-L, but most people had been reserved at best. A few had been hostile. As Nora turned down Main Street, she recalled various comments.

Mrs. Morrow, the dressmaker, had looked her up and down. *I'm in perfect health, miss. You should try another town.*

Winnie Morrow, her daughter, hadn't said a word. She was either shy or unfriendly.

Worst of all had been her visit to the mercantile. Mrs. Johnson had not so subtly questioned her morals. *A woman in medicine? That's indecent.*

Nora had run into *that* criticism before. Yes, she'd seen the male body, but there was nothing handsome about an old man with pleurisy or a young one who'd been gut shot. When it came to matters of life and death, Nora didn't see male and female. She saw suffering.

Last night, exhausted and despairing, she'd opened her Bible to the verse about loving her enemies as herself. She didn't want to be at odds with anyone. Instead, she found herself at odds with almost everyone and especially Zeb Garrison. As his name came to mind, she'd thought of her promise to visit *everyone* and had accepted the inevitable. She had to call on him at the mill.

What she'd say, she didn't know. She only knew she had to make this effort or face going home in failure. At the thought of marrying Albert Bowers, she shuddered. Zeb Garrison had his faults, but being stodgy wasn't one of them. She'd been up half the night arguing with him in her head. Sometimes she won the argument and walked away. Sometimes he winked and asked her to supper. Sighing, she scolded herself for such silly thoughts. Zeb Garrison didn't like her and never would.

As she neared the schoolhouse, Nora recalled her first meeting with Zeb's sister. Pete had asked Edward Gunderson, his helper and brother-in-law, to take her to nearby ranches. At the Circle-L, she'd visited with Emmeline and met Cassandra and a cowboy named Clint. Cassandra had taken a day off preparing for school to visit Emmeline. She'd been friendly and full of questions about New York. The girl had also mentioned Percival Walker, the town attorney, at least five times.

Nora had met Mr. Walker and been unimpressed. He'd

struck her as shallow and vain. On the other hand, she'd enjoyed Cassandra and had promised to loan her a *Godey's Lady's Book*. She had it tucked in her medical bag now.

"Dr. Nora!"

She turned and saw Cassandra waving her arm as she crossed the mill road. Nora stopped in front of the schoolhouse and waved.

When the brunette reached her, she held out her skirt to show it off. "How do I look?"

"Lovely." The rose-colored gown had a striped bodice and white sleeves. A straw bonnet with pink ribbons gave a sheen to the girl's dark hair.

"Do you think Percy will like it?"

"I'm sure he will."

"Good. We're having lunch today." Her eyes shone with excitement. "He asks me every Wednesday. This is the fourth time."

"Are you courting?"

She blushed. "I hope so."

What would that be like, Nora wondered, to blush at the mention of a man's name? How would it feel to be pursued? Maybe someday she'd know, but she had to dampen those thoughts until she succeeded as a physician.

Cassandra adjusted the tilt of her bonnet. "No matter what happens with Percy, I'm taking your advice."

Nora recalled chatting with the girl but not offering guidance. "What did I say?"

"That a woman needs the courage of her convictions."

"That's right."

She'd been talking with Emmeline and Cassandra on the porch. Bess had been with them, listening to every word as Nora described her struggle to become a doctor. Indirectly she'd been reaching out to Bess. Fear had stolen the girl's voice. Only courage could bring it back. Looking at Cassandra, Nora wondered why the comment had hit home.

The brunette took a breath. "You inspired me. I'm thinking of going back to Boston."

"You are?"

"Yes, but don't tell anyone."

"I won't." Nora couldn't imagine leaving High Plains. She already loved the high sky and rolling hills.

Cassandra's eyes lost their eagerness. "Zeb won't like it, but I don't care what he thinks."

Nora held in a groan. Unknowingly, she'd given Zeb Garrison another reason to resent her. He'd no doubt consider her a bad influence on his sister. "Have you mentioned it to him?"

"Not yet."

"It's a long trip," Nora said. "Do you have family in Boston?"

"Not anymore."

"Then how—"

The brunette blushed. "Percy's going back in a month, just as soon as he settles some business."

Nora envied the blush of excitement on Cassandra's cheeks, but she questioned the girl's wisdom. Did she have genuine feelings for Percy, or did she miss Boston? Nora suspected the latter and regretted sharing the *Godey's Lady's Book*. The pictures in the magazine would make Boston shine. She considered reneging on her promise to share it, but Cassandra's eyes drifted to the bag. A promise was a promise, so Nora opened the case. "I brought the *Lady's* book."

Cassandra grabbed it and squealed. "It's so new!"

"It's from June." She'd bought it the day she'd left New York.

"Thank you." The girl clutched it to her chest. "If I *do* go back, I want to fit in."

"You fit here, too," Nora said diplomatically.

Cassandra ignored her. "Who are you visiting today?"

"Your brother."

"I'll walk with you." She indicated a path to the river. "Let's go this way. It's pretty."

Nora appreciated the company *and* the shortcut. The mill road had ruts, dust and the danger of heavy wagons. The river filled her with peace.

As they ambled past the schoolhouse, Cassandra glanced at the color plate in the magazine. They talked about fashion, then the conversation turned to Nora's search for an office. Cassandra said she'd ask Percival to help. Nora appreciated the offer, but she doubted Mr. Walker's integrity. Not so subtly, he'd quizzed her about her father's profession—he owned a brickworks—then he'd suggested investments. If her father took his advice, she suspected Mr. Walker would earn a sizable fee.

He'd impressed her as self-centered, but she'd been wrong about people before. Her father had been quick to set her straight. *Don't judge too quickly, Nora. People aren't always what they seem.*

Walking with Cassandra, she wondered if that observation fit Zeb Garrison and decided it didn't. He was exactly what he seemed to be.

Charming and rude.

Generous but narrow-minded.

Kind to others but arrogant to her. She still hadn't decided what she'd say to him today. The Bible told her to love her enemies. She wanted to honor her faith, but Mr. Garrison and his prejudice tested her goodwill.

With the *Godey's* book tucked against her chest, Cassandra plucked a sunflower from the grass. "I was wondering. Have you ever been to a ball?"

"Just one." She'd been seventeen and Albert Bowers had asked her to dance. He'd smelled like liniment.

"I've been to three." Cassandra stared across the river as if she'd already gone back to Boston. "Zeb was engaged to Frannie, and I—"

"Who's Frannie?"

Her brows shot up. "I shouldn't have mentioned her. Zeb refuses to say her name."

Nora still had questions, but she also had an answer. A woman named Frannie had left her mark on Zeb Garrison's heart. Whether he'd been a cad and she'd left, or Frannie had left and he'd become bitter, she didn't know.

Cassandra rolled the stem of the sunflower between her fingers. It twirled like a dancer. "If it weren't for Frannie, we'd still be in Boston. We'd have a town house, and I'd be going to balls."

Nora didn't want to pry, but she needed information. The more she knew about Zeb Garrison, the better she could cope with his bias against female doctors. "What did Frannie do?"

"She jilted him."

Nora didn't like being called a spinster, but being left at the altar would have hurt more. "That must have been awful."

Cassandra shuddered. "Frannie showed up at the church just minutes before the wedding. She asked me to get Zeb."

Nora cringed for him. "I can't imagine."

"He talked to her, then he came down the aisle by himself, said something to the minister and told everyone to go home, that there wouldn't be a wedding. I've never seen him so…so hurt."

Clearly more than Zeb Garrison's pride had been wounded that day. Frannie had broken his heart.

Cassandra tossed the sunflower to the ground. "He disappeared for three days. He didn't tell anyone where he went, not even me. A week later, he and Will headed West. They scouted out land for this town, and now here I am."

"It's quite a change." A good one, Nora thought. She loved Kansas, but she understood Cassandra's homesickness. Empty meadows and dirt roads were a world away from city shops.

The girl turned wistful. "That first ball—it was wonderful. Even Zeb had a good time."

Nora pictured him dancing to the beat of an orchestra, dressed in black as he matched steps with a woman in fine silk. He had an inborn grace, an aristocratic air that explained his arrogance. She thought of the mill and the capital needed to start such a venture. "You must have been well-to-do."

Cassandra laughed. "Not at all. We grew up poor in a town outside of Boston. My father worked in the mill and so did Zeb."

"It's a big step to go from working in a mill to owning one." Nora respected his effort. "How did it happen?"

"Zeb owes everything to Jon Gridley. Have you heard of him?"

When Nora shook her head, Cassandra told how her brother had apprenticed with a famous millwright and inherited the man's wealth and his love of engineering. Cassandra finished with a sigh. "Don't ask Zeb about the mill. He'll bore you to tears."

Nora didn't think he'd be boring at all. It took a keen mind to design a mill and a bold man to build one in Kansas. Nora loved the open spaces, but she wasn't blind to the risks of weather and Indian attacks. On her list of Zeb Garrison's traits, she had to add courageous. Crazy, too. But no crazier than she'd been for making the same journey.

Cassandra peered at Nora through her thick lashes. "May I ask you something?"

"Sure."

"Why did you come to High Plains?"

"To practice medicine." The oft-repeated words tripped off her tongue.

"Why here?" The brunette waved her arm to indicate the lush meadow. "Why not stay in New York?"

"There's bias against female physicians—a lot of it," she replied. "When I saw your brother's advertisement, I jumped at the chance to start a practice of my own. I'm hoping the need will outweigh the prejudice."

"I hope so, too." Cassandra grinned. "But get ready. Zeb's going to fight you."

"I'll have to fight back," Nora said easily. "It won't be the first time."

As they rounded a bend in the path, she saw a low waterfall. The river spilled over the edge and raced through scattered boulders worn smooth by time. Below the falls stood Garrison Mill. The tall building had wood siding, a pitched roof, small windows and large doors for loading. A wagon stood ready in the yard. Near it she saw a saddled bay gelding. The creak and spill of the waterwheel mixed high tones with low ones, reminding her of Zeb Garrison's quarrelsome ways.

Nora wouldn't be haughty today. She wouldn't be proud, and she certainly wouldn't wink at him. She'd come in peace. To prove it, she'd acknowledge she'd been a bit harsh at their last meeting, then she'd ask him about the mill and how it worked. If she respected *his* work, perhaps he'd respect *hers* in return.

Building a mill was a monumental task, one akin to a woman becoming a doctor. Perhaps she and Zeb Garrison had more in common than she thought. Would that help her cause or hurt it? Nora didn't know, but she intended to find out.

Chapter Seven

"Did you just wink at me?" Pete said to Zeb.

"No!"

Zeb ground the heel of his hand into his eye and rubbed hard. "It's been twitching all morning."

The men were standing on the cutting floor. Pete had just delivered a saw blade he'd repaired, and they'd been talking about the town hall when Zeb's eye went bad.

The tic was driving him crazy. He'd stretched his eye wide. He'd squeezed it shut. He'd rubbed until it hurt, but he couldn't make the twitching stop. He'd been at the mill over an hour now. He'd greased the waterwheel, checked the gearing and inspected the logs delivered yesterday by the Thompson brothers. He'd been about to check the saws when Pete arrived with the blade. As the men attached it, Zeb's crew, including Clint Fuller for the day, had shown up for work and gotten busy.

The mill was going full bore, so he motioned Pete to follow him into the yard. "Let's get out of here."

As they escaped the noise and dust, Zeb tried again to stretch his eye. If it would quit twitching, he could work on the drawings for the dam and trace box. High Plains had enjoyed a fairly wet summer, but the river dropped a little each day. Zeb had to plan for all kinds of weather. A drought would leave the mill helpless unless he upgraded the design.

As they stepped into the sunlight, his eye twitched again.

When they reached the wagon, Pete looked at him thoughtfully. "My grandmother had that happen."

"How'd she get it to stop?"

"She didn't." The blacksmith wiped sawdust off his nose. "She dropped dead on the spot. The doc called it apoplexy."

"Great," Zeb muttered.

Pete kept a straight face, but his eyes twinkled. "You could ask Dr. Mitchell to look at it."

"No way," he answered. "I'm not getting within fifty feet of her."

Pete shrugged. "I like her."

"I don't."

"You don't like anyone from back East," he pointed out.

"I've got cause." His eye twitched again. "She's filling Cassandra's head with nonsense."

"Like what?"

"I don't know, but it's nonsense."

Pete laughed out loud.

"It's not funny." Zeb put his hands on his hips. "Cassandra wouldn't tell me what the woman said, but they met and now she's acting like the high-and-mighty Dr. Mitchell." He still couldn't believe his sister had winked at him. The thought made his eyelid twitch again. Maybe Cassandra had the same problem, but he didn't think so.

Pete rubbed at a clod of dirt on the wagon wheel. "Seems to me the Lord sent a fine woman to take care of this town."

Zeb had another opinion. "He sent a hoyden." Dr. Nora

Mitchell was bold and rude. He couldn't call her tomboyish, but she had that air.

Both men heard feminine laughter and looked toward the river. Zeb saw his sister, dressed in pink and white, coming up the path with Dr. Mitchell. Cassandra looked like strawberries and cream. Dr. Mitchell had on a coppery gown that reminded him of oak. Of all the trees he'd milled over the years, he liked oak the best. It was strong, beautiful and forgiving. Some woods were too brittle for a mechanical saw, but oak could take the pressure.

Pete turned back to Zeb. "Looks like the hoyden's headed this way."

To Zeb's consternation, his eye twitched again. As he rubbed it with his knuckle, Cassandra and Dr. Mitchell reached Pete's wagon. The blacksmith doffed his wide-brimmed hat. "It's good to see you, Cassandra. Doc, how's it going?"

The redhead smiled. "Very well, thank you."

Pete looked at Zeb, daring him to greet the women. To keep his eye from going berserk, he squinted at them. "What brings you ladies here?" He addressed Cassandra, but he was more curious about Dr. Mitchell.

His sister held up a *Godey's Lady's Book*. "Look what Dr. Nora gave me!"

Just what Cassandra didn't need, more fancy ideas about clothes. He didn't care for the silly poetry, either. It reminded him of Frannie. Still squinting, he glared at Dr. Mitchell. She looked mildly pained and he wondered why.

Pete interrupted. "Rebecca likes the recipes. Maybe she could borrow it next."

Dr. Mitchell looked pleased. "I'd be glad to share it. I've got older issues, too."

Cassandra looked at Zeb with a smirk. When had his little sister turned haughty? A few years ago, she'd been as sweet as a kitten. But then he'd taken her to Boston and she'd gotten prissy. Zeb had only himself to blame for her uppity ways. Annoyed, he frowned at her. "What brings you to the mill?"

"Dr. Nora was coming to see you, so I showed her the way." She turned to Pete. "Could you give me a ride back to town?"

"Sure."

When the blacksmith offered his hand to help Cassandra into the wagon, Zeb realized his friend's intention. He planned to leave him alone with Dr. Mitchell and his twitchy eye. With his luck, the eye would wink and she'd think he was playing her game. No way could he be alone with her. He needed his sister to stick around. "Cassandra, wait."

She looked over her shoulder with a gleam in her eye. She had revenge in mind for this morning's spat. She *knew* he didn't like Dr. Mitchell and was forcing him to put up with her.

"What is it, Zeb?" she said too sweetly.

He couldn't ask her to stay. That would be cowardly. He settled for a thin excuse. "Are you going back to the school or heading home?"

"*First* I'm having lunch with Percy."

"I know that."

"Then I'll be home," she added. "But later."

"Not too late," Zeb ordered.

Pete chuckled. "Don't worry, Zeb. They're *lunching* at the boardinghouse. Rebecca will keep an eye on them."

Cassandra flashed a grin. "*And* I want to read the *Godey's* book tonight. Thank you again, Nora."

Dr. Mitchell gave a stiff smile. "You're welcome."

Pete handed Cassandra up to the seat, climbed up next to her and snapped the reins. As the horses lumbered out of the yard, Zeb stared at his sister's back. Only three years separated them in age—he was twenty-five, she was twenty-two—but he felt a lifetime older. Heartache did that to a man. So did hard work. He felt Dr. Mitchell's gaze on his cheek. His eye didn't twitch, but his tongue was ready to give her a lashing. First she'd given Cassandra advice and now the *Godey's* book. How much could a man take?

Being careful to squint, he faced her. "Tell me, Dr. Mitchell. What kind of *advice* are you giving my sister?"

Her eyes—sky blue and sparkling—opened wide. "None really."

"Cassandra told me otherwise."

"She's a confused girl, Mr. Garrison." Dr. Mitchell looked troubled herself. "She heard something I said to Emmeline. I was speaking in regard to Bess, but your sister took it to heart."

"What did you say?"

She squared her shoulders. "That a woman needs the courage of her convictions."

What did *that* mean? The courage to jilt a fiancé and go to Paris? The courage to go to medical college and cut up cadavers? Or did it mean the courage to come West and start a new life? The courage to stare down a thunderstorm after surviving a tornado? Zeb's thoughts turned into a jumble. Wordless, he stared at her.

Dr. Mitchell wrinkled her nose in remorse, the way she'd wrinkled it in Doc's office. "I came today for a fresh start. I showed poor judgment at our last encounter."

"You hoodwinked me with that simpering-female act, so excuse me if I don't believe you now." He opened his eyes extra wide. Hopefully she'd take it as forceful, not an effort to control the tic.

"I won't apologize for staying, but—"

His eye twitched anyway. Not just a tic either. He gave her a full, unplanned and unmistakable wink.

Dr. Mitchell gasped. "You winked at me!"

Zeb held in a oath. "I didn't—"

"I'm so sorry!" She pressed her hands to her cheeks. "I know I started it. I should *never* have winked at you. It was brazen and rude."

Zeb liked her apology. He liked the high color of her cheeks and he liked having the upper hand. He also liked her honesty. Because of it, she deserved the truth. "I didn't wink at you, Doc. My eye's been twitching all morning."

"I see." She regained her composure in an instant and lowered her hands. "I know the cause."

If she looked into his eyes, he'd have to look into hers. Zeb did *not* want to cross that line, but neither did he want to end up dead like Pete's grandmother. He tried to sound casual. "So what is it? Apoplexy?"

Her pretty face crinkled with laughter. The musical tones tripped over him and filled his heart with a lightness he hadn't felt in a long time. The pleasure of it warmed him like sunshine on a cold day, but then he realized he was laughing with *Dr. Nora Mitchell.*

He pulled his mouth into a frown. "It's not apoplexy, is it?"

"That depends." With an impersonal expression, she studied his eye from two feet away. Zeb looked at fresh-cut trees the same way and realized she was seeing a human eye, not necessarily *his* eye. He had to respect her objectivity. She was all doctor as she raised her chin. "Have you been getting enough sleep?"

"Not really."

"Do you read a lot, Mr. Garrison?"

"All the time." He studied books on engineering, records for the mill.

"And coffee." She shifted her gaze from looking solely at

his eye to reading his expression. "I suspect you drink it strong and in large quantities."

As much as Zeb wanted her to be wrong, she'd gotten his attention. "That's right."

"What you have, Mr. Garrison, is a condition called blepharospasm. It's caused by fatigue, some beverages and eyestrain. Adequate sleep should stop the twitching. I'd also recommend turning up the lamp when you read."

Old men needed extra light. The next thing he knew, she'd be telling him to get spectacles. "Thanks," he said coldly. "I'll do fine without it."

"Whatever you say."

He wanted to annoy her. Instead, he saw joy in her eyes, and though she was trying to hide her elation, her lips tipped into a smile. She looked ready to dance and sing and wave a flag. He couldn't stand it. "Why do you look so happy?"

"You, Mr. Garrison, are my first patient in High Plains."

Of all the confounded ironies… Zeb wanted to be mad, but his eye felt better already, maybe because he'd smiled for the first time in a week. He thought of a few other "maybes," like maybe it wouldn't be so bad if she stayed. The thought lingered until he kicked it into next week. Not only did he distrust this woman as a doctor, she reminded him of Frannie. Any fool could see she'd come to High Plains because she couldn't find work anywhere else. If opportunity knocked, she'd be gone tomorrow.

Never mind his twitching eye and that "maybe" in his head. He'd be wise to keep this woman—all women—at arm's length. When it came to finding a wife, Abigail would be a far better choice because he'd never share his whole heart with her. Women, Zeb knew, were self-serving. He'd spent hours listening to Frannie prattle about her paintings, but when he'd talked about *his* work, she'd yawned. He had no respect for ambitious women.

He glared at Dr. Mitchell. "So I'm your first patient. I guess the joke's on me."

"I hope not," she said. "I really do want to apologize for my conduct at the town hall."

She'd come to make peace, but Zeb didn't want a truce. He wanted to find a doctor who didn't wear a dress. He'd already sent a new advertisement to the *Kansas Gazette* with instructions to make the print extra large.

Dr. Mitchell looked at him expectantly. Good manners called for him to apologize in return. Business was business, so he made his voice brusque. "Anything else, Dr. Mitchell?"

"Yes, there is."

"What is it?"

She looked at him from below the brim of her hat. "You owe me for the medical advice."

He had to hand it to her. The woman had guts. "I suppose I do." Zeb reached into his pocket to extract a coin. Doc had charged six bits for advice. He figured Dr. Mitchell's services were worth less, maybe two bits.

As he withdrew the coin, she held up her hand to stop him. "I don't want your money."

His eyes narrowed. "What *do* you want?"

"A tour of the mill."

Zeb's brows pulled together. Most women had no interest in shafts and pivots. "Are you serious?"

She peered through the delivery door. "I like knowing how things work."

So did he.

"Will you show me?" she asked again.

He could turn a tree into lumber and wheat into flour, but as long as he lived, he'd never understand females. Caught by surprise, he shrugged. "Sure. Why not?"

When she smiled her thanks, he knew *why not*. Dr. Nora Mitchell was one hundred percent female and he couldn't forget it. Even with her hair tamed under a brown felt hat, she looked pretty today. He'd show her the mill and how it worked, but that's all. No friendly talk. No walk along the river. No asking her to supper or letting her look at his eye again. To explain how the mill worked, he had to start with the river, the source of power for all the moving parts. He indicated the path to the waterfall with a jerk of his chin. "Let's go."

When she passed him, he smelled lavender. To keep from inhaling more deeply, he held his breath and started counting to ten. When he reached seven, he took a test sniff. Space between them muted the fragrance, but it left a trail in the air. Following it, he noticed the medical bag dangling from her hand.

"Here," he said, indicating his office. "You can leave that thing here."

Expecting her to let go, he reached for the case.

"Oh!" She looked up, but didn't release the bag. Their eyes collided, then their shoulders bumped and the bag hit his knee. Irked, he stepped back. "Fine, take it. But it's a hike to the waterfall."

"I'll leave it," she said hurriedly. "I'm not accustomed to…courtesy."

"I'm not accustomed to denying it," he countered.

"Here." She offered him the bag. "I'd be glad to leave it."

As she loosened her fingers, Zeb took the full weight of the black case. He carried it into his office and put it at the foot of his desk, smelling lavender because Dr. Mitchell had followed him.

"Is this your office?" she asked.

He grunted. "Yep."

As he turned back to the door, he saw her surveying the room. He followed her gaze to the brick hearth with a potbellied stove, then around to the shelves stacked with books and ledgers and finally to the lone chair he kept for visitors. Her eyes came to rest on the desk he'd hauled from Boston. Tall with spindly legs, the standing desk lacked a stool because Zeb never sat down.

Her brows knit together. "Don't you sit down to work?"

"I draw standing up."

"I see."

Zeb didn't need words to read her expression, maybe because he shared the same thoughts. He never rested. He couldn't until every building in High Plains, particularly the town hall, stood tall and proud. No wonder he had a tic in his eye. It twitched now, but Dr. Mitchell politely ignored it.

Zeb motioned at the door. "Time's a-wasting, Doc. Let's go."

The sooner he showed her the mill, the sooner he could get back to standing at his desk.

Chapter Eight

Nora led the way up the trail until they passed the mill. When the path branched into a vee, she paused to let Mr. Garrison take the lead.

"This way," he said, veering to the river.

His stride lengthened and she had to hurry to keep up. She'd been wise to leave her bag in his office. The weight would have slowed her down. She'd always be a physician, but for the moment she felt unburdened.

Ignoring the stir of dust, she followed him around a bend and nearly plowed into his back. He'd stopped at an outcropping of rock that overlooked the High Plains River. Meadows stretched for miles, ending in the rolling hills she'd traveled with the Crandalls. Nora loved the openness and the vast sky. She missed her family in New York, but she didn't miss the city. Inhaling deeply, she savored the fragrance of sunlight and grass.

He gave her a sideways look. "Did that little walk tire you out?"

"Not at all." She smiled. "I'm enjoying the air."

He huffed in a way she didn't understand, then pointed east to the rambling flow of the river. "You're seeing the reason Will and I picked this spot."

Nora studied the pattern of the current. A leaf floated by, gathering speed as it rushed to the waterfall. On the other side of the drop, she saw the waterwheel spinning in time with the flow.

"Do you see what's happening?" he asked.

"The river's pushing the wheel, and the wheel powers the mill." Nora saw a problem. "What happens if the river runs low?"

He turned and pointed upriver to a bulge in the bank where water pooled in a half moon. "When High Plains is back on its feet, I'll dam up that spot to make a millpond."

For the next several minutes, he talked about water flow, gates, traces and types of waterwheels. Garrison Mill had an undershot, the quickest and easiest to build, but he had plans for an overshot design. Instead of the river pushing the bottom of the wheel, an overshot design relied on gravity. Water traveled down a trace box that spilled into slots on the wheel called buckets. Gravity pulled the wheel down and the buckets spilled back into the river, causing the wheel to spin.

"Why the change?" Nora asked.

"An overshot is less vulnerable to drought. Once the millpond is finished, I'll have a constant source of water."

Nora recalled Cassandra's warning about Zeb being boring. The girl couldn't have been more wrong. He had a good mind and the ability to explain complex principles.

Leaning closer to her, he pointed to the opposite bank of the river and the meadow stretching as far as she could see. "Look over there."

As she turned her head, he lowered his chin. Did he realize he'd moved closer to her? She smelled wood and water, grass and his freshly laundered shirt. The sun warmed the dark print of his vest, another paisley with swirls of silver and black. A sudden pounding in her chest matched the rush and spill of the waterfall.

"What do you see?" he asked, challenging her.

"I see grass."

"And?"

He was testing her, but she didn't mind. She enjoyed a match of wits. Pausing, she put herself in his shoes. What would a miller see? He'd see trees, except they'd all been cut down. The grass waved like an open hand. The green blades matched his eyes until the grass bent and the sun bleached the color, leaving a sheen of gold, the color of… "Wheat!" she cried. "I see wheat fields."

"You've got a logical mind, Dr. Mitchell."

She enjoyed the praise, but she wished he'd called her Nora. With the sun warm on her face, she wanted to be a woman first, not Dr. Mitchell. Never shy, she tipped up her chin. "Please, call me Nora."

"Then I'm Zeb." Looking bold and roguish, like the scoundrel Emmeline had called "good," he stepped back and offered his hand.

Clasping it, she noticed the strength of his fingers, how his shirt pulled back on his forearm to reveal a smattering of dark hair. There was nothing clinical about her sense of this man, nor was he looking at her with the hostility she'd come to expect. Their hands stayed locked for a blink too long…until his eye twitched and they each let go of the other, laughing at the irony.

"Was that a wink?" she said playfully.

Turning abruptly, he hooked his hands on his hips and looked downriver. Nora's cheeks warmed with a blush. She hadn't meant to be so bold, but she'd forgotten the tension between them. When he wanted, Zeb Garrison could be charming.

"Let's go." He sounded gruff again. "I'll show you the inside of the building."

"I'd like that."

As they walked back along the trail, he told her more about his plans for the future. If the tornado hadn't struck, he'd have already replaced one of the saw frames with grinding stones. Nora thought of her own dreams that had been delayed. She'd put off marriage for the sake of medicine. Zeb had made a similar choice.

As the building came into view, she tipped her face to his. "You've made sacrifices for High Plains. That's admirable."

He kept his eyes on the mill. "I've done what's necessary."

"You've been generous," she added. "Mrs. Jennings told me how you helped with the children at the boardinghouse. I've gotten to know little Alex. He's special."

"He's a good kid." His expression turned serious. "It's too bad about his brother."

Nora had spent a lot of time with the boy. She knew his parents had died two years ago, and that Alex and his brother, Eli Henning, had been headed to Oregon when the tornado orphaned him a second time. "What's going to happen to him?"

Zeb hesitated. "I'm not sure yet."

Nora wanted to push, but the peace between them hung like gossamer. She had to tread lightly. "I've been visiting families. Some of them still need houses."

"And wood's gotten scarce." He indicated a door on the backside of the mill. "The saws are going full tilt. Come and look."

Nora entered the building and paused. As her eyes adjusted to the poor light, she heard the clatter of gears as they transferred power from the river to saw blades mounted in wood frames. At each of the three stations, she saw a log on a carriage being guided by a team of two men. One of the crews included Clint Fuller, the cowboy she'd met at the Circle-L.

Sawdust filled the air and she coughed. In medical college she'd treated millworkers for a condition called "white lung." It came from dust in gristmills, but sawdust could be just as damaging. A log bucked against a saw. Clint shouted a warning, then manhandled it back into place. She pictured him losing a hand and felt sick. Even from the distance of several feet, she could see circles under his eyes. The cowboy looked exhausted and so did the other men.

Nora thought of Zeb's comment about the mill operating sixteen hours a day. These men—all of them—were on their last legs. Fatigue led to accidents. As much as she'd enjoyed putting down her medical case for a walk along the river with a handsome man, she couldn't stop being a doctor. Someone had to tell Zeb Garrison his mill needed more windows and his workers needed rest.

The *clack* and *whoosh* of the mill filled Zeb's ears, but Dr. Mitchell—Nora now—still commanded his attention. Sawdust overpowered the scent of lavender, but the dim light brought out the ivory of her skin. For all her bold ways, she had a delicate chin and a bow-shaped mouth. Even more attractive to Zeb, she'd asked intelligent questions.

She'd been a good listener, maybe the best he'd ever had. Unlike Cassandra who listened out of obligation, and Will who preferred talk of cattle, Nora had focused on the mill's engineering. She'd also seen his vision of wheat fields, something not even Will had guessed.

Zeb didn't know what to think. One minute he'd been talking to Dr. Mitchell about water and gravity. The next, he'd been calling her Nora. The mill made sense to him. He could identify every sound and explain its cause. What he'd felt at the river made no sense at all. In the middle of his talk about waterwheels, he'd decided he liked the scent of lavender. He liked *her*.

The thought turned in his mind like the wheel powering the mill. It spun in a circle, going nowhere but putting other thoughts into motion…thoughts of a wife, thoughts of children.

If she'd been a farmer's daughter instead of doctor, a woman from Missouri instead of New York, he'd have already asked her to supper.

As things stood, he couldn't cross that line just yet. He didn't trust her judgment, but he was open to a civil conversation. How could he not be? She'd shown him respect. He owed her the same opportunity. As a first step, he'd give her a ride back to town and see what she had to say about finding a new office.

He looked at her profile. Instead of wonderment, he saw worry. He'd planned to show her the lower level, where they'd be alone again, but he changed his mind. To be heard over the noise, he raised his voice. "Had enough?"

She answered by heading for the door to the yard. As they stepped outside, the noise faded but didn't stop. His face felt gritty and he wondered if hers did, too. He didn't think she'd mind. Dr. Mitchell—Nora—had a thick skin.

She squared her shoulders. "I realize I'm not an expert on mills, but I have to ask. Are you aware of the risk of lung disease?"

He'd been expecting a question about the engineering, praise for the efficiency of his design. He'd even wondered if she'd hear the music he heard in the clack of the gears and the rasp of the saws. "What are you getting it?"

"I know millwork is dangerous. It's the nature of it, but there are things you can do for the sake of safety."

"Safety?"

"Yes." She spoke with force. "I'm sure you've heard of white lung disease. It's rampant in millworkers. Inhaling sawdust is just as bad. It can cause lung irritation. And I don't need to tell you that saws are sharp. A fatigued worker—"

"Stop right there, Dr. Mitchell."

"But—"

"But nothing," he said angrily. "You have no right to judge. What do you know about mills anyway?"

"I know—"

"You know *nothing*." He was mad enough to spit. "You said yourself that people need houses. The town hall's only half finished. High Plains won't forget the tornado until that building has four walls and a roof."

"Yes, but—" She bit her lip.

Bitterness flooded through his veins. "You don't know a *thing* about how I run this place. *Safety?* Do you think I don't care? In Bellville I saw a man lose his arm. He nearly bled out on the floor." He held up his hands. "I've got ten fingers. Most millers lose one or two. It's part of the work."

Her expression shifted from concern to outrage. "I'm offering a professional opinion."

"You're interfering." He crossed his arms. "What else do you want to tell me? That dust is explosive? That someone should pour water on the blades to keep them from sparking? That if I don't keep the gears greased, this whole place could go up in flames? Go ahead," he taunted. "Tell me how to run a mill."

"I wouldn't presume." She bit off each word. "I'm addressing a potential risk. Accidents happen when men are fatigued. Clint looks positively ashen! You can't work at this pace without risking serious injury."

"I know that." He worried every minute that someone would get cut, that a log would bounce and crush a man's leg. He worried about sparks and even the dust, because as she'd said, millworkers got bad lungs. He didn't want to be one of them, and he didn't want his men to suffer, either. He cared, deeply. He also cared about the people of High Plains, the ones living in tents who'd freeze this winter if he didn't supply wood for decent houses.

Dr. Mitchell didn't understand. Like Frannie, she saw the world through her own ambitious eyes. Zeb had heard enough. "Look, Doc. Here are the facts. If my men and I don't work long hours, people are going to freeze. Winter's not going to wait for High Plains to finish rebuilding."

"I realize that."

"Do you think I *want* to push this hard? Do you think I'm enjoying it? If you do, you're wrong." His voice had risen and not just from anger. For a few minutes he'd imagined this woman in his arms, his life. He'd enjoyed her intelligence and humor. But he'd been fooled. Deep down, she was a know-it-all female who wanted to tell him how to run his business.

"I know you're conscientious," she said quietly. "I'm sincerely concerned. As a physician—"

He cut her off with a guffaw. "As a *physician,* you should stick to hangnails. I don't want you anywhere near my mill *or* my men. Or my sister," he roared. "You're filling her head with fancy ideas. I won't stand for it."

Dr. Mitchell stepped forward and got right in his face. "I'm doing no such thing, Zeb."

The use of his name cut. He'd let her get too close. Who was she anyway? Frannie's twin or someone else? He couldn't see straight, and it didn't help to have his eye twitch. She saw the wink, and pounced on it.

Staring straight at him, she poked him in the chest. "Look what all of this work is doing to *you!* You, *Mr. Garrison,* need a nap! You should also lay off the coffee and give your men a day off before someone gets hurt."

"That's my problem."

"It certainly is." With her head high, she walked down the mill road.

Zeb thought of his earlier plan to give her a ride. He'd been out of his mind to consider such a thing. Not only did she get on his nerves, she'd gotten under his skin and into his dreams. Oak trees needed to be cut down. Lavender water belonged in big cities. And a woman doctor did *not* belong in Kansas or at his mill.

He had work to do, but he also had a head of steam and didn't want his men to know the lady doctor had gotten to him. He went back to the cutting floor, told the foreman he'd be gone awhile and climbed on the bay he'd been riding when he first saw this land.

Riding steadied him, so he aimed the gelding west along the river. As he passed the bend where he'd taken Nora, his thoughts drifted to the day of the tornado. He still wanted a legacy, children to carry on the Garrison name, and for that purpose he needed a wife. For a foolish moment he'd wondered if Nora Mitchell was that woman. As they'd stood by the river and looked at the mill, watching the harnessed power of the water and then hearing the music of it, he'd imagined her sharing his house. He'd noticed the smattering of freckles on her nose, the easy way she smiled. He'd appreciated her intelligence and her questions. And she'd seen wheat…vast fields of it. She'd seen his dream without him saying a word.

She'd also proved herself to be bossy and uncompromising. He wanted a woman who'd bend her life to his…a woman like Abigail Johnson, a girl like Winnie Morrow.

With the grass rippling, Zeb reined in the bay to a halt and studied the land. Without realizing it, he stopped in the place where the Carter family had been struck by the storm. He thought of Bess and the twins, the people who'd died, the ones who'd moved on and the ones like Emmeline who'd stayed and made a new life. A few weeks ago, she'd married Will in a quiet ceremony at the church. Zeb had never seen his friend happier and had renewed his plan to court either Winnie or Abigail.

He still hadn't decided which one, but the time had come to get off the fence. Looking at the lazy current of the river, he decided to ride into town. Either he'd visit the Morrows to pay Cassandra's bill, or he'd stop by the mercantile and call on Abigail. Maybe both if the mood struck him. Either way, he was done thinking about Nora Mitchell.

Chapter Nine

Nora cut a path back to the river. She couldn't remember the last time she'd been so angry. Stopping for breath, she looked at the waterfall spanning the current. She felt as if she'd crashed over it in a barrel. One minute she'd been enjoying Zeb's attention. The next minute they'd been shouting at each other. She hadn't meant to start an argument, but the truth couldn't be ignored. He and his men were working too hard. As a physician, she had to speak her mind.

"Oh, no," she groaned.

She'd left her medical bag in his office. She couldn't bear the thought of going back to the mill, but she had to have her bag. Dreading the thought of seeing Zeb, she walked back. When she reached the yard, she didn't see his horse and figured he'd gone for a ride. Hoping to avoid him, she knocked on the office door and waited. No answer. She knocked again, then went to the window and peered through the glass. When she saw only shadows at the standing desk, she decided to sneak in and out.

"Dr. Mitchell?"

She whirled and saw Clint holding his hat over his chest. Up close, he looked more exhausted than she'd supposed. Dark circles shadowed his gaunt cheeks, and his eyes were red-rimmed and watery, probably from the sawdust.

"Mr. Fuller." She tried to sound professional, but he'd caught her peeping into his boss's office. She expected him to ask her why and waited.

The cowboy wiped his brow with his sleeve. "I've been wondering… Can you cure a bad throat?"

Another patient… And this one had come to her by choice. *Thank You, Lord.* Her hours of visiting had paid off. "I might. Do you mind if I take a look?" To do a proper examination, she needed an office. She had one…except it belonged to Zeb Garrison.

"It hurts terribly," Clint said. "When could you—"

"Right now." She refused to be shy about a patient's needs. "We could use Mr. Garrison's office. Is he here?"

"He left about five minutes ago."

"Do you think he'll be gone long?" she asked.

Clint shrugged.

Nora took the cowboy's reticence in stride. Women told her everything she needed to know and more, but men grunted or said yes and no. She took the shrug to mean Zeb would be gone long enough for her to examine Clint's throat. Feeling like a thief, she turned the knob and stepped into the office. She needed more light, so she pulled the side chair closer to the window. "Please, sit down."

Clint sat.

Nora took a tongue depressor from her bag. "Open your mouth as wide as you can."

He followed the order and Nora peered at his throat. She saw inflammation but no pustules. She put her hand on his forehead to check for fever. It was evident but slight. Next she checked his neck for swelling of the glands. "How long have you been feeling poorly?"

"About a week now."

When she asked how he'd been feeling overall, the cowboy admitted to working two jobs and skimping on sleep.

She put the tongue depressor back in the bag and removed a folded paper. "This is willow-bark tea. Make it strong and drink it. You can also gargle with salt water, but what you really need, Mr. Fuller, is rest."

"Can't do it, ma'am."

"Why not?"

He shrugged.

"If you don't take care of yourself, a cold could turn into pneumonia and you won't be able to work at all. A day of rest now will save you time later."

"I know, Doc. But I need the money."

Nora waited for more, but Clint headed for the door. At the last minute, he turned. "I saw you with Miss Cassandra."

Nora had suspected he liked the girl. Now she felt certain. To protect Clint's pride, she hid a smile. "She walked with me to the mill."

"She's not feeling poorly, is she?"

"She's just fine."

As the man went back to the cutting room, Nora considered the cowboy's question. He clearly cared for Cassandra. If she went to Boston with Percival, would his heart be broken? Nora had never been in love, but she knew about disappointment. For a moment, she'd let herself wonder about a future with Zeb. Foolishness, she told herself. She pushed the chair back in place and picked up her bag. She had a mind to hunt down Zeb and tell him to send Clint home, but she doubted he'd listen. She'd already risked mayhem by using his office.

As she walked back to town, Nora weighed her options. Only Percival seemed willing to help her find an office of her own. She didn't like him, but she considered Cassandra a friend and they were probably in the middle of lunch at the boardinghouse. Nora wouldn't interrupt, but she hoped to hear from Cassandra later this afternoon.

Still frustrated, she passed the schoolhouse. In front of the mercantile she saw the bay gelding she'd noticed at the mill. Zeb Garrison, it seemed, had gone to call on Abigail. Fine, Nora thought. They suited each other. She didn't care what he did or whom he saw. What had possessed her to drop her guard? To be *Nora* instead of *Dr. Mitchell?* Utter foolishness, she decided again.

Except the choice hadn't been impetuous. She'd asked Zeb to call her Nora because she liked him. In those moments by the river, she'd seen the man who'd built High Plains with love, sacrifice, and the best of intentions.

Passing Dr. Dempsey's office, Nora thought about the odd twists of the day. If she counted both Zeb and Clint Fuller, she'd seen two patients. She also had support from Cassandra, the Logans and the Benjamins. She'd made progress in winning the town's acceptance, but she'd also sent the man who'd hired her into a rage.

The future looked uneasy at best. Thanks to her father, she had money for the fare to New York. She'd promised him she'd keep it, that she wouldn't use it for anything else for at least a year. She'd agreed at the time, but it was only now that she saw the wisdom of his request. When the one-month trial ended, she could very well be on a train back to New York.

As she turned up the street to the boardinghouse, her gaze

strayed to the window of her room, a cozy spot she now considered home. As she looked back at the porch, the door swung open and Mrs. Jennings came to the railing.

"Dr. Mitchell, hurry!"

Nora hoisted her skirts and ran. "What's wrong?"

"It's Alex! He's covered with spots! He could have the pox. It could be diphtheria or—or—I don't know, but he's got a fever!"

Her third patient… This time, she felt no gratitude, only fear for a boy who reminded her of the brother she'd lost. With her bag in hand, she followed Mrs. Jennings upstairs to Alex's room. As soon as she saw his glassy eyes, she went to the side of his bed and sat. Mrs. Jennings stood in the doorway with her arms crossed as if she was afraid the disease would escape.

Alex looked at her with wide brown eyes. "I feel bad," he said.

"Does your throat hurt?"

He nodded.

Nora lit the candle sitting on the nightstand, then raised it to see in the boy's mouth. "Open wide."

When a child obeyed without a bit of protest, she knew the child was truly ill. Alex opened his mouth so wide a train could have gone through it. She peered at his throat and saw redness but no sign of diphtheria.

Wide-eyed, he looked at her with raw hope. "I have spots on my tummy."

"Do you mind if I look?"

He shook his head.

As she lifted the boy's night shirt, she saw sweat-soaked sheets and a mottled rash, the telltale sign of measles. The disease could be serious, but the vast majority of children recovered. She asked Alex a few more questions, then tucked the sheet over his thin body. "Alex, you have the measles."

"What's that?"

"It's a kind of sickness," she explained. "You'll feel bad for a while, and your skin's going to get red and bumpy, but you'll be fine if you do what I say. You need to stay in bed, all right?"

"I will." He looked at her with such trust, such hope. At that moment, all the misery in medical college, the dances she'd skipped and the men she'd ignored, even Zeb Garrison's cruelty, meant nothing compared to helping a child. "I'm going to get some water."

She stood and went to the door. Mrs. Jennings interrupted her. "I need to talk to you." She aimed her chin at the hallway. "Now!"

Nora followed her, but didn't close the door. She didn't want Alex to feel abandoned, but neither did she want the orphan to respond to the obvious fear in Mrs. Jennings's tone. She indicated the door to her room and the two women went inside.

"What can I do for you?" Nora said in a hush.

"That boy can't stay here."

"I know you're concerned about your boarders." Nora respected contagion, but Alex had nowhere else to go. "We'll take precautions."

The landlady shook her head. "Precautions aren't possible. Not when the accommodations are this full. I can't give Alex a room of his own. I can't even give him a *bed* of his own."

"There must be a way," Nora argued.

"I wish there was," Mrs. Jennings replied. "But I don't see what it could be. I can't risk the other boarders getting sick. Either find another place for Alex, or I'll send word to Zeb to take him."

Nora fought to stay calm. If only she had an office with a sickroom, a place where she could nurse ailing children. But she didn't. All she had was a building without a roof. If Zeb took Alex, would he allow her into his home to care for the boy? After today's quarrel, she doubted it.

"I'm sorry," said the landlady, "but the boy has to leave *today*."

"I need time," Nora pleaded. "Tomorrow—"

Mrs. Jennings put her hands on her hips. "And where am I supposed to put the other children who share the room until then? You've got until supper to find a place for him, or I'm telling Zeb to come and get him."

If Mrs. Jennings went to Zeb instead of trusting Nora as a physician, Nora would appear incompetent to the entire town. She had one last hope. "Are Mr. Walker and Cassandra still here?"

"No."

She'd have to send Percy a note. "I need a little time, just a few hours."

"Like I said, you have until supper." Mrs. Jennings left with a worried frown.

Stifling a groan, Nora pressed her fingers to her temples. As she sat on the narrow bed, her eyes went to the painting she'd hung on the wall. A gift from her parents, it portrayed the house where she'd grown up. The artist had captured it on a spring day when the gardens were lush and the windows bright with sunshine. Her father had presented it with a catch in his voice. *No matter what happens, Nora, you'll always have a home with us.*

A home where she'd be expected to marry Albert Bowers. A home where no one respected her skills. Part of her *wanted* to go home. She was tired of fighting for respect, tired of arrogant men and barbed words. Mostly, though, she was tired of being alone. Tears welled in her eyes.

"Why, Lord?" she said out loud. "Why would You lead me here and not provide?"

Even as the complaint left her lips, she heard the falseness of it. Human beings had let her down, but God hadn't left her side. He knew her needs. He knew that a boy named Alex needed a home of his own, and that a woman named Nora needed one, too. Closing her eyes, she sank to her knees at the side of the bed, crossed her arms on the mattress and rested her head on her hands.

Please, God. Provide a place for me. Provide for Alex and all the people of High Plains. She prayed for peace and strength. She named the people she'd met, all the ones she could recall. Last, she prayed for Zeb. *Open his eyes, Lord. Heal his heart from old hurts. Show him Your love and peace.*

She rambled until her throat ached, then she said, "Amen" and pushed to her feet. As she headed for the door to check Alex, she realized she hadn't added her usual plea for a husband. A knot tightened in her chest. Had the Lord said no to that request? Had He brought her to High Plains to be a physician only?

In a final prayer, she bowed her head. "Your will be done, Lord." And it would.

Calm but fighting despair, Nora wrote a note to Percival Walker asking if he knew of a house she could rent immediately. She asked Jonah, Alex's friend, to deliver it, then crossed the hall to Alex's room. If he hadn't been so ill, she'd have taken the note herself. Instead, she stayed at his bedside, doing the things a mother would do. A cool cloth on his brow fought the fever. She changed the damp sheets and rubbed his chest with camphorated oil. She read to him and hummed a lullaby.

As he dozed, she thought of her brother and how suddenly he'd left this earth. A day was like a thousand years to the Lord, but Nora felt the burden of time. She didn't have years or even days to find a place for herself and Alex. She needed a house now.

As he lay asleep, a knock sounded on the door. Expecting Mrs. Jennings, she stood and opened it. Cassandra peered into Alex's room. "How is he?"

"It's measles, but he's strong," Nora answered. "He should be fine."

"I'm glad." Cassandra refocused on Nora. "Could you come downstairs? Percy wants to speak with you."

"Did he get my note?"

She nodded. "I'd already spoken to him at lunch. He has a house that would be perfect. I'll sit with Alex while you talk."

Nora wanted to spring down the stairs, but she feared exposing Cassandra to sickness. "Have you had measles?"

"I had them as a child."

Reassured, Nora brushed by Cassandra and raced down the stairs to the parlor. As she entered the room, Percy stood. "Dr. Mitchell."

"Mr. Walker."

"I have the perfect place for you. It's not common knowledge, but Brice Roysden left High Plains two days ago. I bought his house as an investment. It's on the west side of town, past the mercantile. If you have a minute, I'll show it to you."

"Is it for purchase or rent?"

"Purchase only," he said.

Nora couldn't buy a house unless she spent her father's money. Even with those funds, she might need a loan from the bank, and obtaining one would be difficult. The purchase would be a true act of faith, a risk for the sake of her calling. If she failed to win the town's respect, she'd have to ask her father for help and he'd expect her to marry Albert Bowers without a fight. The risk made her heart pound, but so did the threats posed by caution. Alex needed a place to recover. So would other children who were likely to fall ill. Nora didn't enjoy taking chances, but she'd never regretted being brave.

"I'd like to see it," she said. "What's the price?"

The lawyer named a total beyond her means, then offered to arrange a mortgage if she could manage a down payment. The amount he suggested was slightly less than the amount she had in her trunk for train fare back to New York. If she accepted the offer, she'd have a house and a small nest egg. She considered renegotiating her salary from Mr. Garrison—it presently included room and board—but decided against it. The few dollars he'd have paid Mrs. Jennings for the remainder of the month wasn't worth the risk of having him interfere with the purchase of a house. Later she'd worry about making payments. For now, the Lord had met her needs.

"I'll get my hat and we can go," she said to Percy. If the house would serve as a home and clinic, she'd buy it.

Chapter Ten

Two days had passed since his quarrel with Dr. Mitchell, and Zeb hadn't heard a word from her *or* about her. He'd tried to put her out of his mind, but when his men coughed from the dust, he thought of her and got angry. When his eye twitched, he recalled laughing with her and felt something else.

This morning, standing at the base of the waterfall as he did every morning, he tried to gauge the river's flow, but he couldn't concentrate on the task at hand. The rush of the falls reminded him of *her*. He couldn't call her Dr. Mitchell anymore, but neither did he want her to be Nora. The name rolled too easily from his lips. He liked the hush of it, the soft tones that begged to be whispered.

"You idiot," he said out loud. "Not only is she a doctor, she's just like Frannie."

Standing tall, Zeb glared at the boulder he used to gauge the depth of the river. The volume was decreasing with the summer weather, but he couldn't bring himself to hope for a storm. The thought of another tornado made his belly churn. A town—and a man—could take only so many disasters.

He knew how it felt to love and lose a woman. He'd given Frannie everything—his dreams, his hopes. He'd gone over a cliff for her and had fallen hard. While standing upriver with Dr. Mitchell, he'd wondered if…maybe…but then she'd bossed him and he'd gotten mad. Had she been unreasonable? No. Had she been puffed up? Not until he'd goaded her.

As the water splashed over the rocks, his mind echoed with snippets of their quarrel. She'd been right about everything, particularly the effects of fatigue. When he'd returned from town, he'd send Clint back to the Circle-L to nurse his cold. He thought of men he'd known in Bellville, older ones who struggled to climb hills because they couldn't breathe right. If more windows would clear the air, he'd put them in.

Zeb cared deeply about his men. He worried about everyone in High Plains. So did Dr. Mitchell. He owed her an apology, but hated the thought of making it. He couldn't risk dropping his guard. He'd ask her to supper and he'd start to care about her. Even if they could reconcile their differences about her career, he couldn't trust her to stay. Someday she'd get fed up and go back to New York, leaving him just as Frannie had.

A smart man wouldn't take that chance. He'd court a woman like Abigail. A merchant's daughter, she understood business, and that's how Zeb viewed marriage. After the spat with Nora— Dr. Mitchell, he reminded himself—he'd gone to the mercantile. Abigail had served him biscuits and jam. They'd talked about rebuilding the town hall, and he'd agreed to join the jubilee planning committee. Abigail made life easy, but he had to wonder if the calm would last.

"Zeb!"

He looked at the mill and saw one of his men calling down from a window. "Down here!" he shouted back.

"Reverend Preston's here."

"I'll be right up." Zeb didn't care for church, but he didn't mind the reverend. In addition to pastoring High Plains Christian Church, the man worked as a carpenter. Before the tornado, he'd put the finishing touches on Zeb's house, including cornices, cabinets and a wall of bookshelves. They'd had some interesting talks, but Zeb hadn't changed his mind about God. The Almighty was either cruel or uncaring. Either way, Zeb had no time for religion.

With the sun bright and the river glistening, he hiked back to the mill. He found the reverend dressed in work clothes, looking at the logs the Thompson brothers had delivered yesterday. Rebuilding High Plains had used all the local trees and then some. With each delivery, the Thompsons had to backtrack farther east for good timber. This load of oak, strong and sturdy, had come a long way.

"Good morning." Zeb held out his hand.

The reverend, a tall man in his thirties, pumped it twice. "How are you doing, Zeb?"

"Same as usual."

Preston looked at him a little too long. It was a habit he had, one Zeb found annoying. "What can I do for you?"

The reverend got down to business. "How much for twenty boards of oak? Each an inch thick?"

Zeb named a fair price.

"I'll take it."

The wood still needed to be cut. "When do you want it?"

"As soon as you can do it," he answered. "I'm building shelves for the lady doctor you hired."

Zeb didn't know what to think. Had Nora changed her mind about Doc Dempsey's place? He couldn't stand the thought. Surely she wasn't that desperate. He wanted to ask Reverend Preston for details, but he didn't want to show interest in Nora's activities. If anyone would have the goods on Dr. Mitchell, it was Matilda Johnson. Zeb wouldn't have to say a thing. She'd start gabbing the minute she saw him.

He finished his business with Reverend Preston, then went to his office and lifted his hat from a hook. He had to deliver lumber to the town hall, so a stop at the mercantile made sense. "I'll be back in an hour," he called to his men.

Zeb headed for the yard where he tied down the load, climbed onto the seat and snapped the reins. As the horses lumbered away from the mill, he thought of the oak waiting to be cut. Such fine wood didn't belong in Doc Dempsey's office. Neither did a woman like Nora Mitchell. As he steered down Main Street, he studied the progress made on the town hall. The building had four walls, a plywood roof and the framework for a cupola that would hold a bell. The wood in his wagon would be used for siding. Doors, windows and two coats of white paint would finish the job.

When he reached the building, he reined the wagon to a halt. Briggs called a greeting, then lifted the first of the planks. Zeb usually lent a hand, but today he sauntered across the street to Doc's old place. When he jiggled the doorknob, it didn't turn. Still curious, he peered between the boards covering the window.

Nothing had changed since the day he'd shown the office to Dr. Mitchell, a sign she didn't plan to move in. Relieved but still curious, he crossed back to the town hall where he saw Briggs talking to one of the men. As Zeb approached, they gave him their full attention.

"How's it going?" he said to Tom.

"We're making progress."

"Will it be done before the jubilee?" Zeb had promised the town a big to-do. He intended to keep his word.

"Should be," the foreman replied. "If you keep the wood coming, we'll keep building."

"Don't worry." Zeb spoke with confidence, but his mind echoed with Nora's caution about fatigue. With each day, the river became more sluggish. He needed a millpond and a dam, traces and gates. Instead, he had to hope for a good rain, one that didn't spawn a tornado. If the river didn't go dry, and his men didn't peter out, the building would be done just in time for the jubilee. Zeb counted a lot of ifs, but he'd do his best. He always did.

Except he hadn't done his best when it came to providing a place for Dr. Mitchell. Where had she gone? He considered going to the boardinghouse and asking her directly, but that meant eating humble pie. Instead, he crossed the street to the mercantile. Matilda Johnson accosted him before he passed the pickle barrel.

"Zeb, I'm glad you're here. We have a *terrible* problem."

"What happened?"

"It's that lady doctor. It's indecent, I tell you. It can't be tolerated."

Zeb didn't like her tone at all. "What's indecent?"

"Her living arrangement, that's what!"

Now they were getting somewhere. "Where's she living?"

"Not at the boardinghouse! Not where Mrs. Jennings can keep an eye on her."

"I don't know what happened. Is she moving into Doc's old place?"

"Hardly!" Matilda came around the counter. With her ample bosom and wide skirts, she nearly knocked him over on her way to the window. "There." She jabbed her finger at the Roysden place. "She bought that house. She's living there *alone*."

"What happened to Brice?" he asked.

"He left two days ago." Mrs. Johnson shuddered. "The instant I saw that woman, I knew she'd be a problem. Females do *not* belong in medicine. It's unseemly. She's a hoyden!"

Zeb had used that word himself with Pete, but it didn't fit Nora at all. He couldn't deny her sensitive ways and good character. Yes, they'd had a quarrel. But she'd taken responsibility and apologized. He needed to do the same, but the thought irked him.

He peered at the Roysden place from over Mrs. Johnson's shoulder. Someone had put up yellow curtains. "I have concerns about Dr. Mitchell, but her morals aren't among them."

"They should be."

He flashed to the gossip about Rebecca and Pete. Zeb had been furious then and he was irked now. He had no patience for gossip *or* lies. "She's a decent woman, Mrs. Johnson. Leave it at that."

She arched a brow. "How do *you* know?"

We spoke and she looked into my eyes. I stood close and felt her shyness. He didn't want to say any of those things to the town gossip, so he stuck to business. "She had good references."

Matilda Johnson huffed. "Letters can be forged."

"I have my doubts," Zeb replied. "But you don't need to worry about Dr. Mitchell's character. I don't like the fact she's female, but she cares about people." Did she deserve a chance to prove herself? He'd taken her advice and his eye hadn't twitched in two days. Zeb didn't want to go down that road, but the thought grabbed him and wouldn't let go.

The woman glared at him. "The Ladies Aid Society wants you to get rid of her."

Zeb couldn't think of anything in High Plains more tedious than the Ladies Aid Society. He'd have preferred another tornado to dealing with a herd of hotheaded gossips. In the guise of community service, the Ladies Aid Society bossed the whole town, with Matilda leading the charge. Zeb had heard enough.

"Look here, Mrs. Johnson—"

"Zeb!" He turned and saw Abigail coming from the back room. "Did Mother tell you what that awful new doctor did?"

That did it. He couldn't stand here and listen to Nora being unfairly judged. "She's not awful, Abigail. I'm not happy she's female—" *Liar. He liked her womanly side just fine.* "—but she's not a bad person."

Abigail pouted. "I don't like her. She interferes."

Zeb agreed, but didn't say so.

Mrs. Johnson steered them back to the counter. "As long as Zeb's here, Abigail, why don't you bring him one of those cinnamon buns you made."

Abigail beamed. "Of course."

Zeb held up his hand to stop her. "Thanks, but I can't stay."

Before either woman could protest, he strode out of the mercantile. He had another call to make, this one on Dr. Mitchell.

Chapter Eleven

As he strode toward Dr. Mitchell's new house, Zeb considered what had just happened. He'd taken Nora's side against the Johnsons. There would be a price to pay if he snubbed the store owners, especially after showing interest in Abigail, but which of them would pay it? Nora had bought a house, a sign she intended to stay in High Plains. Zeb held the purse strings for the salary they'd negotiated, but he couldn't force her to leave. Her presence would make finding a male doctor more difficult. What if she refused to leave?

He hated the idea.

He liked the idea…a lot.

He'd gone crazy and it was Nora Mitchell's fault. He paced up the road to the Roysden place. Brice and Annie Roysden had been among the first to arrive in High Plains. Zeb had cut the lumber for their home and helped to build it. The house had five rooms, including two bedrooms on a second floor. Annie Roysden had been nervous since the tornado and had gone back East. The couple had had quite a row and Brice had stayed, though it seemed he'd gotten lonely and had changed his mind.

Zeb thumped across the porch and rapped on the door. No one answered, but he heard humming from an open window. He rapped again, more forcefully. The door opened before he could lower his fist. Instead of Nora, he saw Carolina Samuels. A widow in her fifties, she'd been Doc Dempsey's nurse.

"Good morning, Zeb." She spoke in the even tone of a woman who couldn't be surprised.

"Good morning, Carolina." He removed his hat. "Is Dr. Mitchell in?"

"She's with Alex."

Zeb's brow knotted. If something had happened to the boy, Mrs. Jennings should have informed him. "What's wrong with him?"

"He has the measles."

Zeb put the pieces together. Alex had fallen ill. Instead of telling *him,* Mrs. Jennings had asked Nora for help. Irked, he fisted the brim of his hat. "May I see her, please?"

"That depends," the nurse answered. "Have you had the measles?"

"I had them as a boy."

"Good," she said, smiling. "Come on in."

As Carolina widened the door, he stepped into the parlor. Brice had apparently sold the furniture with the house, but his wife had taken the womanly whatnot when she'd left. Today Zeb saw a wooden bench, two hard chairs, a divan by the hearth and a secretary pushed against the wall. He also saw an oil painting depicting a fancy town house surrounded by a lush flower garden that no doubt included lavender. Memories of Frannie flew like the shingles in the storm. He recalled watching her paint. He thought of the week he'd spent at Cape Cod with her family and how her brushes had caressed the easel when he'd wanted her fingers laced with his. He recalled the day she'd jilted him… The sky had been clear and bright, the sun warm on his face.

As he glowered at the painting, his stomach knotted. Dr. Mitchell, it seemed, had a taste for art like a true city lady. Would she last in High Plains? He doubted it. One good storm and she'd run back to New York. He *had* to find another doctor for High Plains, a *male* doctor who wouldn't cut and run.

With his jaw tight, he looked at the entry to the dining room. A navy blue curtain hung in the doorway. Behind it he heard Nora speaking in soothing tones, then the fussy whimper of a feverish child.

Carolina indicated a chair. "Sit down, Zeb. Dr. Nora will be with you soon."

"Thank you."

She left the parlor, but he didn't sit. Instead, he paced around the room. One minute his temper flared. The next he thought of the oak waiting to be cut and felt a longing for shelves of his own…shelves in the room of a son who'd share his name, a daughter who'd call him Papa. To his consternation, his mind conjured up a picture of a toddler with red hair.

"Stop it," he muttered to himself. He wanted nothing to do with a woman who practiced medicine *and* liked oil paintings.

The curtain fluttered and he turned. In the doorway stood the shy woman who'd arrived in High Plains in a duster and floppy bonnet, except instead of a canvas coat, she was wearing a calico dress. It didn't have a single flounce, not a shred of lace. A row of wooden buttons ran from her neck to the vee of the bodice. Her red hair hadn't changed color, but she'd tamed it into a braid and looped it around her head. As the light struck the plaits, he thought of the swirls in a piece of oak. This woman had stood with him at the river. She'd seen the potential for wheat fields and understood his dream. She'd listened while he'd prattled on about the mill. He'd liked her, in spite of himself.

As the curtain fell back in place, she stepped deeper into the parlor. "Good morning, Mr. Garrison."

Two days ago he'd been Zeb and she'd been Nora. That's how he thought of her, but the moment called for formality. "Dr. Mitchell."

"Has your eye improved?"

He scowled. "I'm not here as a patient and you know it."

She raised her brows. "Then why are you here?"

"I heard you bought this house." He indicated the wall with the painting. "I wanted to know what you're up to."

"I'm not *up* to anything," she said. "I needed an office. Percy kindly found—"

"Percy?" Since when was she on a first-name basis with that Boston sycophant?

Nora indicated a chair. "Please, sit down. I'll explain."

"I don't want to sit." He sounded childish, but he didn't care. "I want to know why you bought a house. We agreed on a one-month trial."

"Not exactly," she answered. "We agreed you'd *pay* me for one month. I never promised to leave."

She had a point. He turned his back and looked out the window. The mercantile lay to the east. His own house sat on a rise a quarter-mile to the west. Dr. Nora had plopped down in the center of his life.

Her voice drifted across the room. "I'd be glad to explain. Perhaps you'd like a cup of tea?"

No way did he want to sit and make small talk. Irked yet again, he faced her. "I don't want tea. I want answers."

Poised and patient, she smoothed her skirts and sat. She looked weary…as weary as he felt himself. An unwanted concern softened his stance, but he refused to sit. Sitting would make them equals.

She folded her hands in her lap. "It started with Alex. When he came down with measles, he had to leave the boarding-house. Percy had the deed for this house and sold it to me. With Mrs. Jennings's permission, I brought Alex here."

"She should have told me," he said irritably.

"Why?"

"I'm paying her to look after him, that's why." If he'd known Alex was ill, he'd have taken him to his house and asked Cassandra to watch him. Or he'd have hired Carolina himself. Since he'd decided to get married, he'd thought about adopting the boy.

"I can't speak for Mrs. Jennings," Nora replied. "But I was there when he took ill. He needed a doctor and she asked me."

Zeb didn't like the implication at all. If Mrs. Jennings trusted Dr. Mitchell, so would others. If she succeeded with Alex, her reputation would improve and he'd never get rid of her. On the other hand, he didn't want Alex to suffer. "How's the boy doing?"

"He'll be fine."

Zeb's next words nearly choked him, but they had to be said. "I'll pay you for your services."

"No." She held up her hand, palm out to stop him. "This isn't about money. I've enjoyed having him."

Zeb didn't like feeling beholden to this woman. Neither did he like the motherly glow in her eyes. If he paid for Alex's medical care, she wouldn't have a claim to the boy. On the other hand, he saw an advantage to *not* paying her. "May I ask you a question, Dr. Mitchell?"

"Of course."

"Your salary runs out in a month. If you're not going to take money for your services, how do you plan on support-ing yourself?"

"I'll accept payment from anyone I treat," she said. "Just not for orphans."

"I see."

"Do you, Mr. Garrison?"

Zeb liked a good fight, but mostly he wanted her to leave High Plains the instant he found a replacement. Matilda Johnson had handed him a weapon this afternoon. He decided to use it. "You should pack your things now, Dr. Mitchell. You don't have a prayer of winning this town's respect."

"I disagree."

"There's talk about you." He sounded grave, even threatening.

"There's *gossip*," she said, correcting him. "And it's unwarranted. As you can see, I've hired Carolina Samuels. She's an excellent nurse and she lives here. At no time will I be alone with a male patient. Does that satisfy you?"

"I'm not the one who's talking."

"But you're *listening*." She arched her brows. "Perhaps to Mrs. Johnson?"

Zeb stayed silent.

"She dislikes me," Nora said quietly. "But it doesn't matter. I'm accustomed to criticism. The Ladies Aid Society has already delivered a letter of concern. It's insulting, but it's just paper. I care about just one thing and that's this town. The people of High Plains deserve a competent physician."

"I can't argue with your logic, Doc. What I question is your competence."

"You didn't question it when you hired me. As I recall, you described my credentials as—"

"I know what I said."

"—as impeccable *and* impressive."

"That was before I met you."

"You met me on paper," she insisted. "We exchanged two letters."

"And not once did you mention your gender."

"Of course not." The woman had the gall to look bored. "It's irrelevant, but we've had this talk before, haven't we?"

Zeb had heard enough of her superior tone. "May I be blunt?"

"Of course."

"If you're such a good doctor, what are you doing in a little town in Kansas? Why aren't you treating rich folks in New York City?"

He expected the question to raise her hackles. Instead, she answered with a tinge of apathy, as if she answered the question every day. "You're not the only person who's prejudiced against women. No one would hire me."

"I can see why."

She pushed to her feet. "You see their prejudice. You don't see *me* at all, and you don't have the knowledge to judge my skills."

She had a point, but he saw another angle. "I know this town. No one's going to respect you."

"I'll have to change their minds."

He chuffed. "You can't. You're female."

She indicated books stacked on the floor, waiting for the oak shelves. "I've read those books. I've studied long hours—"

"A waste of time."

"You're wrong." She raised her hand to her chest in a pledge of sorts. "My younger brother died of asthma. I couldn't save Ben, but I can help others."

Zeb snorted with doubt. "Is that a fact?"

"Yes!"

"Tell me, Dr. Mitchell. Who made *you* God?"

"No one," she said. "But I believe in Him. That's why I'm here, and why I'm not leaving."

"That God you worship," he said mildly. "He sent a tornado to High Plains. He let Pete's first wife die. Back in Bellville, I saw a man lose his hand when a log bucked against the saw. I've—" He almost said he'd loved a woman who'd cut out his heart, but he didn't want to share that information.

Her eyes softened. "You've been hurt, too."

"Who hasn't?"

He felt as if his skin had turned into glass, and she could see his broken heart. Her eyes misted with a sympathy he didn't want and an understanding he feared. They'd met just days ago, yet she knew his innermost thoughts.

"Zeb?" She'd used his given name. Did she want a truce or to remind him of the connection they'd shared at the river?

He kept his voice neutral. "What is it?"

"About Boston…I know you've been hurt. I'm sorry."

His neck hairs prickled. Had Cassandra blabbed to her about Frannie? Nora had made friends with Rebecca and Emmeline. Had they told her he was looking for a wife? The thought made him bitter. He didn't want Nora Mitchell nosing into his heart. He hardened his gaze. "What are you talking about?"

She wrinkled her nose, a sure sign she'd said more than she intended. "Nothing, really."

"Spit it out."

"I'm talking too much."

She waved her hand as if to fan the air. Instead, it fanned his temper. Dr. Mitchell didn't know when to be quiet. She had *that* in common with Frannie. And Abigail. Cassandra, too. Tonight, when he saw his sister, he'd have a few choice words regarding her loose tongue. Right now, he had to deal with Dr. Mitchell. He needed a weapon, something that would send her packing to New York. He pointed at the painting. "See that picture?"

"Of course." Her eyes looked misty.

"That's where you belong, Doc. In a town house in New York with a husband and six kids. With some fool man who'll keep you in your place."

Her cheeks turned redder than her hair. "Stop right there."

"Women don't belong in medicine." His voice rose to a shout. "You should get married and have babies."

"Get out!"

He felt powerful and he liked it. He also knew he'd been meaner to this woman than he'd been to anyone in his life. Why? It hit him... The anger at Frannie had been simmering for two years. Nora Mitchell had turned up the heat and it had reached a full boil. All the words he'd never said to Frannie had swelled into the ugly beast inside him now. He'd turned into a horrible person, a mean person.

Apologize.

His conscience nearly knocked him off his feet. Yet his pride made him walk out the door before she threw something at him. The two parts of his personality were at war. Was Nora the victim or was he? Zeb didn't know, but he felt certain of one thing. The war between them had taken a sharp turn, and it wasn't in his favor. Later he'd decide if he owed her an apology. Right now he needed to pound some nails. Churned up and frustrated, he headed to the town hall where he'd be among men. For today, he'd all the female foolishness he could stand.

Chapter Twelve

The man had the gall to slam her own door in her face. Nora had never felt so shaken in her life. Zeb Garrison had been insufferable, but that's not why her knees had gone weak. She could take being mocked as a doctor. What she couldn't bear was the terrible emptiness, the fear she'd never know the joys of a husband and a family. He'd assumed those joys were hers for the asking. They weren't.

She'd had a beau before medical college, but she hadn't loved him. She'd been kissed, but her toes hadn't curled even a little. As for Albert Bowers, he made her shudder. When it came to real love, she'd never experienced the sweet yearnings her mother had told her to expect.

Until now.

The thought stopped Nora cold. Zeb Garrison had been intolerable, so why did she feel drawn to him? Common sense told her to keep her distance, but another instinct—a brighter one—made her go to the window and watch as he walked away. The sun reflected off the paisley vest he always wore, obscuring the design with a glaring light. She lost sight of him as he rounded the corner, but she could still hear the thunder of the slamming door and the roar of his voice. He owed her an apology, but she didn't expect to receive one.

Carolina came out of the kitchen. "I heard every word. Are you all right?"

"I'm fine."

The nurse put her hands on her hips. "I know Zeb well. Something's bothering him."

"Not *something*," Nora said. "It's *someone* and that someone is me."

"Even so," Carolina insisted. "It's not like Zeb to shout."

Nora thought of the conversation before he'd exploded. She hadn't meant to step on his toes, but she'd trounced all over them. He'd accused her of arrogance—of playing God—and she'd argued back. She'd seen the hurt in his eyes and she'd alluded to Frannie. That's when he'd pointed to the painting, and his attack had turned personal. Nora didn't want to go down that road with Carolina.

"There's always more to a story," she said to the nurse. "I *know* he's working too hard."

"No doubt," Carolina replied. "But I've known Zeb for years. What's got him in a twist isn't hard work."

"Then what is it?"

The nurse laughed. "He's finally met his future wife and he doesn't know it."

"Carolina!"

"I'm serious." She hooked her arm around Nora's waist. "Let's have tea. I'll tell you what Zeb told Pete about getting married. It'll explain a lot, including Mrs. Johnson and her spitefulness."

Nora had no desire to gossip and hesitated.

Carolina gave her a motherly look. "If my daughter had

lived, she'd be your age. If she were alone in a new place, I'd want someone to look out for her."

A longing for her own mother welled in Nora's chest. "Thank you."

Carolina guided her into the kitchen where she'd already set water to boil. Except for essentials, Nora's cupboards were bare. No fancy baked goods. No preserves. She'd planned to purchase jam and eggs from the mercantile, but then she'd received the letter from the Ladies Aid Society and had decided to delay an encounter with the Johnsons.

Carolina filled two cups with tea and sat. "You know about the tornado and how it shook us all up."

"I can see the damage everywhere." She thought of Bess, the twins and the death of Alex's brother.

"It changed Zeb more than most."

"How so?"

"For one thing, he stopped being shy about marriage. He's a handsome man, if I do say so myself." She smiled. "He needs a strong woman in his life, someone who'll take him to task when he acts up."

"Like he just did."

"Exactly." Carolina took a long sip of the steaming brew. "After the storm, he let it slip to Pete that he wanted to get married. Matilda Johnson overheard them, and the next thing Zeb knew, every female in town had set her cap for him. Most dropped out of the fray in a few weeks, but Abigail hasn't given up. Neither has Winnie Morrow, or I should say, neither has Winnie's mother. Winnie's on the timid side. She's not right for Zeb at all."

Neither is Abigail.

Nora kept the thought to herself, but Carolina smiled "You're right. Abigail's an even worse choice."

Nora felt strengthened by the tea *and* the talk. "Now I know why Mrs. Johnson resents me. In addition to the prejudice, she sees me as a rival to her daughter."

"And a worthy one," the nurse said. "I haven't seen Zeb in such a state since that Boston woman jilted him."

"He must have loved her deeply."

"I believe he did." Carolina's voice turned wistful. "My Howard loved me that way, God rest his soul."

Envy flooded through Nora like a river in a storm. Would she ever have a husband and children of her own? Not once in her life had she let her dreams die, but this dream seemed to lay beyond her reach.

A knock sounded on the front door. Both women stood, but Nora motioned for Carolina to remain seated. "I'll get it."

If Zeb had come to apologize, she wanted to meet him halfway. She dared to hope until she opened the door and saw Bess. Nora had been reading up on mutism, and had met with Bess several times at the boardinghouse. Her medical books said criticism and bribes served no purpose, something she'd known instinctively. Instead of coaxing the girl to speak, Nora had taken a different approach. She treated Bess with complete normality. The key to healing, she believed, was making the girl feel safe.

"Hi!" Nora said happily.

Bess waved hello, then handed Nora a note. She took it but looked at Bess instead of opening it. "Carolina and I are having tea. Would you like to join us?"

Bess's eyes flared with anxiety. Frantic, she pointed at the note.

To calm the girl, Nora unfolded the paper. "I'll read it right now." Nora scanned the feminine script. "It's from Rebecca. Another boy has the measles, and his mother wants me to see him."

Relieved to be understood, Bess relaxed. Nora ached for the silent girl, but she also felt a spark of triumph. In spite of Zeb Garrison's dire predictions, she'd just been summoned to see a patient. She put the letter in her pocket, then focused on Bess. "I'll get my medical bag. Would you walk back with me?"

The girl nodded solemnly.

As Nora guided her into the parlor to wait, she glanced at the painting on the wall and thought again of Zeb. He was wrong about where she belonged. New York had stopped being home when she left for medical college. She belonged in High Plains, where children caught measles and Bess needed wisdom. No matter the cost, she refused to let Zeb Garrison chase her away.

After leaving Nora's house, Zeb went back to the town hall. He needed to get rid of the fury in his blood, and pounding nails offered a cure. Later he'd think about his fight with Dr. Nora, but right now the wound was too raw. He needed the company of men, especially men who wouldn't question his foul mood.

As he neared the town hall, he saw Tom Briggs and Edward Gunderson. Every man in High Plains volunteered when they could be spared from their regular work, and Edward, a big Scandinavian who worked with Pete, had helped considerably.

Zeb had worked for an hour when he spotted Winnie Morrow and her mother coming down the street. Winnie had a picnic basket in hand and a stiff smile. Zeb liked Winnie. He liked her more than Abigail because she didn't talk a lot. She also bored him senseless. After quarreling with Dr. Mitchell, though, boredom appealed to him.

"Zeb!" Mrs. Morrow waved at him.

He waved back, then excused himself from the crew of men. As he climbed down the scaffolding, Tom Briggs grinned. "Looks like you're getting lunch."

"I'm not hungry," Zeb muttered.

"I am," said Edward.

Zeb glanced over his shoulder and saw the man doff his hat to Winnie. She looked pretty in a calico dress with flowers that reminded him of the morning glories growing by the river. The flowers were nice, but they didn't last more than a few days. Zeb liked trees better. He liked oak in particular and wished again he'd kept his mouth shut with Nora.

Agatha Morrow nudged her daughter forward. Zeb encouraged her with a smile.

She offered the basket. "Mama thought—"

Mrs. Morrow interrupted. "We *both* thought—"

Winnie sighed. "We thought you'd like some refreshments."

Zeb had behaved badly once today. He refused to do it again. He took the basket and gave Winnie his most charming smile. "Thank you, Winnie. That's thoughtful of you."

Zeb opened the cloth and smelled vanilla. Mrs. Morrow nudged her daughter forward. "Winnie baked snickerdoodles. Didn't you, Winnie?"

Zeb disliked pushy women of any age. He felt sorry for Winnie. "They smell good."

The girl blushed again, but she wasn't looking at Zeb. Her gaze had climbed the scaffolding to Edward's boots. The man was looking down, unsmiling and irritable. Eager to finish with the women, Zeb shouted to the crew. "Break time, men. Miss Morrow's brought us refreshments."

Edward reached the basket first, then Briggs. Zeb helped himself, but he didn't taste a bite as the men praised Winnie. The married ones took cookies and stepped back. Edward staked out the spot in front of her and wouldn't budge. He looked as calf-eyed as Zeb had once gazed at Frannie. What would that be like? he wondered. To admire a woman without a flash of pain?

He didn't remember anymore, but he knew one thing for certain. He wouldn't be courting Winnie. She was too sweet for a scoundrel like him. He also felt Edward's eyes cutting into him. If the man had feelings for Winnie, Zeb would stay out of his way.

When it came to potential wives, that left Abigail Johnson or a red-haired lady doctor. The thought made Zeb's head hurt. He had to get away from cookies and the stupid grin on Edward's face. As graciously as he'd done in Boston, he excused himself with a slight bow to Winnie. Turning, he clapped Edward on the back in manly surrender, then climbed onto the wagon seat.

He needed to go back to the mill, but he felt churned up inside. Instead of heading past the mercantile—he didn't want to deal with Abigail—he drove between the boardinghouse and the corner building and across a patch of dirt to the livery. When he saw Will's sorrel, he grinned. Just what he needed…some healthy complaining about women with his two best friends.

Zeb reined in the horse to a stop, hopped down and strode into the overheated building where Pete was forging a plow blade. Will slapped him on the back. "You've been making yourself scarce."

"Just working," Zeb answered.

"Same here," Pete added.

The three men stood shoulder to shoulder, watching in silence as Pete shaped the metal with hard strokes. Sweat trickled down Zeb's back. Will wiped his brow, then stepped back. "How's the town hall coming?"

"Good," Zeb replied. "We'll be ready for the metalwork in no time." He glanced at Pete. "How are you coming on the hinges?"

The blacksmith turned the metal spike in his hand, inspecting the color. "They'll be ready."

Zeb blew out a sigh. "Once the town hall's done, I can slow things down at the mill."

Will hummed in agreement. Pete said nothing. Standing between them, Zeb shifted his weight. "You won't believe what that lady doctor had the nerve to say."

Both men stared at him.

Will's lips turned up. "What'd she say?"

"She says I'm working too hard, that I'm pushing the men and something bad could happen because we're all worn out."

The blacksmith shrugged. "Sounds like good advice to me."

"Me, too," Will added.

"I'll admit she's got a point," Zeb replied. "But what else am I supposed to do? High Plains needs every board I can cut."

Pete shot a glance from the side. "Is your eye still twitching?"

Zeb ignored the jab. "She's got no right to tell me how to run the mill."

When both men laughed, Zeb felt like the butt of the joke. "What's so funny?"

"You still thinking about getting married?" Will asked.

Zeb scowled. "Sort of."

"Then get used to being bossed." The rancher grinned. "Emmeline bosses me all the time, and she doesn't even know it."

"Same with Rebecca." Pete had the stupid-happy look of a man in love.

Zeb recognized it, because he'd had that look with Frannie. Anger gripped him, but then he thought of Nora and the oak-brown dress she'd worn at the mill. An ache started in his belly and spread to his arms. He felt empty inside, the way he'd felt during the tornado. Two months had passed since that day. He still needed a wife, but he didn't want the grief.

He chortled at his friends. "You're a couple of henpecked

fools. No way is that happening to me. One thing's certain… I'm going to pick a woman who *won't* drive me crazy."

Pete guffawed.

Will stifled a snicker, but it leaked out in a snort.

Zeb glared at them both. "Take Abigail. She knows her place."

Will shook his head. "Don't be stupid, Zeb. She's after your money. If you marry her, you'll regret it."

Maybe, but she'd never hurt him. A man had to love a woman to suffer when she left. He didn't have those feelings for Abigail. A merchant's daughter, she understood business. He figured she could do the books for him. He hated that chore.

Pete rested the blade on the edge of the forge. "Do you *really* want Matilda Johnson for a mother-in-law? That woman—"

"I know." Zeb waved a hand in surrender.

"After what she did to Rebecca—" The blacksmith knotted his hand into a fist and hit the forge. "I've said enough. If you marry Abigail, you deserve what you get."

Will shot Zeb a hard look. "I hear the Ladies Aid Society is going after Dr. Mitchell."

"They are." Zeb thought of his reason for visiting Nora, then he recalled his sharp words to her. He wanted to crawl into a hole. If his friends learned what he'd said to her, they'd slap him upside the head.

"So," Will asked. "What are you going to do about it?"

Will meant the Ladies Aid Society, not the apology Zeb owed Nora. "I don't know."

"You brought her out here," Will said with authority. "Seems to me you owe her a little help."

"You can't let Matilda run amok," Pete insisted. "You've got to do something."

"Like what?" Zeb countered. "Marry her the way *you* married Rebecca? Not in a hundred years, friend. Not *ever*."

Will and Pete traded a look Zeb knew well. His two friends didn't believe a word he'd just said. He wasn't sure he believed them himself. He only knew he couldn't live with the way he'd treated Nora. He had to make amends, but how? Looking at the orange glow of the forging table, Zeb had an idea. Reverend Preston would pick up the oak in three days. Zeb would cut and plane it himself. He'd give the wood to her as a peace offering.

Talk among the men turned to the heat of the day, the need for rain and plans for the future. All the while, Zeb kept seeing the oak and a pair of blue eyes that made him forget Frannie. He wouldn't apologize. He couldn't let down his guard, but he hoped she'd understand.

Chapter Thirteen

Nora felt awkward having Reverend Preston in her clinic building shelves, but Carolina assured her the minister would appreciate the work. The residents of High Plains had pooled their resources to build a lovely church, but they couldn't manage a salary for a full-time minister. Just as the apostle Paul had supported himself as a tentmaker, Reverend Preston built cabinets.

He'd been working on Nora's shelves for three days, and she'd enjoyed chatting with him. Last night she'd invited the reverend and his wife for supper. Susanna Preston had been standoffish, but Nora had enjoyed the story of their trip West. Like most of the residents of High Plains, they'd followed Zeb and Will with a sense of purpose.

As the reverend bent to lift his toolbox, Nora ran her hand over the countertop. The oak had been sanded to the texture of satin. "The shelves are beautiful. How much do I owe you?"

"Not a penny." Standing tall, he lifted the heavy box in one hand.

"I can't accept a gift from you, Reverend. It's too much."

"They're not from me."

Her brows snapped together in confusion. "I don't understand. We agreed on a price."

"And it got paid." He faced her with a twinkle in his eyes. "The person you need to thank is Zeb Garrison."

Shock tingled from her brain to the tips of her toes. When she'd hired Reverend Preston, she'd used a precious bit of her savings. She'd also asked him to build a waist-high examination table. By paying for the carpentry, Zeb had given her breathing room. But why? She hadn't seen him since the day he'd slammed the door in her face.

The reverend headed into the parlor, then lifted his black hat off the peg by the door. Pulling it low, he smiled. "It's been a pleasure, Dr. Nora."

He'd picked up on the nickname Alex used. "The pleasure's been mine."

"If Alex is up to it, I hope to see you both in church tomorrow."

"It's too soon," she said diplomatically.

"For him or for you?"

Nora had to be honest. "For both of us. Alex is still recovering, and I'd like to avoid a fight with the Ladies Aid Society."

She'd received a second letter, this one even more insulting than the first. She'd also treated three children for measles. Mrs. Jennings had given up and let everyone stay at the boardinghouse. She'd invited Alex back, but Nora enjoyed his company. With each day, she became more established as a doctor. With time, she hoped Matilda Johnson and her cohorts would accept her.

The reverend's expression turned wry. "I know all about the Ladies Aid Society. My wife's a member, but some of those ladies enjoy gossiping. I don't allow that kind of nonsense on Sunday mornings. You're welcome in God's house anytime."

"Thank you."

He tipped his hat and strode through the door, leaving Nora with a yearning to hear him preach. She didn't miss New York, but she missed going to church with people she'd known all her life. Here in High Plains, she'd be an unwelcome stranger. Knowing she'd find hostility instead of friendship, she'd put off that first visit and planned to delay it again.

"Dr. Nora?" Carolina came around the corner from the staircase. "Alex wants to come downstairs."

"Sure."

Because of the carpentry work, she'd moved the boy to her room. This morning she'd move him back to the sickroom where she could watch him while she arranged her medicines on the shelves. Later today she'd visit the boardinghouse to see her other patients. The measles outbreak was small and under control. Nora had done a good job, but she couldn't take full credit. She'd learned from Carolina that measles had gone through Bellville three times in the past ten years. Most of the folks in High Plains had acquired immunity before traveling west.

Carolina looked at the new shelves. "Reverend Preston does nice work. I'm sure he gave you a good price."

Nora traced a swirl in the wood. "Actually, he gave Zeb a good price."

"Zeb?"

"He paid for the shelves without telling me."

Carolina hummed with curiosity. "A week ago he left here like a cat on fire. Are you sure it was the same man?"

Nora set a jar on a shelf. "The reverend told me when I tried to pay him. I didn't ask questions."

"It seems to me the shelves speak for themselves."

Nora huffed. "I didn't think *wood* could talk."

"It can't," Carolina said, smiling. "But those shelves are a peace offering if I ever saw one."

"I guess," Nora admitted.

The nurse stepped to the cot in the corner and removed the sheet protecting it from sawdust. As she folded it, she sneezed. "Maybe we should invite Zeb for supper."

The sneeze reminded Nora of quarreling with him at the mill. "He wouldn't come. And if he did, he'd be rude and I'd get angry." She'd also feel the sweet yearnings she'd discovered at the river.

Hugging the sheets, Carolina walked to the doorway and turned. "A thank-you is in order and tomorrow is Sunday. Why don't you go to church. Zeb will be there."

Nora didn't feel ready to see him. "I'll send a note."

"And miss seeing his reaction?" Carolina smiled. "One look will tell you what we're both wondering."

"And what's that?" Nora asked.

"Why he did it."

Nora had the same question, but going to church meant facing Zeb in public. She preferred dealing with her enemies one at a time. "I don't think so."

"Go on," Carolina urged. "Not only do you deserve a day of rest, Reverend Preston has a way with words."

Nora wanted to hear the minister preach, but she'd had her fill of malice from Zeb and the Johnsons. On the other hand, she longed for the beat of a rousing hymn, the peace of a silent prayer. She also saw a chance to chat with the families she'd visited and affirm her presence as a physician. She wouldn't survive for long if she didn't see more patients.

"You need to be there," Carolina insisted. "If people get to know you, they'll trust you. Look at Alex. You helped him."

"I hope so."

"And Bess. She hasn't spoken yet, but she *wants* to. Yesterday when she came to the door, she opened her mouth instead of clamping it shut."

Nora saw progress, but Bess had a ways to go. "I'm trying, but it's not enough."

"You've done plenty," the nurse insisted. "She feels safe with you."

Nora wished she felt as safe in High Plains. Even church posed a danger. The Ladies Aid Society would gossip about her. Even more troubling, she'd see Zeb looking handsome in his Sunday best. She traced a swirl in the oak. It dipped and rose, narrowed, then spread around a knot as dark as Zeb's heart. Only God could remove that hardness. In Nora's experience, the Lord would either soften hard spots with love, or He cut them out with suffering. As a physician, she knew about surgery and scars. She also knew God's ways. She couldn't avoid Zeb just because he upset her. "I'd love to go to church," she said to Carolina. "Are you sure about staying with Alex?"

"Of course." The older woman tipped her head. "I'll press a dress for you. Which one?"

Nora thought for a minute. "The copper silk." The one she'd worn to the mill…the one that had caught Zeb Garrison's eye. Why she cared, she didn't know. If he spoke to her at all, he'd be insufferable. As for the Ladies Aid Society, only the meanest of souls would accuse a woman dressed in brown of low moral character.

Zeb walked into church five minutes late and slid into the back pew. He figured Cassandra would be seated up front with the Logans. When he didn't see her, he scanned the middle seats and spotted her with Percival. Zeb wished he'd dragged himself out of bed sooner. Cassandra and Percy were seeing too much of each other. If Clint didn't wise up, she'd be headed back to Boston as Mrs. Percival Walker, a thought Zeb loathed.

He also loathed church and attended for one reason. It was easier to sleep in the back row than it would be to explain his absence.

He never had liked Sunday services. As a boy, he'd been bored and fidgety. As a man, he knew the weaknesses of his character and didn't need to be reminded. He stumbled every day, though not as badly as he'd fallen in Boston. After Frannie left, he'd disappeared for three days and done things he deeply regretted. There hadn't been any pleasure in that darkness, only a numbness that had burned like fire in the light of dawn. He'd been ashamed of himself and hadn't stumbled since, at least not in that way. No one knew about that ugly time, not even Will. He supposed God knew, but the Almighty didn't seem to care. At least he hadn't struck Zeb dead, which at the time seemed preferable to living without Frannie.

The hymn ended with a tremulous amen and the congregation sat. As the air stirred, he smelled lavender. He looked to his right and saw Nora seated four feet away. Her eyes were riveted to the pulpit, but the blush on her cheeks indicated she'd noticed him.

He had to wonder…did she like the shelves? He'd planed the wood himself and had a splinter in his thumb to prove it. He'd tried soaking it, but it hadn't come out. He'd gone after it with a sewing needle and picked until it bled, but the sliver wouldn't budge. The annoyance seemed fitting. His conscience also had a splinter, the kind that wouldn't come out until he apologized. He'd hoped for a note from her, something to acknowledge the peace offering. Judging by the tightness of her mouth, she didn't have that note in her pocket.

Zeb faced forward. He'd given her a gift, a nice one. Did she want his pride, too? She couldn't have it. He refused to grovel in front of anyone.

Reverend Preston stepped to the podium. "Ladies and gentlemen, let us pray …"

Zeb bowed his head out of habit, not humility. He heard words like *charity* and *neighbor,* but he felt neither charitable nor neighborly. If Dr. Mitchell wanted to make peace, it was her turn to bend.

Reverend Preston cleared his throat. "Please stand for our next hymn, 'Just as I Am.' It's number eighteen in your hymnals."

The book was sitting to his right. So was Nora. When he reached for it, so did she. Their hands stopped in midair just inches apart over the black leather. Zeb's gaze traveled up the sleeve of her brown dress to the high collar, past her jaw to her blue eyes. As their gazes collided, she raised her chin. He indicated she should take the book, then faced forward. She could have the hymnal. He didn't like to sing anyway.

Pages fluttered as books were opened and couples bumped shoulders. The rustling reminded him of the wind. Wind reminded him of the tornado and how empty he'd felt with death a breath away. He still wanted a legacy, a son who'd inherit Garrison Mill, but the thought didn't bring the satisfaction he expected.

His chest felt as hollow as a drum, each beat more lonely than the last. The scent of lavender rushed into his nose and he turned. Nora had stepped to his side with the hymnal open and cradled in her hands. When she tilted her face up to his, he saw the trepidation of a woman who'd had a door slammed in her face. He couldn't blame her for being wary of him. He'd treated her terribly and he knew it. A wry smile lifted his lips. It said *I'm sorry* without words.

She smiled back, then looked down at the page. Zeb

pinched a corner of the book and together they sang the first words of the hymn.

"Just as I am, without one plea..."

Zeb doubted God wanted him just as he was, but he sang anyway. So did Nora. Her voice, a timid soprano, didn't match her hair. With their shoulders nearly touching, she seemed smaller than she had at the mill.

Wanting to bear some of the load, he slid his right hand beneath the hymnal and held it for them both. His thumb grazed the tip of her glove and she pulled back, but only a bit. He felt a sudden lightness at her touch, a lifting of his heart as she sang the words. Did Will feel this camaraderie with Emmeline? Did Pete share it with Rebecca? Zeb recalled his friends laughing at his tirade about women and felt foolish. Instead of chasing Nora out of High Plains, he wanted to kiss her senseless. What a thought to have in church! Surely God would strike him dead...except He didn't. Instead, for the first time since Frannie had jilted him, Zeb felt joy rising as he sang with Nora ...

> Just as I am, Thou wilt receive.
> Wilt welcome, pardon, cleanse, relieve.

He didn't want to think about Frannie and pardon in the same breath, but he very much wanted to be cleansed and relieved of the past. For two years he'd lived with claw marks on his heart. Did he want to feel that sting the rest of his life? No, he didn't. He didn't want to waste two more minutes on Frannie. The thought freed him, but only for an instant. Forgiving Frannie was one thing. Risking his heart on a lady doctor was another.

When the music ended, he closed the book and they sat. Nora folded her hands in her lap. Zeb rested his palms on his knees.

"Good morning!" Reverend Preston boomed. "This is the day our Lord hath made. Let us rejoice and be glad in it."

Nora breathed deeply, as if she were savoring a rose. Zeb tried not to fidget.

The reverend opened his Bible. "More than forty days ago, a tornado ripped our town—and our lives—to pieces. Some of us lost loved ones. Others lost homes. We *all* lost sleep and had bad dreams. We became fearful of the unknown, the uncertainties hidden in clouds on the horizon. Today I want to talk about another storm. This one happened in the days of Noah. It lasted forty days and forty nights and tested the faith of a brave man and the people who trusted him."

Zeb's fingers knotted on his knees. He hadn't built an ark, but he and Will had captained the journey to High Plains. Dozens of families had followed them. He felt responsible for their safety. The reverend had his full attention as he described Noah battling the storm, the rise and fall of the waves, the smell of too much life in small quarters. Zeb thought of families living in shacks. He had to keep the lumber coming for houses.

"What gave Noah his strength?" the reverend asked. "Did he have a compass to find land? Could he meet every need on that storm-tossed boat?"

The reverend paced the length of the pulpit, then looked at Zeb. "Noah couldn't do it alone. That's why he leaned on the Almighty. He prayed. He *believed* God would see them through the storm."

Zeb wanted that assurance, but he didn't have it. In his experience, God cared about Heaven and Hell but not the here and now. Anger welled in his belly, but so did a longing to be proven wrong. He only half listened to the reverend's words about perseverance. Zeb had been persevering his whole life, first to escape Bellville and then to build Garrison Mill.

"So how do we manage in times of trouble?" the reverend asked. "Where did Noah find the wisdom to captain that ship?"

Zeb stopped fidgeting.

The minister kept pacing. "He didn't get it by staying up all night. He didn't get it by working hard, either."

Zeb saw himself as plain as day.

The reverend looked straight at him. "Noah got wisdom by asking the Lord for help. Just like us, he found himself in tough times. He did his best and trusted God to do what he couldn't do for himself."

The minister swept the congregation with his eyes. "The Lord loves us, ladies and gentlemen. And He's given us the capacity to love one another. That's what kept Noah going. He loved God, and he loved the people in his care. We love each other today because God first loved us."

Zeb didn't feel loved by God. He felt worse than empty, as if his soul had turned to dust. Had the dryness started with Frannie? He wanted to blame her but couldn't. As long as he could remember, he'd had a yearning he couldn't satisfy. He'd thought success would fill it, but it hadn't. He'd thought marrying Frannie would make him happy, but she'd left. He'd once asked Will if he felt that same lack. His friend, a godly man, had said no.

Zeb wanted that peace. How did he get it? *Show me, Lord. What do I have to do?*

His mind traveled back to the church in Bellville. *Ask and it will be given to you. Seek and ye shall find.*

Was it that easy? Could he ask God for help and get it? As a millwright, Zeb lived by logic. To be effective, the millworks had to be powered by the river. The waterwheel transferred the energy to the saws. What connected man and God? Nothing Zeb could see.

In the next breath, Reverend Preston looked right at him again. "What is it that connects us to God?"

Zeb got chills.

"I'll tell you what that connection is," the man said. "It's love. A mother will go hungry to feed her child. A man will die to save his family. It's love that keeps us looking for the missing children, and it's love that gives us the power to rebuild this town."

A prickling raced up Zeb's spine and put his thoughts in motion as surely as the flow of the High Plains River powered the mill. God was the river, the source of power. Love was the waterwheel, the connection between God and humanity. Love had put Christ on the cross and given mankind the hope of eternity and new life. As understanding dawned, Zeb felt a trembling in his belly. Without God, he was as dead as a mill in a drought. He couldn't explain why bad things happened, why tornadoes struck and children got snatched, but he could trust in rivers and waterwheels—in God and His love—the way Noah had trusted during the storm.

Zeb had some amends to make and he knew it. *I'm sorry, Lord, for my pride.* Peace filled his soul, but only halfway. He owed Nora a real apology, not one made of wood.

Reverend Preston rocked back on his heels. "We share God's love in many ways. We're friends. We're neighbors." His eyes twinkled. "We're also male and female. Like the animals on Noah's ark, we do better in pairs than we do apart."

The minister smiled at his wife in the front row. Will turned to Emmeline and smiled. Pete and Rebecca tipped their heads together like lovebirds. A yearning for more than work, something beyond a legacy, pulled at Zeb's gut. He wanted to be in love again, but how could he take that chance?

He looked down at Nora's hands, loose in her lap and covered with ivory lace. He imagined curling his fingers around them, but in the next breath he called himself a fool. Medicine would always come first in her life. He knew, because he had the same drive when it came to milling. Never mind her keen intelligence and fetching blue eyes. He'd be a fool to do more than apologize. With his jaw tight, he decided to make amends immediately after church. A few words would suffice.

Instead of feeling relieved by the decision, Zeb felt cheated. He didn't want to have feelings for Nora, but he did. Tough by nature, he was accustomed to fighting for what he wanted. Right now, he wanted to take this pretty, intelligent woman for a walk by the river. He wanted to take her hand and hold it, just to see what she'd do. Did they have a future together? He wouldn't know unless he kicked that rock down the road. He couldn't think of a better place to test their feelings than by the waterfall.

Reverend Preston closed the service with a prayer. As the crowd filtered to the door, Zeb turned to Nora. Her gaze held a challenge, but she didn't speak.

Keeping his voice level, he matched her stare and held it. "I'd like a word with you, Dr. Mitchell. Would you take a walk with me?"

With his heart plinking against his ribs, Zeb waited for her answer.

Chapter Fourteen

Nora matched his gaze with a tough one of her own. "Certainly. I have something to say to you, too."

"Then we're of the same mind."

She doubted it. Zeb Garrison detested her. What she felt for him defied explanation. When he'd slid into the pew next to her, she'd imagined a string pulling them together. She'd seen his jaw, freshly shaved with a small cut, probably because he'd hurried, and she'd wanted to dab it with her handkerchief. She hadn't thought twice about sharing the hymnal with him. She could no more shun Zeb and his troubled heart than she could leave Alex in a ditch.

He crooked his elbow and offered his arm. With a glint that dared her to accept, he waited for her to slip her fingers into place.

With a defiant gleam of her own, Nora took his arm as they stepped into the aisle, blending into the crowd waiting to greet Reverend Preston. Zeb said nothing, but she sensed his every breath. He seemed different than when he'd slid into the pew without noticing her. Standing at his side, she understood why the people of Bellville had followed him to High Plains. He had the poise of a confident man, someone they could trust because he'd fight for what he believed in.

Nora admired his bearing, but she knew it came at a cost. As a doctor she maintained the same poise. Only a few people knew how profoundly she wept when she lost a patient. She tightened her grip on Zeb's arm. When his biceps bunched, she recalled the brush of their fingers on the hymnal. As her nerves twittered, he looked down with the hint of a smile. Nora let go of his arm and stared straight ahead. She owed him a thank-you for the shelves, not a glimpse into her wayward thoughts.

The line moved steadily until they reached Reverend Preston. The minister shook her hand. "Welcome, Dr. Nora. I saw you in the back row." His eyes twinkled. "That's Zeb's special place, you know."

"I'll remember that." In the future she'd avoid him. "I enjoyed the sermon very much."

"Thank you." He released her hand. "I look forward to seeing you again."

"You will," she replied.

The minister gripped Zeb's hand next. "You, too, Zeb. Even in the back row."

When Zeb chuckled, Nora felt it in her bones. She'd grown accustomed to his tense moods. Today he seemed at ease. Why had he invited her for a walk? Her mind tripped down a strange and twisting path that ended at the top of a waterfall. Her stomach went over the edge, but she forced herself to weigh the facts. She had no reason to think he'd seen the light when it came to female physicians. Until she heard what he had to say, she'd be wise to maintain a polite distance.

As they walked into the churchyard, he spoke so only she could hear. "Let's walk around back."

"All right."

As he guided her to a side path, Cassandra waved at them. "Zeb! Nora! Come here."

He kept walking, but Nora stopped. "You can't just ignore her."

"Sure I can." He flashed a grin. "She's my sister."

His expression left her breathless, but her mind stayed engaged with her surroundings, especially people noticing them. Zeb didn't need to earn the town's respect, but she did. Leaving with him, especially in a secretive manner, would lead to gossip.

He looked at her thoughtfully. "All right, we'll stay a minute. But I want to talk to you alone."

"Zeb!" Cassandra's voice rose to a whine. "Hurry up!"

When he grimaced, Nora smiled. "She's determined, isn't she?"

"Very," he said dryly.

Together they walked to a circle that included Cassandra and Percy, Winnie Morrow and Will and Emmeline Logan. Several feet away she saw the Benjamins chatting with Clint, who looked uncomfortable in a starched collar. Nora looked for Bess and spotted her on the outer edge of a group of children playing tag. She recognized Johnny and Glory Carter, the younger siblings of Emmeline and Bess. When a girl with pigtails caught Johnny, Bess clapped, but made no other sound.

Will waved at Zeb, motioning them forward. Percival stepped closer to Cassandra to make room for them. As Cassandra beamed, Winnie scanned the crowd as if looking for someone else. Several feet behind her, Nora saw Clint watching Cassandra's back with a dark expression. When Rebecca said something to him, he shook his head and turned to leave.

When Mrs. Jennings joined Rebecca and Pete, Zeb called to him. "Clint! Come over here."

The cowboy gave a tight shake of his head, tugged his hat low and headed for his horse. He swung into the saddle with an angry grace, turned the bay and galloped out of town.

Nora wished he'd accepted Zeb's invitation. If he didn't fight for Cassandra, he'd lose her to Percy. Nora thought of her own mixed feelings concerning Zeb. Did the same advice apply to her? As her mother had cautioned when she'd chosen medical college over dances, pride made for a lonely bed.

Emmeline looked from Zeb to Nora with a question in her eyes. "Did you two enjoy the sermon?"

"I did," Zeb replied.

Will's brows shot up. "Did I hear that right?"

Nora wondered about Will's reaction until the rancher looked at her with a lopsided grin. "You have to know Zeb to understand why that's a surprise. As long as I've known him, he's slept through every sermon he's heard."

"Not today." Zeb spoke with authority. "If Noah were alive, I'd shake his hand."

Will looked at his friend thoughtfully. "Me, too."

Emmeline glanced in Bess's direction, then turned to Nora. "Rebecca tells me Bess visits you. Thank you for helping her."

"I wish I could do more." Nora focused on Emmeline. "As I mentioned when we met, I've written to a colleague in New York. He's an expert in psychiatry."

"What's that?" Cassandra asked.

The subject had been among Nora's favorites. "It's the study and treatment of disorders of the mind."

Percival cleared his throat. "The field is just being explored, isn't it?"

"In this country, yes."

Zeb huffed with derision. Whether he'd aimed his opinion at Percy or herself, Nora couldn't tell. Neither did she care. She respected Dr. Zeiss and hoped his work would help Bess.

Cassandra looked at Percy with pride, then smiled at Nora. "Did you study psychiatry in medical college?"

"I was privileged to study with Dr. Gunter Zeiss from Berlin. He's an expert in the field."

Zeb said nothing. Emmeline looked doubtful and so did Will. Cassandra, taking a cue from Percival, tried to appear sophisticated. Nora wondered if she'd ever belong in this town. In New York she'd grown accustomed to doubt, so why did it hurt in High Plains?

"Zeb! There you are!"

Nora turned and saw Abigail Johnson approaching with her parents. Nora had met Mrs. Johnson, but Abe Johnson had been away when she'd visited the mercantile. She saw a portly man with flushed cheeks and a bulbous nose, signs of a skin disorder called acne rosacea. "Good morning," she murmured as everyone exchanged greetings.

Abigail gave her a cold smile. Mrs. Johnson refused to make eye contact. Mr. Johnson looked past her and clapped Zeb on the back. "How's the town hall coming along?"

"Fine." Zeb shot Nora an irritated glance, then spoke to the others. "If you'll excuse me, we were about to—"

"You can't leave," Abigail insisted. "Didn't you hear?"

"Hear what?" he asked.

"The jubilee committee is meeting right now."

"That's right," Mrs. Johnson said. "Abigail baked the pies herself. Mr. Johnson and I are leaving now to put on the coffee."

Mr. Johnson looked surprised, but he followed his wife without a word. Abigail stared at Zeb as if she had the right to ask questions. Nora watched Zeb for a reaction but didn't see one. She wanted to know why he'd asked her to take a walk, but she'd understand if he backed out for a prior obligation.

Without a glance in her direction, he spoke to Abigail. "I won't be there."

"You *have* to come!" Abigail said with a pout. "We're planning the games. We need a man's perspective." She turned to Cassandra and Emmeline. "Isn't that right, ladies?"

Cassandra gripped Percival's elbow. "Percy and I will be glad to help."

He patted her hand. "Of course."

Emmeline shook her head. "My mother's feeling poorly. Will and I have to get home."

Cassandra looked at Nora. "You'll come to the meeting, won't you? We need new ideas, especially ideas from New York."

Nora didn't want to be labeled an Eastern debutante, but neither did she want to be unfriendly. Abigail wanted to keep her away from Zeb, and Zeb looked fit to be tied. An excuse seemed in order. "I'd love to, but Carolina's expecting me."

"Of course," Abigail said too eagerly.

Cassandra bounced on her toes. "Please, Nora." It came out in a whine. "You're the only person I know with a *Godey's Lady's Book.*"

Abigail snickered. "We don't need a *magazine* to plan the jubilee."

Nora would have been glad to leave graciously, but she refused to be chased off by Abigail. She also wanted to be part of the community. Working on the jubilee would be a way to make friends. She smiled at the group. "I'd be glad to volunteer."

Abigail shot daggers with her eyes. Nora glanced at Zeb. Instead of irritation, she saw amusement dancing in his green irises. She didn't know if he liked boxing, but he looked like an enthusiast on his way to a match. Fine, Nora thought. It wouldn't be the first time she'd fought to be accepted.

Abigail wormed her way in next to Zeb. "Everyone's here, so let's go."

Nora hung back, but Zeb motioned for her to walk at his side. Ignoring him, she paired off with Winnie and followed behind Cassandra and Percy. After saying goodbye to Will and Emmeline, the six of them strolled down Main Street to the mercantile. Outside stairs led to an apartment stuffed with a sofa, two curio cabinets, a dining room table and mismatched rugs. Nora figured the Johnsons had owned a big house in Massachusetts and planned to build again, but the current arrangement made for a gaudy display.

Abigail dropped down on an armchair upholstered with rose-colored silk. "Please, everyone, sit down."

Winnie sat with Percy and Cassandra on the sofa. Abigail indicated that Zeb should take the seat on her right. Everyone except Nora had a place in the circle. She spotted a spindly chair off to the side and moved in that direction.

"Hold it," Zeb said to her back.

Nora turned and saw him holding out the chair next to Abigail. She had no desire to take the spot meant for him, but he'd already detoured to the little chair and was carrying it into the circle. He set it down next to the seat meant for him, putting Nora directly between himself and Abigail. Smiling politely, she smoothed her skirts and sat. As Zeb sat on the side chair, it creaked.

Abigail disguised her irritation by starting the meeting. "Considering how hard Zeb's worked to finish the town hall, I want the jubilee to be spectacular."

Zeb shifted in the chair. It creaked again. "It's not *my* hard work, Abigail. The whole town is chipping in."

"Don't be modest," she insisted. "Without you, we'd all be living in tents. High Plains wouldn't be on the map. You're one of the founding fathers. You're—"

"I'm just one person," he said. "It's like Noah and the ark. Will and I captained the ship, but everyone helped."

No wonder Zeb had enjoyed the sermon. He understood storms.

Winnie glanced from Zeb to Abigail. "Everyone's helped with the town hall. I see Edward Gunderson there almost every day."

"Edward's a good man," Zeb acknowledged.

Winnie's expression turned wistful, a sure sign that she liked the man. Nora wondered why Edward, Pete and Rebecca hadn't joined the circle after church, and why Rebecca wasn't included in planning the jubilee, then she recalled Mrs. Johnson's ugly accusations after the tornado. The cook had wisely kept her distance. With a little luck, she'd have her revenge by winning the baking contests.

Cassandra looked at her brother. "I'm tired of dust and dirt and old clothes. Instead of opening the town hall with an afternoon social, let's have a dance."

The girl looked to Nora for support, but Nora had no desire to take sides. She enjoyed dancing, but she preferred long walks to noisy parties.

Abigail smiled at Zeb. "That's a *wonderful* idea! My father plays the fiddle. I'm sure we can find some other musicians."

Cassandra looked up at Percival. "It won't be as nice as an orchestra, but we'll have fun."

"I suppose," Percy replied.

Nora owed him for finding her a house, but her opinion of the attorney sunk lower with his patronizing tone. Nora loved High Plains. Boston had ballets and intellectual pursuits, but High Plains had people with good hearts and big dreams.

Zeb started tapping his boot in an ominous rhythm. Nora glanced to the side and saw him glaring at Percy. "What about games? Any ideas?"

The attorney lifted a brow in challenge. "A test of strength, of course."

"Like what?" Zeb asked.

"Arm wrestling." Percy flexed his biceps.

The gesture struck Nora as silly, but Cassandra looked ready to swoon. If Zeb had an opinion, he kept it to himself. Instead, he turned to Abigail. "I'll set up a log-sawing contest. Pete can help with horseshoes."

Nora thought of Rebecca and decided to chime in. "How about a baking contest? Maybe for the best pie?"

"And pie eating," Winnie added.

Nora smiled. "Alex would like that one. How about something for the younger children?"

Abigail looked smug. "Don't trouble yourself, Dr. Mitchell. I've already planned something for the children."

Cassandra interrupted. "I'm the teacher. You said I'd—"

Abigail glared a warning. "I said it's handled."

Nora knew a fib when she heard one. The blonde hadn't done a thing for the children. The woman's expression turned thoughtful, then she looked straight at Nora. "If you really want to help, there *is* something you could do."

Nora sensed trouble. "What do you have in mind?"

"We're going to have a mess after the pie-eating contest. Someone might even be sick." She looked straight at Nora. "You can be in charge of clean-up."

The insult bounced off Nora like a drop of rain. She'd heard worse. "If that's what you need, I'd be glad to do it."

Cassandra gaped at Abigail. Percy arched a brow, and Winnie looked confused. Silence reigned until a rumble started in Zeb's throat. It grew in intensity until all eyes were on him and he turned to Nora. "No, you won't," he said in low tone. "I'm in charge of cleanup."

Abigail huffed. "You can't be. Cleanup is women's work."

Nora didn't know whether to pity Abigail for her lack of sense, or to challenge her bigotry. In Nora's experience, messes were like suffering. They had no gender.

Zeb wrinkled his brow, then stared at Percival. "What do you think, Percy? Shall we stick the ladies with *hauling trash?*"

"Of course not," he said gallantly. "We'll hire someone. Maybe that cowboy—"

Zeb cut him off. "Clint's helping me."

All eyes turned to Nora. She appreciated Zeb's effort on her behalf, but she didn't want to add to Abigail's hostility by siding with him. To avoid more bickering, she pushed to her feet. "I'll be glad to do anything, but I can't stay any longer." She focused on Cassandra. "Will you let me know what the group decides?"

"Of course, but—"

Nora held up her hand. "I'll do whatever has to be done."

As she stood, so did the men. Nora turned to Abigail. Good manners called for a polite goodbye, but Abigail's insults had to be addressed. Nora spoke in a drawing room tone she'd used with professors. "Thank you, Miss Johnson, for your hospitality. I can't remember the last time I felt *this* welcome anywhere. In fact, I've *never* met anyone with such a *gracious* demeanor."

With a dip of her chin, Nora glanced around the room. Cassandra looked pleased and so did Winnie. Percival's brows had shot up and were locked in place. Last, she looked at Zeb. His mouth stayed straight, but his eyes were dancing with laughter. He'd wanted a fight and he'd gotten one. But who had he been rooting for? Nora didn't know and she didn't care. At least that's what she told herself as she headed for the door.

No one moved as it closed behind her. She needed to go home to Alex, but she didn't want to see him with her temper high. Zeb had promised her a walk by the river. Leaving him to Abigail, she decided to take the walk alone.

Zeb gave Nora a ten-minute head start, then excused himself from the silly meeting. He'd have run after her when she left, but he knew how spiteful Abigail could be. She'd start ugly rumors. Matilda would launch an all-out attack, and Nora would have more problems than she did now. Zeb didn't like the idea of a woman doctor any more than he had a few weeks ago, but he had to admire the way she'd stood up to Abigail's snobbery.

He didn't want to look too closely at the reason he'd bristled on Nora's behalf, but he couldn't deny the reaction. He thought of the apology he owed her and tensed again. Irritated by everything, he shoved to his feet. "I'm leaving. I have work to do."

Abigail sulked. "But Zeb. We haven't had pie."

"No, thanks."

"But I'm not finished!" she whined.

Yes, you are. And in more ways than one. No way could he consider marrying Abigail after today's little show. The woman had a mean streak just like her mother. Will was right. Zeb had been crazy to consider such a plan.

"Work comes first," he said, dismissing her.

He went to Nora's house, knocked politely and learned from Carolina that she hadn't come home. He wondered if she'd gone to the river. Determined to speak with her, he cut across the meadow to the path that led to the mill. He spotted her near the waterfall, perched on a flat stone with her back to him. The river muffled his steps, giving him time to gauge her mood as he sauntered down the path. She sat ramrod straight, but her shoulders had a feminine grace. She looked at ease, but he suspected the battle with Abigail had exacted a price. Zeb knew how he reacted after a quarrel. He was prickly for hours.

He felt prickly now, but not from anger. Unaware of his presence, Nora poked a finger into her coiffure and scratched an itch. She must have missed the spot, because she raised her arms and unpinned her hat. Turning slightly, she set the hat on the rock and removed a pin. A loop of hair fell to her shoulder.

Suddenly transfixed, he watched the sun turn her hair into copper. With the waterfall pounding in his ears, he imagined the loose curls tumbling down her back. Somewhere in the past two weeks, he'd stopped disliking this woman and had become intrigued. Except for Will and Pete, people in High Plains did what he said. Nora stood up to him without hesitation. He didn't trust her medical skills and doubted she'd stay in Kansas, but he had to admire her spirit. He also had to make his presence known before she caught him looking and accused him of bad manners.

He raised his voice to be heard over the river. "Hey, Doc. Got an itch?"

She shot to her feet and faced him. The hank of loose hair bounced like a spring until she tucked it above her ear. "You were spying on me!"

"No, I wasn't." He ambled forward. "If I'd been spying, I wouldn't have spoken up."

Hatless, she looked less like Dr. Mitchell and more like Nora. He wasn't sure what to call her, but she'd assumed a formal pose. A breeze caught the tendril behind her ear and tugged it loose. It must have tickled, because she jammed it deeper into her coiffure, then looked at him with an expression that was all business.

"You wanted to speak to me," she said evenly.

"I do," he said. "But first I've got to hand it to you, Doc. That tongue of yours is sharper than my best saw."

He was trying to be friendly, but her expression hardened. "What do you mean?"

"You put Abigail in her place. She had it coming."

Nora raised her chin. "I took no pleasure in the exchange, Mr. Garrison. It was a silly argument."

"I rather enjoyed it." Hoping to show his goodwill, he grinned.

She answered with a cold stare.

The expression irked him. He wanted to laugh with her about the silliness, maybe hear a thank-you for how he'd stepped in. In Zeb's view, Abigail had earned her comeuppance.

Come to think of it, so had he. He still owed Nora amends. After wiping the smirk off his face, he approached her. His shadow fell across the hem of her dress, turning the copper to a dull brown.

She stepped back into the sun, causing the grass to wave at her feet. "Why are you here?" she demanded.

"We had plans."

"For what? Another quarrel?" She sighed with disgust. "I've had enough bickering for one day. That includes arguing with you about my competence as a physician."

"That's not why I'm here." He held out his hand to indicate the rock. "Sit. This won't take long."

"I'd rather stand."

Did she have to argue about *everything?* He'd hoped to find the woman who'd held the hymnal with him, the one who hadn't pulled away when their fingers touched. The woman in front of him looked mad enough to spit on his boots. Zeb understood anger. It made him strong, but it also got him in trouble. Dr. Mitchell, it seemed, had the same bad habit. If she wanted to fight, he'd be glad to oblige. He crossed his arms over his chest. "What's got you in a twist?"

"You know very well."

He saw the shine of hurt feelings in her eyes. "Actually, I don't. Perhaps you could enlighten me?"

"You wanted a catfight and you got it."

"You and Abigail?"

"Exactly."

He wrinkled his brow. "Why would I want that?"

"I don't know *why* you do anything, Mr. Garrison! One day you're berating me for being a doctor. The next day you've paid for shelves for my office. Half the time you're glowering at me. The other half, you make me feel—" She sealed her lips as if she had nearly spilled a secret.

Zeb knew how *he* felt around *her.* He breathed deeper around this woman. He felt stronger, even hopeful. "Go ahead," he said, prodding her. "How do I make you feel?"

"You make me furious!"

"Likewise, Dr. Mitchell." He put his hands on his hips, then grinned at her with the full force of a determined man. "Since we're of one mind, would you have supper with me tonight?"

Chapter Fifteen

"Supper?" Nora stared in disbelief.

"Sure. Why not?"

A dozen reasons crossed her mind, starting with the one that confused her the most. She had to say no because she wanted to say yes. While sitting on the rock, she'd weighed the events of the day and come to a harsh conclusion. Before she opened her heart to anyone in High Plains, she had to establish herself as a physician. Why make friends if she'd be gone in a few weeks?

Even more dangerous, why give her heart to a man who didn't like her? Or did he? Nora didn't know what to think. Zeb had just rescued her from trash duty. Considering his opinion of female doctors, the gesture made no sense. Earlier, looking at the mill, she'd made a silent vow to ignore him. She had to stand on her own and she would.

Having supper with him would only complicate the situation. "Thank you," she said. "But I can't accept."

"Why not?"

The reasons seemed obvious. "For one thing, we don't like each other."

His eyes twinkled with amusement. "Speak for yourself, Doc."

Baffled, she matched his stare with one of her own. When the corners of his mouth hinted at a grin, she thought of the shelves and the brush of his arm in church. She also recalled his sharp tongue and the way he'd slammed the door when he'd left her house. Zeb confused her in the most fundamental ways. Her heart felt drawn to him. Her experience with male arrogance told her to push him away.

He indicated the boulder with an open hand. "Please, Nora. Sit and listen. I have some explaining to do."

The hush of her name stole her breath. So did the hint of an apology. Intrigued, she dropped down on the warm granite. As she looked up, the sun burned into her eyes and she squinted. Zeb stepped in front of her, shading her face as the blue sky turned his head into a silhouette. He could see her plainly. She couldn't see him at all.

"I'm listening," she said evenly.

"I want to apologize for my behavior when you first arrived. Regardless of your gender, I had an obligation to provide an office for you. I didn't do that, and I'm sorry."

The apology stunned her. Was he sincere? Could she trust him? "I don't know what to say."

"There's more." He pointed again at the rock, indicating he wanted to sit next to her. "May I?"

"I suppose."

As he lowered his lean body to the slab, Nora scooted to the side but only an inch. There was nowhere to go. She didn't know which posture she found more disconcerting—Zeb looming over her, a black silhouette with broad shoulders, or Zeb sitting next to her, a flesh-and-blood man with bristly cheeks. Hoping to appear unruffled, she sat with her hands primly laced in her lap.

Zeb sat with his forearms on his knees, steepling his fingers as he looked past her to the river. "I'm sorry about the other day at your house. I'm not usually that much of an ogre."

She'd already forgiven him, but she didn't want to cheapen the apology by making light of it. "*Ogre* fits. You left in a rage."

"I know."

She waited for an explanation, but he answered by staring into the distance. The breeze stirred his dark hair and the grass rippled with lazy ease. In the distance she heard the river tumbling over the waterfall. Some things in life were unstoppable. Gravity pulled a rock down a hill. Love pulled men and women together the same way. From the minute she'd seen Zeb Garrison, she'd felt drawn to him. She felt the pull now and it scared her to death.

He didn't like her.

He didn't respect her work.

He had a bad temper and a prideful disposition.

He'd also loved a woman and been deeply hurt. He'd seen his hometown blown to bits and his neighbors die.

Nora knew about wounds. Pain made even the gentlest souls cry out in rage. The deeper the cut, the longer it took to heal. The longer the healing, the more prominent the scar, whether it was visible or not. She thought of Bess locked in a silent world. Zeb didn't have trouble speaking his mind, but he'd stifled his feelings as surely as Bess stifled her voice. Nora couldn't leave him dangling any more than she could abandon Bess. She smiled at him. "Were the shelves a peace offering?"

"Yes."

"I accept." To seal the deal, she held out her gloved hand. Zeb took it, and their fingers meshed like reeds making a basket. Neither of them spoke. Neither twitched a muscle until the lingering turned into a question. Startled, Nora ended the handshake with a quick squeeze of her fingers.

Zeb winced.

"What's the matter?" she asked.

He tried to pull away, but she turned his hand palm up so she could see what had caused the pain.

"It's nothing," he said, drawing back.

"Then you won't mind if I look."

Frowning, he turned his hand to the side so she could see his thumb. A red bump had formed below the knuckle. Shiny and hard, the infection looked ready to burst. "What happened?" she asked.

"It's just a splinter. I get them all the time."

"This one's festering." Nora didn't want to be a doctor today, but she couldn't ignore her training. "How long have you had it?"

"About a week."

As she poked at the boil-like lump, she thought of the shelves lining her clinic. Someone had spent hours sanding them smooth, and it hadn't been Reverend Preston. She looked at Zeb with a new understanding. His gift had been more personal than she'd realized. "You cut the wood for the shelves, didn't you?"

He shrugged.

She wished he'd speak up, but she recognized the gesture as agreement. Not only had he paid Reverend Preston, he'd spent time thinking about her, trying to please her. She felt warm all over. She also knew what an infection could do. "The splinter should be removed. I could—"

He tried to take back his hand, but Nora held tight. Zeb pulled until she let go. "It'll work its way out," he said. "They always do."

"This one's deep."

Zeb shook his head. "I'll deal with it later."

"Let me help you." She saw him considering the offer and

decided to be charitable. "This isn't even real doctoring. Anyone could take it out."

He hesitated. "No, thanks, Doc."

They were talking about more than a splinter. If he accepted her help, he'd be sacrificing his pride. Nora had a quandary of her own. If she accepted his supper invitation before she earned his respect, she'd be denying the call on her life. They sat in silence, each listening to the river, until she couldn't stand the closeness. She dropped his hand and stood. "If you change your mind, I'll be at the clinic." She snatched her hat from the rock, turned her back and headed up the path.

His boots scuffed the earth. "Nora, wait."

Again he'd used her given name. The hush of it made her warm all over. It also made her furious. Who was she to this man? A woman or a doctor? She wanted to be both. She *needed* to be both. Hurting and frustrated, she raced down the path. He followed her, his boots slapping against the dirt. Intending to tell him to leave, she pivoted. Her heel caught on a rut and she stumbled.

He caught her in his arms, steadying her until her legs stopped wobbling. Common sense told her to step back, but she didn't want to snap the thread of silent connection. From the distance of inches, a foot at the most, she felt the tug and pull of being female. This man needed her. He had splinters in his heart as well as his flesh, but how could she trust him, even as a friend, when he didn't respect her work? She couldn't, but neither could she look away from his green eyes, bright and glittering like the broken glass in Doc Dempsey's office.

Her chest rose and fell with three quick breaths. His throat twitched and his hands tightened on her elbows. They stood face-to-face, breathing in a matching rhythm as seconds churned into an eternity, until the corners of his mouth tightened and his eyes glinted. "I do believe you're daring me to kiss you."

Her tongue refused to move.

"Are you?" he murmured.

"It's not a dare," she answered. "It's… I don't know what it is."

"I do," he said in a gravelly voice. "You're wondering."

Nora couldn't lie, not even with silence. Almost imperceptibly, she nodded her head.

"I'm wondering, too."

Slowly, giving her time to object, he drew her into his arms. His lips came together and his eyes closed as if he were dreaming, then his mouth found hers and he kissed her. He brushed her lips once, then again. The sweetness of it made her senses reel. The danger made her heart pound. She didn't dare love Zeb until he respected her work, but neither did she want to stop kissing him.

In that moment, Nora faced a painful truth. She cared for Zeb Garrison. Whether he respected her work or not, she'd gone over the waterfall in a rush.

Zeb wasn't surprised when Nora broke from his arms and stepped back gasping. He felt the same way. Not since crossing the Mississippi had he felt the strange and wild daring of uncharted territory. He felt it now with Nora and he liked the amazement.

Far too much, he realized.

As usual, he'd gone too far and too soon. Unless they resolved their differences, they'd fight all the time. He didn't want to love a woman with a career. He wanted the mother of his children to be home. Zeb had other doubts, too. He still didn't trust her competence, and he doubted her commitment to High Plains. She'd come West because she'd been rejected everywhere else. What would she do if she was offered a position at a New York hospital? Frannie had faced a similar choice and she'd left him.

The thought of Frannie riled him, but not as much as the memory of kissing Nora. He needed to calm down. So did she. He wanted to put her at ease, but didn't know how. If he acknowledged the wonder of the kiss, where would they be? She wanted his respect for her work, but he couldn't give it. He wanted guarantees of her loyalty, but medicine would always take precedence in her life. Before they took another step, he needed to know he'd be first in her heart, not playing second fiddle to her medical bag. The thought angered him.

Before he found his tongue, Nora steadied herself with a sharp breath. "I'm not wondering anyone. That answers my question."

She sounded clinical, as if she were diagnosing a sore throat. Zeb kept his voice matter-of-fact. "So what's the answer?"

"Poison ivy."

He frowned. "I don't understand."

"Have you had it?"

"Once."

"As a physician, I've seen it many times." She sounded calmer. "People touch the ivy without knowing it. The next thing they know, they're red and itchy and the rash spreads."

Zeb didn't know if he'd been insulted for the kiss or paid a strange compliment. He'd never made a woman feel red and itchy before, but he supposed it was better than feeling nothing. A *lot* better, he decided. At least she was as unsettled as he was. "So what do you do for poison ivy? I'm asking because I've got it, too."

"Avoid it in the future."

"I'll try," he drawled. "But I can't say poison ivy's all bad."

"Me, neither." She looked him in the eye. "I'll be blunt, Zeb. I like you. I know I'm being too bold, but that's who I am."

"I like boldness."

Her gaze hardened with determination. "I'm also a doctor.

Until this town accepts me—until *you* accept me—I have to keep my eyes on why I'm here."

"I see."

"I'm not sure you do. My work—"

"—matters to you," he said for her. "You have a burden you never put down. I know, because I have the same burden with the mill. People need me."

"And they need me."

"I agree they need a doctor," he said. "But I still don't think you're the doctor they need."

Her lips pulled tight. "That's why we have to forget that kiss. It takes time, but poison ivy goes away."

She had a point, but Zeb wasn't ready to back down. This mess had started because he'd asked her to supper. She hadn't said no, but neither had she said yes. "You still haven't answered my question about supper."

She lifted her chin. "Thank you, but no."

"That's what I thought." Medicine would always come first in her life. She wouldn't even risk a meal with him.

After a long look, she turned her back and headed down the path. He wanted to follow her, but what could he say? One of them had to have a change of heart and it wouldn't be him. He'd learned the hard way not to trust ambitious women, and Dr. Mitchell would always put her career before anything—or anyone—else. The splinter in his thumb hurt, but he could live with it. It would take more than a little piece of wood to make him ask Dr. Nora for help.

As for the so-called poison ivy, only a fool touched it twice. He was no fool. He'd go back to the mill and shove logs through the saws with his men. In Zeb's experience, hard work cured anything, even poison ivy.

Chapter Sixteen

Alex picked up a wooden horse and ran it across the blanket covering his legs. He made it whinny and rear, then galloped it toward Nora, who was cleaning a window. The toy had arrived yesterday along with a note addressed to Alex in Zeb's handwriting.

Both had been delivered by Clint, who looked as worn out as he had a week ago. Apparently Zeb hadn't taken her advice about safety at the mill. She'd counseled Clint to rest, but he'd shaken his head. She hadn't liked his cough at all, but he'd refused to let her listen to his lungs. Instead, he'd pulled himself onto his horse and headed for the Circle-L. Nora let out a sigh. Would she ever gain the town's respect? It didn't seem like it.

As Alex galloped the horse over his knees, Nora thought again of Zeb. She'd never forget kissing him, though it seemed unlikely the moment would be repeated. He'd kept his distance and she'd kept hers. Unless something happened to turn the tide of public opinion, she'd be headed home to New York in a matter of weeks.

Alex stopped playing with the horse. "It stinks in here. I want to go outside."

She didn't blame him for being quarrelsome. He'd been in bed for ten long days. The rash had faded from red to brown, and light no longer bothered his eyes. He needed to be careful, but sunshine would do him good. She liked the idea of fresh air herself.

"Let's go right now." She draped the rag over the washbowl. "We can work in the garden."

"I guess so." He sounded forlorn.

Nora sat next to him on the bed. "Is something wrong?"

"I used to help my ma in the garden. I pulled weeds."

"You miss your family."

"A lot."

Nora smoothed the boy's hair. She'd come to love him the way she'd loved Ben. No matter what the future held, she hoped to adopt him and give him a good home. She hadn't mentioned her hopes to Alex because she didn't know where that home would be. She'd seen an appallingly small number of patients. In addition to Zeb's eye and Clint's cough, she'd treated four children, including Alex, for measles. One of the families had paid her, but the father of an ailing baby had ignored the obligation. He'd been well dressed and so had his wife. His failure to pay her had been blatant disrespect, but she'd visited the child again this morning.

If she didn't earn the town's confidence soon, she'd have to wire her father for money. She'd end up in New York married to a man who smelled like liniment. Every night she asked God for help. She'd visited several families again, but nothing had changed. Zeb's mistrust had infected all of High Plains. If he wouldn't let her remove a splinter, how could she gain respect from anyone else?

Frustrated but determined, she focused on Alex, the one person who believed in her. She tickled his cheek with her knuckle. "Instead of pulling weeds, how about we bake cookies?"

"Yeah!"

"I'll have to get more sugar at the mercantile." She had no desire to speak with Abigail or Mrs. Johnson, but she hadn't heard from Cassandra since the committee meeting. She needed to know if she'd ended up with trash duty. She also wanted to check for mail. She expected to hear from Dr. Zeiss any day.

Alex picked up the horse and made it rear up. "I love cookies!"

"Me, too." She stood, then lifted the bowl of vinegar water. "Go ahead and get dressed. I'll be back soon."

She took the bowl to the kitchen, removed her apron and went in search of Carolina. She found the nurse in the exam room dusting the books spread on the counter. Nora had perused them again last night in search of information on mutism.

As Carolina lowered the duster, Nora put on her brown felt hat. "I'm going to buy sugar for cookies. Do we need anything else?"

"Not a thing," the nurse replied.

"Would you watch Alex?"

Carolina smiled. "The boy's climbing the walls. Zeb did well to bring him that toy horse."

Nora said nothing.

"It's none of my business," the nurse said, "but what happened between you two?"

"Nothing important."

"It doesn't look that way to me." She flicked the duster over a shelf. "When it comes to Zeb, you've been as quiet as Bess."

Nora decided to change the subject. "Maybe I'll hear from Dr. Zeiss today."

"I hope so," Carolina replied. "That girl has me worried."

"Me, too." The longer Bess went without speaking, the deeper the mental scars. "No one really understands mutism, but Dr. Zeiss might have some insight."

"It's like her mind's bruised," Carolina said.

"Exactly."

After they traded worried looks, the nurse put the books back on the shelf and Nora left for the mercantile. With a smile plastered to her face, she ambled down Main Street. Children were playing in the meadow by the schoolhouse, and she saw women talking as they strolled past newly opened shops. In the distance she heard hammers as men pounded nails at the town hall. She thought of Zeb and felt bleak.

"Dr. Nora!"

She turned back to the mercantile and saw Will shouldering a sack of floor. He heaved it into a wagon, then tipped his hat to her. "It's good to see you, Doc. How are you doing?"

"Fine, thank you."

He indicated the door to the mercantile. "Emmeline's inside. I'm sure she'd like to say hello."

Nora welcomed the friendship. "I'd like that."

Will lowered his voice. "We appreciate what you're doing for Bess."

Nora saw the girl frequently, but she hadn't been out to the Circle-L since her first visit. "How is she at home?"

"She hasn't spoken, but I think she wants to." He told her about Bess moving her mouth in front of a mirror. "It looks strange, but it's a start."

"I hope so." Nora didn't mean to sound despondent, but she had a heavy heart today.

Will looked at her thoughtfully. "Stay strong, Doc. Before you arrived, Bess didn't even *want* to speak. She's going to talk again, and it's because of you. You're a good doctor. Don't ever doubt it."

"I wish others felt that way." She thought of Zeb and the splinter.

Will kept his voice low. "Still no patients?"

"A few." She tried to sound hopeful. "Alex is living with me now."

"He's a good kid." The rancher's expression turned grim. "Kids shouldn't suffer. I wish we could find the twins."

"Me, too." Nora's heart broke for Mikey and Missy. "Any sign of them?"

"Not a one."

Their disappearance haunted everyone in High Plains but especially Bess. Finding the twins—even if it meant burying bones—would help the girl recover. Nora hadn't seen her for a few days and wanted to say hello. "Is Bess with you?"

Will pointed down the street to a group of girls. Bess stood among them. "She just listens, but it's something."

The door to the mercantile opened and Emmeline came down the steps. "Dr. Nora! It's nice to see you." She walked forward and held out her hand.

Nora took it in both of hers. "I'm glad to see you, too. Your husband's been telling me about Bess."

Emmeline's eyes clouded. "We're doing what you said. We treat her as if everything's perfectly normal. It's just so—"

A scream cut off her next words.

Emmeline gasped. "That's Bess!"

A second scream filled the air. Longer and more determined, it sent shivers down Nora's spine. Some people ran from danger. Nora didn't run from anything, especially not a cry of pain. As she hiked up her skirts to run, so did Emmeline. Will grabbed them both by their elbows. "Stay here," he ordered. "It could be an Indian attack."

"I can't!" Nora insisted. "Someone could be hurt."

Emmeline pulled from his grip. "That was Bess! I *know* it."

Will knew better than to try to stop two determined women. "All right," he said. "But stay behind me."

He grabbed his shotgun from under the seat of the wagon. With the weapon loose and ready in his hand, he strode down the street with Nora and Emmeline following in a cloud of dust. Pete Benjamin emerged from between two buildings. He had a shotgun that matched Will's and the look of a man who'd use it. The two men met in the middle of the street. Shoulder to shoulder, they neared the town hall where Zeb, holding a matching weapon, fell into line. Briefly his eyes clashed with hers, the first time since the kiss, and she knew he hadn't forgotten.

As the men strode forward, Nora looked in the direction of Beth's shrieking. The cries were panicky now, long and full and rich with terror. A crowd had gathered in a half circle. The armed men shouldered through the throng. Nora and Emmeline followed until they saw an Indian woman mounted on a buckskin mare. In her lap sat a little girl with blond hair, feverish cheeks and blue-tinged lips.

Behind the woman sat a boy with the same blond hair but healthy coloring. With his arms tight around the woman's waist, he leaned to the side to look around. On the corner stood Bess, her hands pressed to her face as she screamed yet again.

"Mikey!" she wailed. "Missy!"

The shriek had turned to words. Hunching forward, she shook her head over and over as if she was reliving the tornado. As Nora ran to help her, Bess fainted. With Emmeline in her wake, Nora dropped to her knees at the girl's side, checked her pulse and felt a steady heartbeat. Bess had fainted from shock. She'd be fine when she woke up, but would she speak again?

"Dr. Mitchell!"

Will had called out to her. As Nora stood, Rebecca pushed through the crowd and crouched next to Emmeline. "Go! It's the twins! I'll stay with Bess."

As Nora and Emmeline moved into the circle, the boy slid

off the horse's rump. His sister lay limp in the Indian woman's arms. Her eyes, glazed and unfocused, had rolled back in her head. Each breath rasped as the girl struggled to get enough air. Nora suspected an asthma attack, the disease that had killed Ben. Or maybe quinsy, a swelling of the tonsils that blocked the airway. Quinsy had killed a man as formidable as George Washington. Missy didn't stand a chance without help.

The Indian woman searched the crowd. Even with shotguns aimed at her chest, she showed no fear. When her gaze landed on Emmeline, she said something in Kansa to Mikey.

"That's her!" the boy cried. "That's Emmeline!"

Emmeline raced to the horse's side, her arms outstretched to take Missy. The Indian woman kissed the girl's cheek, then handed her to Emmeline with a few soft words in the Kansa tongue.

Emmeline sagged beneath Missy's weight, but she didn't stumble. "Thank you," she said in full voice. "Thank you for saving them."

The woman said something to Emmeline, then eyed the men and their guns with a stoic expression. Will lowered his weapon first, then Zeb. Pete lowered his shotgun last. The woman looked at Mikey with a tender smile. When he reached up to hug her goodbye, she leaned down and kissed the top of his head. After a final nod, she turned her horse and rode out of town.

The crowd erupted in shouts of joy. Nora hurried to Emmeline's side and touched Missy's forehead. "She's burning up."

A terrible rasping came from Missy's throat. Emmeline gasped. "She can hardly breathe!"

Nora opened the girl's slack jaw with her fingers. In the back of her throat she saw a pustule the size of a walnut. "It's quinsy."

"She'll die!" Emmeline wailed.

"Not if I can help it." Nora sounded calmer than she felt. "We need to get her to my office. The abscess has to be lanced *now*."

Emmeline turned and ran with the child in her arms. Will pushed out of the crowd. "Give her to me!"

Emmeline handed over Missy and they all ran to the wagon in front of the town hall. Zeb leaped up to the seat and lifted the reins. The women vaulted into the back with petticoats flashing and no thought of modesty. Will laid Missy in Emmeline's lap, then climbed up next to her. Pete and Rebecca ran up behind Will. Pete was carrying Bess's limp body in his arms, and Rebecca had Mikey by the hand. Will gripped Bess's shoulders and hauled her into the wagon. Mikey jumped into the back on his own.

"Go!" Nora cried. "We don't have much time!"

Zeb shouted "Ya!" and the horses bolted. The wagon jerked violently and Emmeline toppled into Nora. Nora hit her head on the side of the wagon. Ignoring the pain, she tore off her glove and felt Missy's forehead. A feverish heat penetrated her palm. Missy opened her mouth wide to clear the airway, but it did no good. Each breath was weaker than the last.

Mikey started to sob. "She's going to die and it's my fault!"

Emmeline touched his cheek. "Don't say that, Mikey. Dr. Nora will fix her. You'll see."

The boy turned to Nora. "Are you really a doctor?"

"I am."

"But you're a *lady*."

Under less dire circumstances, Nora would have laughed at his baffled expression. Right now the boy needed reassurance. "I've been to school and everything."

Wide-eyed, he stared at her. "Can you fix Missy?"

"I'll do my best."

She knew not to make promises only God could keep. She'd watched helplessly when Ben died of asthma. He'd turned blue just like Missy. Her father had summoned a physician in the middle of the night. The man had done his best, but he couldn't save Ben.

To honor her brother, Nora had studied breathing ailments with particular interest. Most of the time, quinsy could be treated with rest, good food and herbal teas that helped the patient fight the infection. When those treatments failed and an abscess formed in the throat, the pustule had to be opened with a lancet and drained. The surgery itself posed little danger, but Missy had only minutes before her airway was blocked completely. When that happened, she'd be beyond help.

The wagon careened up the street to her house. Zeb reined the horses to a halt and jumped down from the seat. Carolina burst through the door. "What happened?"

"It's Missy," Nora shouted. "She has quinsy."

"I'll lay out your instruments!"

Carolina hurried inside, leaving the door open for them. Zeb raced to the back of the wagon and scooped up Bess. She was closest to the tailgate and blocking the way.

"Where do you want her?" he said to Nora.

"On the divan for now." She had one examination table.

As he left with Bess, Will lifted Missy and raced up the steps with Emmeline and Mikey behind him. Nora brought up the rear, praying for God's mercy for them all. Missy's life was on the line. In a way, so was Nora's. If the child died, no one would trust her. It wouldn't be her fault, but people would consider her a failure. She had no control over the final outcome. Only God could give and take life, and she knew Missy's symptoms were dire.

"It's in your hands, Lord," she said out loud. With the prayer still alive on her lips, Nora walked into the exam room to perform the surgery.

Chapter Seventeen

Zeb lowered Bess to the divan, then looked around for help. Nora and Carolina were with Missy, the more seriously ill of the two patients. Emmeline had followed Will into the surgery, leaving Zeb alone with the unconscious girl.

He felt as helpless as a babe.

Nora would know what to do. From the moment he'd seen her running to the commotion, he'd been aware of her confidence. Emmeline had been trembling with fear. Nora had stayed steady, though he wondered if she'd get the shakes when the crisis ended. That happened to him sometimes. It had happened three days ago when he'd kissed her. He'd been matter-of-fact about her attitude until he'd put his head on his pillow, then he'd realized what he'd done. He'd opened a floodgate of feelings. He didn't want them. Neither could he stop them.

Right now, he didn't have time for such thoughts. He needed help with Bess. As he considered what to do, the curtain blocking the exam room fluttered open. Emmeline emerged holding Mikey's hand. Alex came next, with Will bringing up the rear. Zeb hadn't seen his friend this grim since the tornado.

"How's Missy?" he asked.

No one answered.

Emmeline, still clinging to Mikey, dropped to her knees at Bess's side. The girl looked at peace, as if she were sleeping. Emmeline turned to Alex. "Would you get a damp towel for me?"

"Sure," he answered.

"Take Mikey with you," she said, sounding calm.

As soon as the boys left, Zeb looked to Will for news about Missy. After two months of searching, finding the twins should have filled them all with joy. The thought of losing Missy now felt like a slap in the face. Zeb had thought a lot about God since last Sunday. He saw God in the big things like rivers and storms, but he had to wonder if he cared about the small things like a man's broken heart and one sick child.

Will planted his feet and crossed his arms. To Zeb's surprise, his friend gave him the hardest look they'd ever shared. "I'm sure glad we have a *doctor* in town."

Zeb said nothing.

Will's voice went deep and low. "Missy wouldn't have a chance without Dr. Nora. If you'd chased her off, the little girl would already be *dead*."

Emmeline looked up from Bess. "Stop it, Will."

"No!"

"This isn't the time." The words hissed off her tongue. "We have to pray—"

"Yes, we do," he said calmly. "But Zeb needs to hear the facts. That *woman*—" he aimed his thumb at the curtain "—is doing something *you* can't do, something *I* can't do. When are you going to wise up and give her a little help?"

If he trusted Nora as a doctor, he'd have no reason left to keep her at a distance. He'd start to love her. He'd worry about her leaving High Plains and taking his heart with her. The thought chilled his blood. Questioning her medical skills kept a wall between them. It also saved his pride. Zeb didn't like eating crow. That's why he still had the splinter in his thumb.

Alex and Mikey came back with a damp rag. As Alex handed it to Emmeline, Mikey looked at Bess. "Is she dead?"

"She's just sleeping." Emmeline looked over her shoulder at Will. "I'll stay with Bess. Take the boys outside, okay?"

Will glared at Zeb, daring him to continue the talk out of the children's earshot. Zeb had no desire to fight with his friend, but he knew Will. The man was a dog with a bone when it came to right and wrong. Zeb motioned for the door. "Let's go."

As he turned the knob, Bess moaned. He froze in midstep. So did Will and Alex. Mikey ran to her side. "Bess!"

Her eyes fluttered open. The moment of truth had come. Bess would speak or return to her silent world. She looked at Mikey, blinked once, again, then gasped. "It's really you!" Her voice sounded rusty, like an unused gate, but she'd spoken. She ran her hands over Mikey's face and down his arms. She gripped his hands, squeezed, then playfully chucked him under the chin. "You're alive," she murmured. "I was so scared."

"Me, too," the boy said.

Bess looked around the room. Confusion clouded her eyes. "I saw Missy. She's sick."

Mikey nodded solemnly. "The lady doctor's going to fix her."

"Yes," Bess answered. "She will. I know it."

Zeb envied the girl's trust in Nora. If he'd been able to share it, he wouldn't still have a sore thumb.

As Emmeline stroked her sister's hair, Will stepped behind his wife. "Hi, Bess."

"Hi, Will." She smiled timidly. "I'm glad you married my sister."

"Me, too."

It was the first time Will and Bess had exchanged words. How long had the girl wanted to voice her thoughts? How long had she fought the urge? Zeb thought of his reluctance to speak with Nora when she first arrived. Silence made a thick wall, but love could climb over it. The Logans had that kind of love for Bess, and Nora had it for her patients. Zeb didn't want to think too much about love right now. He felt safer behind his wall.

Footsteps tapped behind the curtain and they all turned. Nora stepped into the parlor with a smile that lit up the room. "Missy's going to be fine."

Emmeline closed her eyes. "Thank You, Lord Jesus!"

Mikey hugged Nora's knees.

Alex grinned.

Will clasped her hand and shook it hard. "Thank you, Dr. Nora. We're in your debt."

"Not at all." Her gaze skipped Zeb and went to Bess.

The girl grinned. "Hi, Dr. Nora."

"Bess!" Nora crossed the room and hugged the girl hard. "It's so good to *hear* you!"

Tears welled in every eye in the room, including Zeb's. Looking at Nora with Bess, he felt the tug he'd felt at the river and wondered how things might be between them. He didn't wonder about kissing her. They were good together. He wondered about trusting her as his wife, the mother of his children. The thought terrified him.

Emmeline touched Nora's shoulder. "Tell us about Missy."

"She has quinsy." The lady doctor described the throat infection in simple terms, then explained how she'd lanced and drained the pustule. "As soon as the swelling went down, she took a deep breath and her color came back."

Mikey looked forlorn. "But she's still sick, isn't she?"

"Yes, she is." Nora spoke to the boy with the respect she'd

have given an adult. "She needs rest, nutritious food and lots of love. If we all help, I think she'll be fine. She's sleeping right now, but you can see her later, okay?"

"Okay." Visibly relieved, Mikey sagged against Emmeline.

Will pulled up a chair. "So, young man, where have you two been?"

A mystery was about to be solved. Zeb took a seat on the outside of the circle. Alex sat on the floor at his feet.

Emmeline put her arm around Mikey's shoulders. "Can you tell us what happened?"

The boy's eyes filled with tears. "It was my fault."

"What was?" Will asked.

"I made Missy come with me. She didn't want to, but I said we could get away and now she's sick."

"Away from what?" Emmeline hugged his shoulders.

"We didn't want to go with new families when we got to Oregon. We were going to run away, but then the tornado came and it picked us up."

"I saw that," Bess declared.

Mikey's eyes rounded with fear. "I didn't know where we were. I heard people calling, but I was afraid. If we went to new families, we couldn't be together. Missy didn't want to leave, but I talked her into it."

Emmeline riffled his hair. "You must have been very scared."

The boy raised his eyes to the ceiling as if he was considering a grave question, then he looked back at Emmeline. "I was, but just a little."

Zeb knew bravado when he heard it. He used the same tone himself.

The boy kept his eyes on Emmeline. "We were walking back to the town we'd been in. The lady at the store didn't like us, but we thought maybe someone would let us do chores for food. Before we got there, some Indian children found us. They took us to their tribe, and we lived with them."

Emmeline broke in. "The woman who brought you—"

"We called her Ni-Wako," he said. "I don't know what it means, but she was nice. She was *real* scared when Missy got sick. She tried to heal her, but the medicines didn't work. Today Missy's lips turned blue. That's when the Indian lady brought us here."

Bess reached for Mikey and hugged him. "I'm glad you're safe."

"Me, too."

As he squeezed back, Emmeline rubbed Bess's shoulder. "The storm hurt you, too."

Bess let go of Mikey, sat up and looked at Nora. "I don't know why I couldn't talk. I tried, but nothing would come out. At first, I couldn't even think."

"You had a trauma," Nora explained. "In a way, your mind went to sleep so it could heal."

Emmeline shuddered. "The storm was terrible."

Bess's eyes misted. "Even before the tornado, I was scared all the time. Do you remember the Indians on the hill? I thought they'd eat us alive."

Zeb understood the girl's fear. Kansa warriors plucked their scalps bald except for a strip down the middle. With their stoic faces and unfamiliar clothing, they had a fearsome presence.

Bess took a breath. "I remember the noise from the tornado and looking for Mikey and Missy. The next thing I knew, we were at a cemetery burying Papa. I couldn't think. I just knew I was afraid."

Emmeline hugged her sister. Together they rocked and grieved until Bess sniffed and they broke apart. Will put one hand on his wife's shoulder, then tugged at Bess's braid with the other. He made a good big brother. "Hey, kid. I'm glad you're here."

"Me, too," she replied.

Zeb's gaze went to Nora. She'd put an apron over her dress and looked relaxed. She could have been baking bread instead of saving a child's life. He didn't know what to think until he saw a scrape on her temple.

"What happened to you?" he said, almost growling.

"This?" She raised her hand to the lump. "I hit my head in the wagon. It's nothing."

Zeb's thumb was nothing. A hit on the head could have been serious. What if she'd suffered a concussion? Who'd take care of *her?* Startled by his protectiveness, he looked back at the Logans and saw Will drilling him with his eyes. Zeb knew what his friend wanted. He expected Zeb to tell her she had the doctor job permanently, and he expected him to do it now. When Zeb stayed silent, Will blew out a disgusted breath.

Emmeline went to Nora and gripped both her hands. "I can't thank you enough, Dr. Nora. I'm going to tell *everyone* that you saved Missy and Bess."

"Thank you," Nora replied. "But I don't want to cause a stir. I just want to be a good doctor."

Will gave Zeb a hard look. "It seems to me you *are* a good doctor. You're the only doctor this town needs."

Zeb couldn't deny Nora's skill, but he didn't like being put on the spot. "She's good with children," he finally said. "Women, too. But don't expect men to see her."

"Mr. Garrison?"

He heard Nora's voice, but he kept his eyes on Will. Will looked ready to punch him.

Nora waited with the patience of Job until Zeb gave up and faced her. "What is it?"

"I'm in the room," she said mildly. "Rather than speaking *about* me to Will, please address me directly."

Zeb didn't like being corrected, but he had it coming. Neither did he like the scrape on her temple, or the memory of kissing her. Everything about this woman confused him, especially the gentle tone of her voice. It disarmed him. "You're right," he said sincerely. "I apologize."

"Apology accepted," she replied. "Now I have an offer for you."

He dreaded hearing her plan. "What is it?"

"I'd be glad to serve the women and children of High Plains. When it's convenient, we'll negotiate a new salary. If a man falls ill or gets hurt, of course I'd help."

Will grinned. "Trust me, Doc. It won't be long before some tough guy stubs his toe and comes running."

"It won't be me," Zeb argued. He'd let his thumb fall off before he asked Nora for help. He glanced at her. "We can talk about it."

Someone rapped on the door. Zeb was closest, so he opened it. "Come in," he said to Pete and Rebecca.

Rebecca's eyes snapped to Bess. The girl grinned from ear to ear. "Hi, Rebecca!"

"Glory be!" Rebecca hurried to the sofa. Bess pushed to her feet, and the females hugged for a solid minute, rocking and crying like babies. Zeb snuck a peek at Nora and saw tears of joy in her eyes.

Carolina stepped out from behind the curtain. "Dr. Nora? Missy's awake."

"Thank you, Carolina." Nora crossed the room to where Mikey was huddled against Emmeline. She crouched next to him and smiled. "Would you like to see your sister?"

He nodded.

She stood and held out her hand. As Mikey took it, Nora turned to Emmeline. "We'll give them a few minutes, then you and Will can see her."

"Me, too!" Bess said.

Zeb's throat tightened with awe. Bess was speaking. The twins had been found. He'd witnessed two miracles today. He'd also just seen a side of Nora that rocked him to the core. Mikey was only eight years old, but she'd treated him with respect. The boy had been taking care of his sister, and he needed this time with her. Didn't Nora deserve the same consideration—a chance to express herself without being judged?

As Nora and Mikey stepped behind the curtain, Carolina turned to Emmeline. "I'm going to heat some broth for Missy. Would you like to bring it to her?"

"Very much," Emmeline answered.

As she went with Carolina, Rebecca sat with Bess on the divan. They were chattering like magpies, a welcome sound compared to silence. Alex looked up at Zeb. "I'm glad Mikey and Missy are back." The children had been friends on the wagon train.

"Me, too." High Plains had much for which to be grateful. Zeb thought of the town hall. He'd finish it in time for the jubilee or eat a bucket of sawdust.

Will slid his gaze to Pete. "Zeb's come to his senses. Dr. Nora's staying."

Pete clapped him on the back. "It's about time."

"Hold on!" Zeb protested. "I said I'd talk to her, but we haven't agreed on anything."

Will put his hands on his hips. "What is *wrong* with you?"

Zeb aimed his chin at the curtain. "If she wants to see women and children, fine. But we still need a male doctor." He hadn't planned on taking such a hard stand, but Will had goaded him. He almost said he'd be paying her half just to make a point, but his conscience stopped him. Zeb could be spiteful, but he wasn't *that* bad.

Pete shrugged. "As long as we've got a doctor, I'm happy."

Rebecca smiled at her husband. When Pete grinned back, Zeb wondered if they had a baby on the way. He understood Pete's hope for children. He had the same dream himself. Blinking, he imagined a little girl with red hair and blue eyes. The thought made him crazy and he shot to his feet. He had to get out of the parlor before he started liking oil paintings again.

He looked at Alex. "How about a trip to the mercantile? We'll get licorice for everyone and bring it back."

"I have to ask Dr. Nora."

Before Nora had interfered, Alex had looked to *him* for guidance. He'd been thinking about adopting the boy. Now Alex considered Nora his guardian.

The boy peeked into the sickroom. "Dr. Nora? Can I go with Zeb to the store?"

Zeb heard her voice through the curtain. "May I," she corrected. "And yes, you may. Just don't overdo it."

"I won't."

Alex popped out from the curtain, grinning like a prisoner loosed from a jail cell. As Zeb opened the front door, he heard Will talking to Pete. "I don't care what Zeb says. Once word about Missy and Bess gets out, anyone in town'll be happy to go to Dr. Nora—male or female. And when that happens, Zeb will have no choice but to admit she's the only doctor we need."

Will had that know-it-all tone that had irked Zeb for years. "Not a chance," he said, turning back to face his friend.

"I say Dr. Nora has her first male patient by Sunday."

Zeb laughed. "That's just three days away."

"So you have nothing to lose by agreeing." Will rocked back on his heels. "If you say that you'll accept Dr. Nora if she gets a male patient in the next three days then there's nothing on the line except your pride."

"It's a deal," Zeb said. "With one condition. *You* can't be the patient and neither can Pete."

"Fair enough," Will acknowledged.

Rebecca and Bess looked at him with a giggle in their eyes. Zeb felt like an adolescent fool for fighting over Nora, so he pushed open the door. "Come on, Alex."

Side by side, they walked to the store. Instead of chattering about candy and wooden horses, Alex talked the whole way about Dr. Nora. Zeb's thumb throbbed. So did his heart. He ignored them both.

Nora stood back as Emmeline spooned the last drop of soup into Missy's mouth. Will and Bess stood on one side of the bed, and Mikey was perched on the foot of the narrow cot.

Nora couldn't have been happier for the twins. Will and Emmeline had just promised to adopt them. Mikey and Missy wouldn't have to worry about being separated ever again. Counting Bess and Emmeline's other siblings, Glory and Johnny, plus Emmeline's mother and her new husband, the Logans had a huge family and the promise of babies of their own.

A bittersweet joy tightened Nora's chest. She wanted a husband and children. But she wanted them with Zeb. Considering Zeb's tone, that dream seemed as impossible as flying. Needing distraction, she turned to the counter where she kept her apothecary jars, spooned sumac leaves into a bowl, then searched the shelf where she kept small bottles of liquid medicine. She needed tincture of myrrh, found it and excused herself.

"I'll be back in a few minutes," she said to Emmeline. "I'm going to brew a tea for Missy." The family barely noticed when she left.

Nora went to the kitchen. Carolina was filling the teakettle, and Rebecca and Bess were chatting at the table. Nora loved her new friends, but she couldn't stop envying the Logans and their big family. She blinked and imagined a boy with Zeb's dark hair. She wanted a girl, too. Nora loved dolls and games. She'd done her first doctoring on a rag doll with a torn arm.

"Hi," she said as she set down the medicines.

All three of them smiled at her. Rebecca spoke first. "If this doesn't show people you're a good doctor, nothing will."

Bess's face lit up. "I want to shout it from the rooftops, at least the ones that are fixed."

"Thank you both," Nora replied. "We'll see what happens."

Rebecca's eyes twinkled. "After you left the room, Zeb and Will got into it again. They made a deal about you."

Nora was afraid she knew what they'd talked about. She'd heard Will's dig about male patients. "What's the deal?" she asked Rebecca.

"Will thinks you'll have a man for a patient by Sunday. If you do, Zeb has to admit you're all the doctor we need. Zeb says it'll never happen."

Nora groaned. "If word gets around, no man will want to be first. I'll never have male patients." She thought of Clint and his cough. He'd be sure to avoid her now.

As Nora put the leaves to boil, someone knocked on the door. Carolina was filling a basin with boiling water, so Nora waved for her to stay. "I'll get it."

Walking across the parlor, she wiped her hands on her apron. Putting on a smile, she opened the door and saw a woman she recognized from the visits she'd made her first week in town. Lanie Briggs was married to Tom Briggs, the man working on the town hall with Zeb. She had her little girl with her, a toddler with a lazy eye. The woman studied Nora with a mix of hope and suspicion.

"I've come about Ginny." She hoisted the little girl into her arms. "Can you fix her eye?"

"Maybe," Nora replied. "If you patch her good eye, her lazy eye will have to do more work. It might straighten on its own. But I won't give you false hope, Mrs. Briggs. Patching doesn't always work."

"It's worth a try, though. Isn't it?"

"Yes," Nora replied. "If you do nothing, the eye will go blind."

"Will you do it, Dr. Nora?" the woman asked. "Would you try?"

Nora opened the door wide. "I can't make promises, but I'll do my best. Come in."

As Lanie Briggs crossed the threshold, joy bubbled in Nora's heart. The seeds she'd planted were breaking through hard earth and reaching for the sun. Soon she'd have a harvest of patients. Her practice would flourish and she'd be able to stay without a salary from Zeb. One of her dreams had come true. The other—the desire for a husband and children—hung beyond her grasp.

As she stepped back into the parlor, she heard laughter coming from the Logan clan. Fighting a heaviness in her chest, Nora smiled at the little girl with the crooked eye. "Hi, Ginny. I'm Dr. Nora. I'm going to try to fix your eye, okay?"

When Ginny gave a solemn nod, Nora patted her head and prepared to go to work. It was enough. It had to be.

Chapter Eighteen

Every time Clint coughed, Zeb thought of his deal with Will. The cowboy looked more peaked with each passing day. Yesterday Zeb had ordered him to go to the Circle-L and not show his face until he could talk without wheezing. Clint had gone, but this morning he'd come back. He was on the cutting floor now, getting ready for the day's work.

If Doc Dempsey had been alive, Zeb would have hauled the cowboy to the man's office. Doc had faltered after the tornado, but he'd done well enough with fevers. At the very least, he'd have ordered Clint to stay in bed. Dr. Mitchell could give the same advice, but Clint wouldn't listen to her. Men didn't respect lady doctors and never would.

Alone in his office, Zeb considered ordering the cowboy to see Dr. Nora in spite of the deal with Will. He hadn't started up the saws yet, and the Thompsons were late delivering timber. He could do without the cowboy today, so he walked from his office to the cutting floor. The building was silent until Clint started coughing up his lungs. Zeb put his hands on his hips. "I told you to stay home."

"Can't stop working." Clint headed for the keg of vegetable oil they used for lubrication.

"Hold up!" Zeb ordered.

Clint glared at him, but his expression had no force. Standing with his shoulders hunched, he looked as if every breath hurt. Not a speck of sawdust filled the air, but later the room would be awash in it. How much worse would he feel then?

"Get out of here," Zeb said gently. "You're as sick as a dog."

Clint shook his head.

Zeb took another approach. "You're a good man, Clint, but right now you're not worth spit." The next words pained him, but they had to be said. "Go see Dr. Mitchell."

"No way, boss."

Zeb wiped his hand through his hair. "I know she's female, but she can handle a silly cough." Anything more serious, and he'd think twice about sending his best worker.

"I don't care about her being a woman." Clint backhanded feverish sweat from his brow. "I have to work because I need the money."

Zeb didn't see why. The man worked two jobs. Will paid him a decent wage and so did Zeb. Clint didn't waste a dime on anything. "I know you've been saving up. You've earned a day off."

"I don't have much time," Clint argued. "I need every cent."

"For what?"

Clint looked at him as if he were stupid. "She's gonna leave with him, Zeb. I tell you, she's—"

"You mean *Cassandra?*"

Clint's cheeks flushed. "Who else would I do this for? I love her, but I can't marry her until I can take care of her. And I can't do *that* until I can buy a ring that's *twice* the size of what Percy has in mind."

He spat the man's name. Zeb shared his dislike. "I see."

"No, you don't."

Zeb heard an insult. "What do you mean?"

"Have you ever loved a woman? I mean really *loved* her? Loved her so much it hurt to say her name?"

Instead of Frannie, he saw a redhead with blue eyes. He didn't want to love Nora, but he did. The thought rocked him to the core. Love, like the river, couldn't be stopped. Could he learn to respect her career? He could tolerate her seeing women and children, but how would he feel when she took off in the dead of night to care for a stranger? And what about her New York roots? She'd come to High Plains out of desperation. Would she stay no matter the cost? He didn't know.

Clint started to pace. "Percy's got Cassandra tied in knots. He's nothing but a big talker, I tell you. I'd like to—" Clint sealed his lips.

"You should be talking to my sister," Zeb replied. "Not me."

"I'd marry her tomorrow if I could." Clint looked as starry eyed as a moonless sky.

"What's stopping you?"

"Money."

Zeb saw a solution, a quick one that would save Clint's health and keep Cassandra in High Plains. "How much to you need? I'll loan it to you."

Clint shook his head. "Borrowing's not my way."

"You're being prideful," Zeb insisted. "Take it."

The cowboy's eyes glinted with unexpected wisdom. "You're one to talk about pride."

"What do you mean?"

"I like Dr. Nora. So does Cassandra and everyone else. You just can't admit you're wrong about her."

Zeb's thumb throbbed. "What's your point?"

"None, I guess." Clint coughed. "I better get busy."

"Forget it. I'm loaning you the money. You can pay me back later."

"I said no."

Zeb wanted to argue some sense into him, but he saw another way out. "I tell you what," he said. "I'll give you a way to earn it fast."

"How?"

"I hear you're the strongest man at the Circle-L."

"That's right."

"At the jubilee, sign up for the arm-wrestling contest. There's going to be a prize."

Clint's eyes widened. "How much?"

Zeb did some quick calculations. Clint clearly already had some saved, but he needed money for a ring, a place to live in town and a bit extra for Cassandra's taste in clothes. "The winner's going to walk off with twenty-five dollars. Think you can win?"

He put his hands on his hips. "You bet I can."

Zeb saw another problem. "Do you think you can outdo Percy when it comes to romancing my sister?"

The cowboy looked sheepish. "Don't tell anyone, but Mrs. Rebecca's been giving me lessons in being mannerly."

Zeb admired Clint's effort. "That's good."

"She's taught me about using a napkin and not gobbling down my food. I'll never be a high-class man from Boston, but I know how to treat a lady."

"I'm counting on it," Zeb said. "Now get some rest."

"All right, I will." Clint indicated a saw frame, the one without a blade. It had broken, again, and Pete had repaired and delivered it late yesterday. "Before I go, how about I help you mount the blade? It'll be ready when the crew gets here."

"Thanks."

Zeb and Clint put on heavy leather gloves, lifted the blade

and attached it to the frame. Zeb insisted on doing the balancing himself, then he checked the fasteners.

"Want to test it?" Clint asked.

Zeb didn't want to keep the cowboy around, but Clint knew the millworks better than the workers scheduled for the day. "Sure. Go pull the brake."

Clint went outside, unlocked the waterwheel and came back. With Zeb watching, the gears picked up speed and the blade spun in a perfect circle.

Satisfied, he shouted to Clint. "Shut it down, will you?"

"Sure." The cowboy went outside to set the brake. A rattling drew Zeb's gaze to the pivot above his head. The pivot transferred power from a horizontal shaft to the vertical one turning the blade. He looked up and saw a loose pin.

Zeb had tremendous respect for freshly honed metal, but he also knew the continued motion would cause the pivot to fly apart. The blade would wobble and possibly break. Fighting impatience, he eyed the shaking wood. With each spin of the waterwheel, the wobble increased. He looked down at the blade. The speed had slowed, but it was still spinning at a dangerous rate. As Clint came around the corner, the blade slowed enough so that Zeb could see the metal teeth in a two-toned blur. In a minute, it would come to a halt.

He set his foot on the frame. At the same instant, the pivot broke and the saw went askew. Metal sliced through his boot, then into skin and muscle. As a cry exploded from Zeb's lips, he fell back on the floor. With a shout of his own, Clint sprinted to his side.

Blood ran from the gash in the boot. Dark and sticky, it soaked Zeb's pant leg and formed a maroon pool. He tried to wiggle his toes and felt only searing pain. With each beat of his heart, blood poured from the gash, widening the puddle into a circle. If he didn't get help, he'd die. He'd bleed out on the floor of the mill.

Clint yanked off his shirt, ripped off a sleeve and tied it above Zeb's knee. The gush turned to a trickle, but Zeb was already light-headed.

Clint's face turned from feverish to ashen. "We've got to get you to Dr. Nora."

Zeb tried to sit up, but the room spun in a crazy mix of black and white, the same color as the debris-filled wind of the tornado. Fighting to stay conscious, he sucked in air. As his stomach rebelled, he shouted a curse. Of all the foolish things… A cry exploded in his mind. *Why, God? What more do You want from me?* He wanted to shake his fist at the Almighty. Instead, he felt Clint's strong hands hoisting him upright and balancing him on his good leg.

Clint half carried, half dragged Zeb into the yard where he'd left his horse. He put Zeb's good foot in the stirrup, hoisted him on to the gelding, jumped up behind him and gave the horse free rein. With each stride, Zeb felt more light-headed. Shock faded to unbearable pain and he moaned like a baby. The cry destroyed the last of his pride. He no longer cared about Dr. Nora Mitchell's gender. He just wanted to keep his leg.

"Doc!"

Nora didn't recognize the male voice bellowing in the yard, but she knew terror when she heard it. Dropping the bandage she'd been rolling, she hurried out the front door. In the yard she saw Clint on the far side of a black horse, but she couldn't see who he'd hauled from the saddle until she rounded the horse's rump.

"Zeb!" she cried. "What happened?"

"He's cut," Clint answered. "A blade clipped him below the knee."

Nora looked down and saw the tourniquet, Zeb's flapping boot and the bloody pant leg. "Get him inside," she ordered.

She sounded in control, but her thoughts buzzed like a swarm of frightened bees. This was Zeb—the man she was starting to love, the man who didn't trust her to remove a splinter. When Clint sagged beneath his weight, Nora wedged herself under his other shoulder. As she took his weight, he moaned through gritted teeth. Together she and Clint carried him into the house.

As they thudded into the parlor, Carolina burst out of the kitchen. "What happened?"

"He's cut." Nora clipped the words.

Carolina flung back the curtain to the exam room. With the nurse's help, Nora and Clint maneuvered Zeb onto the exam table. He tried to stifle a moan, but it came out in a hiss through his clenched teeth. Carolina looked to Nora for direction. Nora looked at Zeb's leg. The tourniquet seemed to be holding.

She touched his cheek. "I have to remove your boot. Do you want laudanum?"

"Not now." His body tensed against the table. "I want to know what's happening."

They both understood the magnitude of the injury. If the saw had severed tendons and arteries, he'd lose the leg now. If the blade stopped short of the bone, he'd be in for a battle against infection. Carolina retrieved the amputation kit from the cupboard. Nora prayed she wouldn't have to use it.

She took a knife, slit the boot from top to bottom and removed it as gently as she could. Pain hissed through Zeb's teeth, but he didn't cry out. As she dropped the boot to the floor, Clint shuddered. Nora had forgotten about him. He looked helpless, pale and flushed. She aimed her chin at the door. "Go get Cassandra."

"No!" Zeb said. "I don't want her here."

Nora stood over him, matching her eyes to his. "I might have to make a hard decision. If you pass out, I want her here."

Clint took off like a rifle shot.

Zeb shook his head. "No—"

"Yes." Nora clamped his face between her hands, forcing him to look at her. Tears sprung to her eyes. Of all the tests she'd faced as a doctor, this one pushed her to the edge of her faith in a loving God.

"Listen to me, Zeb." She kept her voice steady, but her heart was fluttering like a trapped bird. "I haven't seen the leg yet. We might be able to save it, but—"

"Save it," he muttered. "Please."

The plea tore at her heart. "I'm going to try, but if it's impossible—if the bone is broken and the arteries are severed—I'm going to save your life instead."

She waited for a nod of agreement. Instead, he looked into her eyes, then touched her hand with his. "I lost the deal with Will, didn't I?"

Nora smiled through a haze of tears. "If you can make a joke at a time like this, you're going to be fine."

His eyes drifted shut. "Don't do it, Nora. Not yet."

"I might not have to," she answered. "I have to clean the wound to see the damage."

Zeb clenched his jaw, then nodded.

Nora and Carolina blotted blood with white rags. Red stains bloomed like roses. Zeb groaned, but he didn't thrash. Nora had to admire his self-control. Other men would have cursed and kicked. When she finished cleaning the wound, she forgot everything except her anatomy class.

"How bad is it?" he asked.

The blade had cut an inch into the side of his calf, closer to the knee than the ankle. Mercifully it had missed the Achilles tendon and the tibial nerve and artery. If he survived the inevitable infection, Zeb would walk again. Healing would take time and he might have a limp, but for now she had hope. "The cut's deep," she told him. "But it doesn't go to the bone."

Zeb panted for breath. "That's good, isn't it?"

"Yes."

"So you don't have to…amputate."

"Not yet," she said quietly. "But we both know what lies ahead." Infection would set in. He'd grow feverish and the wound would fester. He'd be at risk for blood poisoning. If the infection spread, she'd have to cut off his leg.

She looked into Zeb's eyes. His pupils, dilated with pain, turned his green irises into narrow bands. She prayed she wouldn't have to amputate his leg. Zeb would never be the same.

She tried to give him a reassuring smile, but the corners of her mouth turned down with suppressed tears. Zeb touched her cheek. "Cheer up, Doc. You're going to save my leg."

The words of respect should have thrilled her. Instead, she felt the burden of truth. The odds were against them. If she waited too long to amputate, Zeb would die. If she took off the leg to save his life, would he still trust her? She doubted it. She took his hand and squeezed. He had a long, painful journey ahead of him, one that could still end in tragedy. "Close your eyes," she said. "I'm going to sew up your leg."

As trusting as a child, he obeyed. Nora went to work with a needle threaded with catgut. As she sutured muscle to muscle and skin to skin, she heard Alex on the porch. Aware of Zeb's injury, he told everyone who came to see her about the accident. Within an hour, all of High Plains knew Zeb had been seriously injured and could lose his leg.

As she placed the last suture, a buggy rattled into the yard.

When a man coughed, she recognized Clint. An instant later, she heard Cassandra speaking with Alex, then the *whoosh* of the front door as the girl raced inside, calling her brother's name.

"I'll be out in a minute," Nora called through the curtain.

It opened anyway and Cassandra came into the exam room. Her eyes went to the bloody leg and she gasped.

"Get out of here," Zeb growled.

The color drained from Cassandra's face. Fearing the girl would faint, Nora spoke firmly. "Wait in the parlor. I'll explain everything when I'm done."

As Cassandra left, she pressed a white handkerchief to her eyes. Nora thought of the cotton she'd use to bandage Zeb's leg. It wouldn't stay white for long, but she'd work day and night to keep the wound clean and free of infection. With Carolina's help, she wrapped clean bandages around Zeb's leg. Satisfied she'd done all she could, she washed her hands and took off her bloody apron. Before leaving to speak with Cassandra, she rested her palm on Zeb's forehead. She felt perspiration but no fever. The infection would come later.

He swallowed hard. "Thanks, Doc."

Emotion clogged her throat. She nodded and went to the parlor where she saw Cassandra huddled on the sofa. Clint was standing across the room, staring out the window.

"How is he?" Cassandra asked.

As Nora sat next to Cassandra, Clint cleared his throat. "Clint, sit down," Nora said. "Considering you saved Zeb's life, you're part of this."

The man turned but didn't budge. "I've got a cough. I don't want Miss Cassandra to catch it."

"Of course." Nora thought of the toll today had taken on him.

Cassandra looked at him with a new respect. "You saved Zeb's life?"

Clint shrugged.

Nora jumped in. "Clint's too modest to tell you, but he made a tourniquet out of his shirt. If he hadn't been there, Zeb could have bled out. At the very least, he'd have gone into shock."

Cassandra looked at Clint with a new respect. "You should have told me."

His face turned even redder. "I did what had to be done."

"And you're sick, too." Cassandra's voice filled with sympathy. "*And* you're working too hard…just like Zeb." She turned to Nora. "I was at the Circle-L. Clint brought me, but he should be in bed himself!"

The cowboy stifled a cough. "Don't baby me, Cassandra. I can take care of myself."

"I'm trying to help you!"

"I don't want help," he argued. "I want to take care of *you*." He sealed his lips, but a moment too late. Embarrassed, his eyes hardened as he looked at Cassandra. "I do what has to be done. Right now, that means helping you and Zeb."

Nora recognized the curious lift of Cassandra's brow, the question lurking in her mind. She'd worn a similar expression just before Zeb kissed her. Whether Cassandra knew it or not, she was in love with Clint, not Percival Walker. The attorney had filled her head with the glamour of Boston, but he didn't leave her spinning like the cowboy did.

Envy made Nora tremble. Today Zeb had shown respect for her work, would the respect last if she had to amputate his leg? She doubted it. No matter the cost, she'd save Zeb's life. She could only hope saving his life wouldn't cost her a chance at his love.

Nora focused on Cassandra. "I'd like to keep Zeb here for a few days, maybe a week. He needs bed rest."

"He won't like that."

"No, but the wound will heal best if we keep the leg still. I don't want him hobbling around on crutches and risking a fall."

"Of course not," Cassandra agreed.

Clint interrupted. "Tell him not to worry about the mill. I'll see to things."

"But you're sick!" Cassandra protested.

Clint looked pained by his weakness but pleased with her concern. "Don't worry about me, Miss Cassandra. I'm going to be fine. I feel better already, as a matter of fact."

Cassandra wrung her handkerchief, then gave Clint a hard look. "You take care of yourself, Clint Fuller! I don't need to be worrying about *two* men."

"I will." He sounded solemn.

Their gazes met from across the room. Clint lowered his arms to his sides. Cassandra took a breath and her lips parted. Quietly Nora stood and went back to the exam room. As the curtain swished behind her, she heard Cassandra telling Clint to sit down, then the creak of a chair and the soft hush of a man and a woman getting to know each other.

Nora wanted that sweetness for herself and Zeb. Would it grow between them? Maybe, but first she had to save his life…and his leg.

Chapter Nineteen

Several hours later, Zeb woke up in a bed in a small room next to Nora's surgery. The only part of his body that didn't hurt was his thumb. He held it up and saw one small stitch. Nora had taken advantage of his exhaustion and removed the splinter while he slept. He could only shake his head at his stupidity. He should have asked her to remove the splinter days ago.

Leaning back on the pillow, he thought of his bias against female doctors and felt ashamed of himself. The woman was far more competent to practice medicine than Doc Dempsey had been. Zeb had been a fool to think she couldn't face the rigors of medicine, and a bigger fool to think she'd leave High Plains at the first sign of trouble. The woman ran *to* problems, not away from them. A smile curled on his lips. She wasn't timid and she wasn't Frannie. She never had been.

Zeb felt a peace he'd never known before now. For the first time in his life, apart from being a babe in his mother's arms, he could do nothing to change his circumstances. For years he'd striven to succeed. He'd fought his way out of the Bellville Mill. He'd worked night and day to build High Plains, not once but twice. With his leg a bloody mess, he could do nothing but ride out the storm as Noah had ridden out forty days and nights on the ark. Zeb's fate was in God's hands, not his own. He could only pray for a mercy he didn't deserve but desperately wanted.

Somehow he'd found peace in Nora's sickroom. He'd forgotten Frannie, which he supposed was a kind of forgiveness. As the anger left him, he saw Frannie's rejection in a new light. What he'd considered to be a terrible loss had led to the best things in his life. If he'd married Frannie, he wouldn't have come west with Will. He wouldn't have the dreams and friends he now treasured. Most important of all, he wouldn't have fallen in love with Nora Mitchell, a fine doctor and a woman to be admired.

Humbled and full of gratitude, Zeb bowed his head. Thank You, Lord, for steering me to Kansas. Thank You for protecting me from my own stupid mistakes and stubbornness. I'm not a perfect man, Lord. But from now on, I'll do my best to honor You. Amen."

Contentment washed over him, but it disappeared with a stabbing pain in his leg. Zeb had made peace with the Almighty, but he had another problem. He loved Nora and he wanted to marry her, but only if he survived the infection as a whole man. No woman, even a doctor, should be saddled with a cripple, especially a cripple who'd be as cantankerous as he'd be. Zeb didn't think he could stand himself if he lost the leg. No way would he ask the woman he loved to put up with his foul moods.

As he looked out the window above his sickbed, he made a decision. He'd thank Nora for saving his life. He'd absolve her of responsibility in case the worst happened. He'd give her the respect she'd earned, but he wouldn't tell her how he felt until he could walk.

As he heaved a sigh, Zeb saw Alex in the doorway. "Hey, kid."

The boy handed him a familiar wooden horse. "Being sick is boring. I brought you something to do."

"Thanks." Zeb made the horse gallop down the length of the bed, making clopping sounds with his tongue until Alex laughed. The sound of it, high and bright, made his chest ache with the longing he'd felt during the tornado. He wanted children, and he wanted to have them with a certain lady doctor. He brought the toy horse to a halt, reared it up and imitated a stallion ready for a fight.

Alex grinned. "I named him Ranger."

"It's a good name."

Nora came through the door with a tray holding a bowl of water and fresh bandages. When she smiled at Alex, Zeb felt a longing so strong he could barely breathe. For this single moment, they were a family and he liked it.

She set the bowl on the nightstand. "Out you go, Alex."

"Can I help?" the boy asked.

"Nope," she answered. "This is my job."

The boy hugged her for no reason except that he could, then he scampered out of the room, blessedly unaware of the dangers lurking in Zeb's flesh.

Nora pulled the chair closer to the bed and sat. "I'm sure you want to go home, but I'd like you to stay for a while."

Zeb didn't mind at all. "How long?"

"Maybe a week." She raised her chin the way she always did, but the gesture had no pride. "I've done my best, Zeb. But infection is inevitable."

"I know," he said quietly. "How soon?"

"Maybe a week." She knotted her fingers in her lap. "The wound will turn red, and the sutures might be puffy. Pus will form, and you'll have seepage. If we're lucky, you'll fight off the infection before it spreads."

"And if I don't?"

"You'll run a fever. You know the rest."

Yes, he did. The damaged flesh would rot. Gangrene would set in and she'd have to amputate before it poisoned his blood. By nature, Zeb made plans. He wanted facts. "When will you know?"

She reached for his hand. "If you can go two weeks without a fever, I'll be relieved. I'll do everything I can. I promise you—"

He squeezed her fingers. It was a handshake of sorts, a sign of trust and more. "No matter what happens," he said, "you're not to blame. I trust you completely."

"Do you mean that?"

"I do." He meant every word. Aching inside, he grinned at her. "You're hired. Permanently. For men and women alike."

He expected her to smile back, maybe gloat at her victory. Instead, she unwound the soiled bandage from his leg and replaced it with a swath of white cotton. She looked disappointed, as if she'd wanted something more. Zeb understood because he wanted more, too. He wanted to tell her he loved her. He thought of the kiss at the river, how she'd revealed her feelings but held back because of her principles. Now *he* had to hold back because of his. As she headed for the door, he fought the urge to tell her he loved her. She deserved a whole man for a husband, but he couldn't let her leave in silence. "Nora?"

She turned, but dipped her chin to hide her eyes. "Yes?"

"There's something else I want to say, but I don't want to say it here." He indicated the sickroom with its bowls and bandages. "I want to be standing on my two feet, and I want to be wearing pants, not a nightshirt."

Her eyebrows arched but instantly settled. She looked pleased. "You look fine to me."

"No, I don't." He rubbed his bristly face. "I need a shave and a bath." Put more simply, he stank. "When I say my piece, it's *not* going to be lying flat on my back in a sickroom."

A smile touched her lips. "Where will it be?"

Zeb knew just the spot. "There's a hill two miles west of here. Wildflowers grow in a blanket so big you can't see the end. If you look hard enough, you can see the future. We'll take a long buggy ride, have a picnic."

He watched her eyes, gauging her expression to see if she'd understood. When he saw a sparkle, he knew she'd gotten his drift.

She raised her chin in that saucy way of hers. "Will we have to worry about poison ivy?"

"You bet," he said, deadpan. "Where I'm taking you, there's poison ivy everywhere. But don't worry, Doc. I promise to keep you safe. We won't touch it. Not until we've said a few things to each other."

Her cheeks turned a shade of pink only slightly less red than her hair. "I see."

"I hope so." He wanted to tease her some more, but he'd already said more than he'd intended. His heart beat faster and his fingers ached to touch her hair, to caress her cheek before he kissed her. Until he could propose marriage as a whole man, he had to fight such thoughts. But neither could he deny them. He loved this woman and wanted to bring her joy. He let his eyes linger on her face. "So will you go with me for that ride?"

She blushed. "I'd like that very much."

He took a breath.

So did she.

With hope binding them together, she left the sickroom with a bounce in her step. Zeb closed his eyes and prayed the fever would never come.

On the second day of his recovery, Zeb hurt so badly he couldn't see straight. Nora offered him laudanum, he took one dose, slept all day and decided to never take it again.

On the third day, he woke up with less pain and felt hopeful.

Nora cleaned the wound four times a day with whiskey. It stung, but then she'd coat it with lavender oil and he'd feel better. The smell alone relaxed him because it matched her special soap. Like the whiskey, the lavender fought putrefaction. Every time she replaced the bandage, they both checked for signs of infection. He saw some redness and the stitches itched, but he took it as a sign of healing.

He and Nora were having a good time together. Instead of asking Carolina to serve his meals on a tray, Nora brought them herself. She'd set up a table where she and Alex joined him for supper. They made a nice family.

As much as Zeb enjoyed supper, he liked her morning visits even better. Along with fresh nightshirts, Cassandra had brought his shaving tools. On the fourth day of his recovery, Nora showed up in his room before breakfast, carrying a bowl of steaming water. When she offered to shave him, he accepted. Looking rosy, she mixed soap and scraped his jaw clean.

Shaving him had become a ritual, one he appreciated considering the number of visitors he had. Cassandra came several times a day. Clint had been banned from his sickroom, but he sent word about the mill through Nora. Zeb's construction-crew foreman had everything under control, and the town hall was close to finished. From Nora he learned that Clint had shaken the cough. Zeb expected the cowboy to win the arm-wrestling contest hands down, pun intended.

On the fourth day of his recovery, Will and Emmeline visited with Bess and the twins. Zeb envied his friend and hoped to follow in his path.

On the fifth day, Pete and Rebecca arrived with a pie that made Zeb's mouth water. He'd enjoyed it with the evening meal, but he'd enjoyed the second helping even more. Unable to sleep, Nora had wandered downstairs after midnight. She'd brought two plates into his room and they'd shared the sweetness by lamplight.

On the sixth day, Zeb had company he *didn't* want. Judging by the aroma wafting from the parlor, Abigail and her mother had brought cinnamon rolls. Without asking him, Cassandra refused the baked goods and told them to leave. Ever since the committee meeting, his sister had been bold in her criticism of Abigail. Zeb kept his mouth shut, but he shared Cassandra's opinion. He wanted nothing to do with Abigail. With time on his hands, he'd searched his conscience to see if he owed her an apology. Considering he hadn't asked for permission to court her, hadn't kissed her or even thought about it, he felt right about letting the flirtation die a natural death. He didn't care about his pride, but he worried a clear rejection would send Abigail into a snit.

As the seventh day dawned, Zeb rubbed his hand over his jaw in sweet anticipation of Nora's arrival. He hadn't slept well, and he had a headache behind his eyes. His skin felt prickly and his bones ached. Groaning, he leaned forward and touched the bandage covering the wound. Heat resonated to his fingers. The cotton felt damp but not from blood. Yellowish pus had oozed into an ugly oval.

He dropped back to the pillow. "Please, Lord," he prayed. "Don't let this happen now." In another week, he could take Nora on that buggy ride. He'd use crutches. He'd use a cane. He didn't care as long as he still had a leg.

Nora came through the door with a bowl of steaming water and a smile. "How's my best patient?"

His tongue stuck to the roof of his mouth.

As she stared into his fever-glazed eyes, the bowl wobbled in her hands. She set it down, then pulled the sheet back from his leg. A sickly-sweet smell wafted to his nose. Nora inhaled sharply, then looked into his eyes. "The fever started, didn't it?"

"I think so."

She touched his forehead. "You're burning up."

Before he could protest, she left the room. In minutes she came back with the willow-bark tea he'd grown to hate. She cleaned the wound, prepared a poultice and assured him—too many times—infection was to be expected. When visitors came, Nora sent them away herself. She allowed Cassandra to help at his bedside, but Zeb told his sister to leave. The leg smelled of infection and it looked even worse. He'd been relieved when Clint had offered to take her to the boarding-house for a meal, then got annoyed when she'd said no because she had plans with Percy.

Zeb *had* to live. He had to protect Cassandra from mistakes like the one he'd made in Boston. He wanted to marry Nora and love her right. He wanted to adopt Alex and see High Plains prosper. He wanted the legacy he'd imagined during the tornado.

He dozed throughout the day.

At midnight he woke up drenched with sweat. He'd been dreaming of wolves and realized the howling had come from his own throat. As fever burned in his bones, lamplight spilled into the sickroom. He opened his eyes and saw Nora. She had on the same blue dress and white apron, but she'd let down her hair. It brushed her shoulders in waves. Tendrils wisped around her ears and he thought of all the things he wanted to whisper.

She set the lamp on the nightstand, sat on the chair next to the bed and put her cool hand on his brow. "You're still feverish."

"I know."

She left and came back with a bowl of water and a towel. As she bathed his face, water ran in rivulets down his neck and throat. Avoiding his eyes, she spread a wet towel over his chest. It soaked the nightshirt and felt good, but an instant later the towel was as hot as the infection in his blood and she removed it.

Carolina approached from the door. "Do you need help?" she said to Nora.

"Yes, thank you." Her objective tone scared him to death. "Zeb needs fresh sheets and a dry nightshirt."

"I'll do it." The nurse pulled the linens off a shelf, then rested a hand on Nora's shoulder. "There's hot water on the stove. Go drink some tea."

Nora touched his cheek, then offered a smile. "I'll be right back."

Zeb nodded and she left. He was glad she'd asked Carolina to tend to his basic needs. He didn't want her to see him helpless. If he lived and they got married, he'd be glad to bare his soul and everything else, but not now. He'd never been so needy in his life, so dazed by fever and pain. And fear, he admitted.

When Carolina finished her ministrations, Nora came back and sat by his bed. For the next several hours, he floated between consciousness and a tortured slumber. Not once did she leave his side. She cooled his brow with damp cloths. She checked the bandages. She held his hand, softly humming melodies from church and childhood to comfort him.

Near dawn, he felt a spike in the fever. The room spun in clouds of black and white. He imagined the infection surging up his leg, entering his blood and brain. He blinked and imagined a stump in place of his leg. Fearing he'd pass out, he gripped Nora's fingers. "When will you know?"

She raised his hand to her lips and kissed it. "The biggest danger is blood poisoning. I'm watching the wound for red lines. If they spread upward, I'll have to take your leg."

A man could argue with God, but he couldn't shout at rotten flesh and expect it to obey. Zeb had no control over his fate. He could only hope, pray and prepare himself. "Tell me what to expect."

She swallowed so hard her throat twitched. "If I have to amputate, I'll give you chloroform." She sounded matter-of-fact, as if they were talking about a bad tooth. "I'll make the cut above the knee."

Zeb groaned. *Why, God? Just when I've found Nora...*

She laid her hand on his brow. "There's still time, Zeb."

But her voice had a quiver. He'd never been so close to death. Without Nora, he'd have gone mad. With her, he had hope. Clutching her fingers, he whispered, "Pray for me."

"I am. I won't stop."

An hour later, the sun came up. When morning had a firm hold on the day, Nora excused herself to see to her own bodily needs. With gold light pouring in the window, Zeb begged God for mercy. Helpless and tortured by feverish images, he rubbed his jaw. Nora wouldn't be shaving his face this morning. He could only pray she wouldn't be cutting off his leg instead.

Chapter Twenty

Nora slipped into the kitchen and collapsed in a chair by the window. She'd done everything she could to save Zeb's leg. She'd made poultices. She'd cleaned the wound with whiskey and lavender. She'd brewed teas, kept him warm and prayed with every breath. Unless he turned a corner before dusk, she'd be forced to do the unthinkable.

Nothing—not her training, not her faith—had prepared her for this moment. If she took the leg, she'd save Zeb's body but scar his soul. Aching, she bowed her head. "Please, Lord. Don't ask me to—"

"Dr. Nora?"

She looked up and saw Alex in dungarees and a misbuttoned shirt. Nora motioned him forward and fixed the buttons. "Are you hungry?" she asked.

"I'm scared," he said in a small voice. "Is Zeb going to die?"

Nora never lied, not even to reassure a frightened child. Honest questions deserved honest answers. "I hope not, Alex. But he's very sick."

"My ma died from fever. Zeb looks worse than she did."

Nora pulled the boy into a hug. With his head nestled on her shoulder, she made the only promise she could keep. "I'm doing my best, but we have to pray. Okay?"

Alex pulled back. "Eli's dead, too. Everyone dies."

A small truth… A painful truth. Nora ached to comfort him. "My brother died when I was a little older than you. I'm sad, but I'm going to see him again in Heaven. You'll see your ma and Eli, too."

"Really?" Alex looked hopeful.

"Yes, really." When she hugged him again, he snuggled against her. She wanted to be this boy's mother. She wanted to marry Zeb and give him children, but if she had to amputate his leg, the buggy ride would never take place. He wouldn't offer marriage. No way could she stand loving Zeb without the hope of a future. She'd have to leave High Plains.

As her throat closed, she squeezed Alex tighter. The boy hugged her back, then let go. "Can I go play with Jonah?"

Nora recognized his friend at the boardinghouse. "Sure."

As Alex scampered out the back door, Nora bowed her head. "Only You can heal, Lord. Only You can save us from disease and pain." *And death.* The thought humbled her. It also reminded her of the most basic truth of all. A man's soul mattered more than his body. As she'd tended to Zeb, she'd sensed a new peace in him. Just as the splinter had been removed and his thumb had healed, Zeb's pride had been broken and the bitterness had left his heart. Would the bitterness return if he lost his leg? She didn't know. And what about her own faith? How could she honor a God who asked her to do such a terrible thing? She felt as if God had dangled candy—a husband and children—in front of her nose and snatched it back.

Carolina came into the kitchen. "Zeb's asleep. Why don't you get some air."

Nora desperately needed to think, to pray. "Thank you. Maybe I'll walk by the river."

"That's a fine idea," the nurse answered.

Nora went upstairs to change her dress. She put on her walking shoes and a hat, then slipped out the front door. The river beckoned to her, but so did the steeple of the church. If she went to the river, she'd see the waterfall and boulders scraped raw by the current. She'd see the inevitability of a hard choice. The church had miraculously survived the tornado. Nora needed a miracle, so she turned up Main Street.

As she passed the mercantile, Winnie Morrow came through the door. "How's Zeb?"

Nora searched for hope. "He's struggling."

"I'm so sorry," Winnie replied.

A sweep of the broom drew Nora's attention to the front of the mercantile. Mrs. Johnson, broom in hand, glowered at her through the dust, but didn't call out a greeting. Nora refused to be insulted. "Hello, Mrs. Johnson."

The woman gave a curt nod. "Dr. Mitchell." She swept more dust, then gave in to her curiosity. "How's Zeb?"

"He's fighting the infection."

Mrs. Johnson planted the broom like a flag. "You can tell me the truth, Doctor. Zeb and Abigail are *very* close. I hear he's dying."

Nora had to bite her tongue to keep from lecturing the woman. "Cassandra is Zeb's only family. I'll discuss his condition with *her.*"

"Of course," the woman said too sweetly. "I just hope you don't have to cut off his leg. That would *certainly* kill him."

Nora didn't trust herself to speak. "Good day, Mrs. Johnson."

With her temper seething, she left Winnie with a nod and paced down Main Street. Everyone she passed asked about

Zeb, and she began to wonder if she'd been foolish to come to town. Over and over, she gave the same report. Yes, the leg had become infected. No, he wasn't dead. Desperate to escape, she raced to the church. The bell tower pointed to an azure sky and the white paint gleamed in the sun.

Tense and trembling, she walked up the steps. As she opened the door, cool air rushed from the shadows. She took in the diamonds of light on the floor, then she dropped down in the back pew, the same pew she'd shared with Zeb before he'd kissed her, before she'd fallen in love with him.

Nora buried her face in her hands. *Please, Lord. Save his leg. Save his life!*

Her prayers came in silent waves. She wanted to trust in the God who made the blind see and the lame walk. She *did* believe. She believed in God's sovereignty, His wisdom. Heaven offered joy and freedom, untold beauty, everything good in this life and more. It was a far better place than the here and now, but she couldn't bear to see Zeb leave for eternity just yet. High Plains needed him. *She* needed him. And Zeb needed his leg.

"Please, Lord," she whispered. "Be merciful."

Tears ran down her face, taking with them the tension that had kept her upright from dusk to dawn. Exhausted, she curled on her side on the pew, closed her eyes and fell into a dreamless sleep.

Sometime later, Nora awoke to the creak of the door. She heard footsteps, manly ones, and figured they belonged to Reverend Preston. She started to sit up, but stopped when she heard female footsteps.

"Thank you for seeing me," Abigail said to the minister. "It's urgent."

"Of course," he answered. "I'm sure you won't mind if Mrs. Preston joins us?"

"That would be fine," Abigail replied.

"I thought she'd be practicing the piano," he said. "I wonder where she is."

"Here I am," his wife called. "I was sorting through the music in your office. What can we do for you, Abigail?"

Nora didn't want to eavesdrop, but neither did she want Abigail to see her looking grim and disheveled. It seemed likely the blonde had come to discuss the jubilee, so Nora stayed hidden on the pew.

"Shall we step into my office?" the reverend asked.

"No," Abigail said hurriedly. "If what I'm hearing is true, we don't have much time."

"Time for what?" Mrs. Preston asked.

"I'm so embarrassed." Abigail's voice cracked. "I—I made a mistake. That is, Zeb and I—we did something we shouldn't have. Something…personal."

Nora's eyes popped wide.

"You can tell us," Mrs. Preston said in a low tone. "Even good people make mistakes."

Abigail sniffed. "It happened after the tornado, we were both upset and worried. We—He—Now I'm—I could be—" A choked sob finished the confession.

Nora's body turned into a bag of sand. Heavy and lifeless, she fought to drag in air.

"You poor girl!" The words came from Mrs. Preston. Nora heard the rustle of skirts and imagined Abigail clinging to the minister's wife. Tears filled her own eyes. Not for Abigail but for Zeb.

The reverend cleared his throat. "We need to be clear, Abigail. Are you with child?"

"I—I could be."

Trembling inside, Nora weighed the facts. The day she'd arrived, Abigail had swooned and Nora had suspected pregnancy. She'd seen how Zeb had looked at the blonde, the familiarity between them. Most haunting of all, she knew him to be a passionate man. Nora didn't doubt his character, but she knew the frailties of being human. If Abigail offered temptation, especially in the aftermath of the tornado, Zeb could have fallen. To keep from crying out, she crushed her knuckles to her mouth.

"It'll be all right," Mrs. Preston crooned to Abigail. "I'm sure Zeb will do the right thing."

Nora cringed with the obvious truth. If she didn't lose Zeb to death or the amputation, she'd lose him to Abigail and his sense of honor.

Reverend Preston cleared his throat. "Does he know?"

"I haven't told him," Abigail confessed.

"I see," said the minister. "Before we move forward, I'd like a word with Zeb in private."

"There's no time!" Abigail cried. "He's dying!"

The reverend interrupted. "I saw him a few days ago. The leg was healing nicely."

"The infection is spreading. Mother heard it from Percival."

The attorney had no doubt heard the news from Cassandra. Nora wanted to lecture him on respect, privacy and real civility.

Abigail continued in a whine. "That awful lady doctor is going to amputate his leg. If the infection doesn't kill him, *she* will!"

Reverend Preston took a breath. "Now, Abigail—"

"You *have* to help me," she cried. "If Zeb doesn't marry me, I'll be ruined. I'll have a child! *His* child. That baby deserves to inherit all that he's worked for."

Nora's hackles rose. So did her suspicions. Was Abigail lying to get her hands on Zeb's money? She wouldn't put anything past the woman, even scheming to deceive a man on his deathbed, then later claiming a miscarriage.

Mrs. Preston's voice broke in to her thoughts. "What would you like us to do, Abigail?"

"I want Reverend Preston to come with me to see Zeb. He could marry us on the spot."

"I see." The reverend sounded wary. "Shall we go now?"

"Yes, please." Abigail sniffled. "He *has* to marry me. If he doesn't, I don't know what I'll do!"

"I know Zeb," Reverend Preston said with confidence. "He'll do what's right."

Nora knew him, too. Zeb had his flaws, but he'd keep his word. When a man took advantage of a woman before marriage, even if he surrendered to her seduction, he made a promise of sorts. Spoken or not, Zeb would keep his word.

The Prestons left with Abigail, but Nora stayed in the church. She didn't want Abigail to upset Zeb, but the woman deserved to be heard. If she was carrying his child, he needed to know. As much as Nora wanted to protect him, she didn't have the right to deny him this knowledge…if it was true. In the gloom of the church, Nora prayed. "Please, Lord," she said out loud. "Let Abigail be lying. Save Zeb's life and let the truth be revealed."

Zeb felt like a corpse on fire. He didn't want visitors, but someone was making a commotion in the parlor. Carolina spoke with calm authority. He heard a faint rumble of a male voice, then the door to his sickroom opened and Carolina came in looking distressed.

"It's Miss Johnson," she said curtly. "I told her to leave. She says it's urgent. Reverend Preston is agreeing with her."

"Not now," Zeb muttered.

As the nurse backed out of the room, Abigail pushed through the door. "I have to see you, Zeb. It's important." She charged to his bedside as if she belonged there. She didn't. He had to make that point clear. If he was going to die, he wanted to do it without loose ends.

He looked at Carolina through the haze of fever. "It's all right. I'll speak with her."

The nurse's brows hitched. "If you're sure—"

"I am."

Propriety called for Carolina to leave the door ajar and she did. Abigail waited a moment, then tiptoed to the door and closed it. She had that look in her eyes, the one he'd ignored in the foolish weeks he'd entertained thoughts of marrying her. Trepidation swept over him. "What do you want?"

"I want what you promised." The words rattled off her tongue.

"I didn't promise you anything."

"We were courting," she said in a rush. "At least we *were* until that lady doctor showed up. You owe me, Zeb."

"I don't owe you a thing."

"Oh, yes, you do!" Her face darkened with anger. "You've humiliated me! Everyone's talking behind my back."

Zeb focused on Abigail through his fever-glazed eyes. "I don't care what people are saying. I *considered* courting you, but we never even kissed. You *know* that."

She looked smug. "No one else does."

A chill shook his bones. "What are you saying?"

She spoke in a hissing whisper. "I want to be Mrs. Zebulun Garrison, and I know how to make you say yes."

"That's impossible."

"I don't think so," she said, sounding coy. "I told Reverend Preston I'm carrying your child. He's outside. He can marry us right now."

"You *what?*"

"You heard me."

Zeb pushed up to a sitting position. Pain shot through him, but he didn't care. "That's a bald-faced lie and you know it!"

"*I* know it, but people will believe me. After we're married, I'll have a convenient miscarriage—"

"Abigail, you're crazy!" Zeb had never witnessed such selfishness. Had he ever thought she had pretty eyes? A pleasing smile? He'd been dead wrong. Looking at her now, he saw raw greed. Abigail wanted more than his name. She wanted his money. What he didn't understand was why she thought she could pull it off. "You're not carrying my child and we both know it. There's no way I'll marry you."

Her face turned ugly. "Face it, Zeb. You're going to die. If the infection doesn't kill you, the amputation will."

Blood leached from his face.

"If you don't marry me, I'll make life *miserable* for your beloved Dr. Nora." Sarcasm curled her lips into a snarl. "She humiliated me. So did you. You'll be long gone, but I'll make her pay in your place."

Zeb stared in disbelief. "You're serious, aren't you?"

"Very."

"So am I." He would have given a year of his life to be able to stand. He settled for aiming his finger at the door. "Get out."

"But—"

"I said *get out!*" When she didn't move, he shouted at the top of his lungs. "Carolina! Get in here!"

The nurse whipped through the door. Zeb saw Reverend Preston behind her. He considered calling Abigail a liar in front of the minister and the nurse, but he didn't want to repeat her ugly lies for fear of gossip. Carolina wasn't known to be a talker, but juicy tidbits had a way of spreading like a prairie fire.

The best way to stop gossip was to shut up, and that's what Zeb intended to do with one exception. He'd speak his mind to Reverend Preston.

He focused on Abigail. "Leave. Now."

She burst into tears and ran. Zeb made eye contact with the minister. "I need a word with you."

"Of course."

He told Carolina to leave and shut the door, then he indicated the chair. "Sit down, Reverend."

The man dropped down on the seat. "Is she lying, or do you have an obligation?"

"She's lying." Suddenly dizzy, Zeb settled back on the pillow. "I'm not a perfect man, but I *never* touched her."

"It's your word against hers."

"Yes."

"So she wants your money," the reverend surmised. "And your good name."

"Exactly." How could he have considered marrying such a woman? He'd been crazier than a loon.

The reverend's brows knit together. "Have you considered the possibility that she's carrying another man's child?"

"She's not," Zeb answered. "She admitted she's planning a miscarriage."

"I see." Reverend Preston tapped his fingers on his thigh. "It seems to me your path is clear. You need to live and you need to wait. The truth will come out."

"It's not that simple. She's threatening to make trouble for Nora."

Reverend Preston grimaced. "Maybe you should tell Nora what happened today."

Zeb thought for a minute. If he lived, he could handle Abigail himself and not involve Nora. If death approached, he'd tell her everything, including how much he loved her. "Not yet," he said to the reverend. "But if something happens to me, I'm trusting you to make things right."

"I'll look out for Nora," he answered in a solemn tone. "Right now, I'm concerned for you."

Pain knifed up Zeb's leg and he groaned. "The leg's bad. I might not make it."

The minister had preached at a dozen funerals after the tornado. He knew death well. "Is there anything you'd like to get off your chest?"

"Plenty." Zeb felt the weight of every mistake, every regret. "I settled my differences with the Lord the other night, but I've stumbled. If I could change anything, I'd treat Nora with respect from the day I met her. We'd already be married."

The reverend smiled. "I figured as much."

Zeb thought of the night ahead. "I don't want to die, and I don't want to lose my leg."

"And if you do?"

"I don't know." He licked his dry lips. "I have to be ready. I need to make a will. Would you write it for me?"

"Sure."

Zeb indicated a tablet and pencil on the nightstand. Until a few days ago, he'd been using it to jot down notes about the mill. "Use this."

The reverend propped the tablet in his lap.

"Write this down." Zeb's voice stayed strong. "I, Zebulun James Garrison, hereby leave half my worldly possessions to my sister, Cassandra, and the other half to Dr. Nora Mitchell."

The reverend's brow shot up. "Are you sure?"

"Don't say a word to anyone," Zeb cautioned. "I love Nora. If I die, I want her provided for." Even more important, he wanted her to know how he felt. If he died, naming her in his will would say that he loved her in the best way he knew. He'd be taking care of her.

Zeb continued with instructions for Will to look after Cassandra and to keep the mill or sell it, whichever he preferred. Zeb's heart sank at the thought. If he died, he wouldn't even leave sawdust behind. He'd have no legacy at all.

The reverend must have read his expression, because he lowered the tablet. "You're staring down the road to eternity, aren't you?"

"I am."

"It's dark now, but it won't be that way in the end."

Zeb's heart pounded. "How do you know?"

The minister sat back in his chair. "I could quote Scriptures to you, Zeb. I could tell you about my own brush with death. But mostly I believe in Heaven because of my ma. Just before she passed, she cried out the name of her Lord. The smile on her face was a sight to behold. I haven't doubted since."

Zeb didn't doubt in Heaven anymore. He just wasn't ready to make the trip. "Cassandra needs me. The *town* needs me."

The man lowered his chin. "So does Nora."

Zeb's heart beat like crazy. All his life, he'd fought to be the best man he could be, to make choices that would lead to a better life. Sometimes he'd been right, and sometimes he'd been wrong. Either way, he'd been in control until he'd put his boot on the saw frame and the pivot had broken. At that moment he'd been knocked flat in body and soul. Lying in Nora's sickroom, he faced a humbling truth. He had no control over life, death and the hard times in between. All he could do was fight for what he loved.

He looked at Reverend Preston. "Promise me something."

"What is it?"

"If I don't make it, protect Nora. Don't let Abigail get away with her lies."

"I promise," the reverend answered. "But I want a promise in return."

"What?" Zeb asked.

"Don't die with regrets. Tell Nora how you feel."

Zeb grimaced. "I'll tell her I love her, but I won't ask her to marry a cripple."

"That's pride talking." The minister spoke with quiet wisdom. "I won't push you, Zeb. But I'm urging you to think long and hard about what you say to Nora. I guarantee you, she's a lot less interested in your leg than she is in your heart."

"I know, but I…" Zeb couldn't think. It hurt too much.

The reverend stood. "If something happens, I'll take care of things for you. But I'm praying you'll live and do it yourself."

"Me, too," Zeb answered. He wanted to live and he wanted to walk. He wanted to marry Nora, have children and leave that legacy he treasured. After the reverend left, Zeb tried to pray but couldn't. Instead, tears leaked from his eyes. He hoped God would hear a prayer without words.

Chapter Twenty-One

The instant Nora got home, Carolina asked for a private talk in the kitchen. The nurse told her about Abigail's visit, how Zeb had ordered the blonde to get out, and how the reverend had spoken to him in private.

"I tried to stop her from upsetting him," the nurse said. "But he wanted to speak with her."

"It's his business," Nora answered. Her throat felt parched, so she poured herself a cup of water. She'd slept longer on the pew than she'd thought, then she'd waited awhile before coming home. She'd wanted to give Zeb privacy while he dealt with Abigail, and she didn't want him to see her face until she'd composed her thoughts.

She drained the cup of water, but the liquid didn't wash away her worries.

Carolina gave her a motherly look. "Sit. You need to eat."

"I have to check Zeb."

"I just did," she answered. "He's dozing. Have some of Rebecca's pie."

The last time Nora had tasted the pie had been with Zeb.

Would they ever share meals as man and wife? As Carolina put a wedge on a plate, tears pushed into Nora's eyes. As she took a bite, the sweetness hurt her tongue.

Carolina touched her shoulder. "Talk to me, honey. It'll help."

"I can't." Not about Abigail and what she'd overheard. She didn't want to spread gossip. Maybe the blonde had lied. Maybe Zeb would keep his leg and they could take that buggy ride. She wanted to believe, but she couldn't see through a sudden veil of tears.

Carolina sat in the second chair. "Pretend I'm your mother. Tell me what's wrong."

Tears spilled down Nora's cheeks. She imagined her mother's smile, the scents of lavender and linen. For the first time in weeks, she wanted to go home. She wanted to be twelve years old and full of dreams instead of wisdom. Her resolve crumbled like a dam made of sand. In a choked murmur, she told Carolina what she'd heard in church.

The nurse gripped her hand. "I know people stumble, but I don't believe Abigail for a minute. She's told lies before."

"As big as this one?"

"I don't know," the nurse answered. "But I wouldn't put anything past her. Before you came, folks figured Zeb would marry her. That all changed when you arrived. He loves you, Nora. But something's holding him back."

"I thought it was because of his leg."

"It could be," Carolina replied. "You deserve the whole story. I think you should ask him straight out if Abigail's claim is a possibility."

Nora couldn't stand the thought. "If there's a child, he'll have to marry her. His honor would demand it. So would mine."

Carolina nodded in that calm way of hers. "The truth will come out."

Nora's temper flared at the injustice. "It would come out *now* if Abigail would let me examine her. I can just see it…she'll fool Zeb into marrying her and claim to have a miscarriage."

The nurse nodded. "You need to speak with Zeb."

"I will," Nora answered.

"Tonight?"

"It depends on the leg, the fever." She shuddered. "I don't want to have this conversation when he's fighting for his life."

"You'll know when it's right," the nurse said. "Maybe Zeb will tell you about the visit."

Nora hoped he would. If he told her about Abigail's claim and disputed the lies, Nora would be at peace. Instead, her insides were in a jumble. She stood up from the table. "I need to check Zeb."

"One more thing." Carolina stepped to the counter and retrieved an envelope. "Pete stopped by. He picked up a piece of mail at the mercantile."

As she took the envelope, Nora recognized Dr. Zeiss's penmanship and opened the envelope eagerly. He'd written a missive on hysterical mutism. Later she'd read it more carefully and write back about Bess. At the end of the letter, he'd added a P.S.

> I have another reason for writing. Geneva Medical College has received a sizable endowment, and I've been given permission to hire an assistant. I'd be honored if you'd return to New York and share my work. I can offer you a respectable salary and a chance to serve all humanity with our research.

Nora stared at the letter. A few months ago, she'd have danced around the room with joy. Now it held a consolation prize. As much as she appreciated Dr. Zeiss's offer, she wanted to stay in High Plains and marry Zeb. The two desires were completely entwined. If she and Zeb couldn't be man and wife, she'd have to leave High Plains.

Shaking, she left the letter on the table, excused herself from Carolina and went to examine Zeb's leg. The minute she stepped into his room, she smelled the sweetness of increased infection. With her stomach churning, she sat on the chair next to his bed.

He opened his eyes. "Hi."

"Hi," she answered. "How are you feeling?"

He stared at her face as if he was memorizing it. She felt the same need, but instead of seeing his handsome features, she saw the glassiness of fever. A bead of sweat swelled on his temple, broke away and trickled into his thick hair.

He aimed his eyes at the ceiling. "The fever's worse."

"I can see." She raised the sheet from his toes and rolled it up to expose the wound. The smell gagged her, but the sight of an abscess filled her with hope. Her gaze went to his knee. This morning she'd seen a tiny red line, a sign of blood poisoning, snaking up his leg. Now she saw a slight receding in the redness. The fever was high, but Zeb's body was rallying against an enemy. If she lanced the wound, the infection would drain. She'd have to cut away dead tissue, but she saw a real chance to save his leg.

"What's the verdict?" he said to the ceiling.

Was he hiding his eyes because of Abigail, or because he feared her answer? Nora resisted the urge to hold his hand. She no longer had that privilege. "I see improvement."

His throat twitched. "How much?"

"Enough to put off amputation." She wished he'd look at her, but she feared what she'd see. Guilt over Abigail…the lost cause of their future. "I'm going to drain the wound and debride it again. If the fever breaks, you have a good chance at walking out of here on both legs." He'd be on crutches and he might have a limp, but he'd *walk*.

He closed his eyes. "Do it now."

"It's going to hurt," she said. "Do you want chloroform?"

"Save it."

They both knew he could still lose the leg. If she had to amputate, she'd use the drug then. She ached to comfort him with a touch. Instead, she carried her instruments to the kitchen where she instructed Carolina to boil them for five minutes. Next she put on a clean apron and washed her own hands in the hottest water she could stand. The nurse plucked the instruments from the boiling pot with a pair of tongs and placed them on a tray covered with a white towel. Together they went to Zeb's room.

Nora tried to make eye contact, but he'd sealed his eyelids and was breathing deep. When he heard the clatter of the instruments, he turned to Carolina. "Cassandra's not here, is she?"

They all knew he'd do some yelling in the next hour.

Carolina wiped his brow. "Will and Emmeline are in town. They took her to the boardinghouse for a meal."

"Good."

And so the procedure began. For what felt like an eternity, Nora cleaned the wound of pus and rotting tissue. Zeb moaned like a dying animal, but he didn't fight. Twice tears pushed out of his eyes. It took a lot to make a man cry, but Zeb had entered that humbling darkness where a man turned into a needy child. Pushing her feelings aside, she did what had to be done.

By the time she finished, her body ached with tension. Instead of suturing the wound, she left it open in case she had to debride it again, and so air and sunlight could dry the tissue. She had one more painful task to perform. "Hold tight, Zeb. I'm going to wash it with whiskey and then we're done."

Groaning, he clutched the bedsheets. As she irrigated the wound with the alcohol, he arched his back and cried out the Lord's name in a forsaken prayer. Tears filled Nora's eyes. Causing pain served a purpose, but it shook her to the core. Attempting to ease the sting, she rapidly fanned the leg with her hand. If the rush of air helped, she couldn't see it. Seconds of groaning turned into a full minute. When the worst of the stinging subsided, Zeb relaxed against the mattress. "Nora?"

"Yes?"

"Thank you…for everything."

"I just hope the fever breaks for good."

"Me, too." He looked at her then. "I need to talk to you. Not now. I can't think straight. But soon."

Why had he said *talk?* Why had he sounded so defeated? Her heart clenched. Surely he'd have said something more promising if they had a future together.

"We'll talk when you're able." She sounded like a doctor addressing a patient, not a woman in love.

In the next breath he surrendered to exhaustion and passed out. Carolina touched her shoulder. "I'll stay with him. Go change your dress."

Sweat trickled down her back. "Thank you, I will." Nora left the room, passing through the parlor where she saw an unexpected gathering that included Cassandra, Percival, Emmeline and Will.

Will looked ashen, but he stood tall. "How is he?"

"I'm hopeful," Nora said. "The fever spiked, but the wound is draining. I think he'll make it."

"And his leg?" Cassandra asked in a hush.

"It's looking good."

Will blew out a breath. As Cassandra wept into her hankie,

Percy patted her back. Emmeline reached for her husband's hand and squeezed. "We're all grateful."

Nora felt near tears herself. "Would you like some tea? I could make—"

"No." Emmeline waved her hand in protest. "We're here to help, not make work. Rebecca came by. She left supper on the stove."

The food smelled wonderful. Nora surveyed Zeb's friends with a lump in her throat. They were her friends, too. She'd lose them if she lost Zeb to Abigail. "Let's all have supper."

Percy stood. "I appreciate the offer, but I have a commitment."

"Are you sure?" Cassandra protested.

"Sorry, Cassandra." He touched her shoulder. "Business comes first."

Nora wondered what Zeb would say about the easy way Percy touched Cassandra. She figured he'd be annoyed. As the attorney left, Nora and the women went to the kitchen. Cassandra spotted the letter from Dr. Zeiss on the table. The job offer was in plain view for the girl to see. Her eyes widened. "You've been offered a position in *New York!*"

"That's right." Nora turned to the cupboard to hide her face. The offer filled her with a mix of pride and dread. Dr. Zeiss's respect pleased her, but she didn't want to leave High Plains.

"Are you taking it?" Cassandra asked.

Nora weighed her options. If Zeb had to marry Abigail, she would go back to New York with her heart in tatters. She'd pour her soul into her work. If Abigail's claim proved to be a lie, Nora would turn down the offer. Right now, she didn't know what the future held.

"I don't know," she said to the women. "I love High Plains, but a person has to do what's right."

"Of course," Emmeline answered. "But we want you to stay."

Cassandra sighed. "I'd go to New York in a *heartbeat*."

"Don't be so sure," Emmeline replied. "If you loved a man in High Plains, you'd stay forever."

Emmeline had been speaking of Will, but Nora felt the same way about Zeb. She reached for the supper plates stacked neatly on a shelf. She wanted to be putting a meal on the table for a family—for Zeb and their children. She also wanted to adopt Alex. If she had to leave, she hoped to take him with her to New York. Surely Zeb would grant her that consolation.

Cassandra came to her side and took the plates. "I want you to stay, but a woman has to have the courage of her convictions. *You* told me that."

Nora thought back to that early visit to the Circle-L. Today the words cut deep. "I did, didn't I?"

Emmeline stirred the stew warming on the stove. "When will you decide?"

"I don't know."

Mercifully, someone knocked on the parlor door. Nora opened it and saw Bess. The girl hugged her hard, and together they went to the kitchen. Nora, Emmeline and Cassandra traded looks that finished the conversation about her possible departure. No one wanted Bess to worry, so they talked about Rebecca's good cooking, Zeb's recovery and the summer jubilee.

For Nora, supper passed in a nerve-racking storm of small talk. She loved these women and the details of their lives. She loved Zeb and wanted to stay, but only if he could love her back. When the meal ended, the women did the dishes and left. Nora checked on Zeb. He was snoring soundly and the wound looked clean, so she went upstairs to bed.

In spite of her exhaustion, she couldn't sleep. Between Zeb's health and Abigail's claim, she spent the night considering a list of what ifs. At best, she could hope to catch Abigail in a lie. At worst, she'd be going back to New York alone, without Alex for consolation. At dawn she dressed and crept down to Zeb's room. In the dim light she stood in the doorway, watching him sleep. Pewter light bathed his face in shadows, softening his features beneath the bristle of his dark beard. His skin looked cool and dry. Closing her eyes, she listened to his soft snores filling the room. The fever had broken. He'd live. He'd keep his leg. But the fight for their future remained treacherous.

The woman in her wanted to awaken Zeb with a touch of her hand, a kiss to his forehead so she could feel the coolness on her lips. The doctor knew he needed his rest, so she went to the kitchen and had a cup of tea. When she finished it, she checked Zeb again and saw him sprawled on his back. Out of the blue, he let out a snore that raised the roof. The rumble made her smile. It also filled her with a longing for a future with this man and the knowledge that her hope could be lost.

She went back to the kitchen, where she met Carolina. "I'm going to visit Cassandra," she said. "Will and Emmeline stayed with her in town. They'll want to know how Zeb's doing."

"Enjoy the fresh air." Carolina had already washed Nora's dishes. "I'll keep an eye on our patient."

Nora thanked her, then left through the front door. Zeb's house lay to the west, but she had to pass the mercantile before she turned on the road that led to the two-story home she'd only seen from a distance. The sight of the store filled her with disgust. She wanted to go inside and demand to confirm Abigail's claim with an examination. The allegation could be proved or disproved in minutes, though another angle had to be considered. She could be pregnant, but not with Zeb's child.

As her stomach twisted with worry, Nora looked down Main Street. Thanks to a community effort, work hadn't stopped on the town hall. She could see glass windows and the first coat of whitewash. The building stood strong and bright, a tribute to the people of High Plains. Nora ached to be part of this town. She wanted to put down roots and stay forever.

"Dr. Nora?"

She turned and saw Winnie Morrow approaching from across the street. She had a basket on her arm and a sweet smile on her face. Nora smiled back. "Good morning, Winnie."

"How's Zeb?"

"The fever broke." Nora enjoyed sharing happy news. "He's going to be fine."

"Oh, good!" Winnie shifted the weight of the basket. "The jubilee committee met last night. We were deciding what to do about the celebration. If Zeb had died…" She shook her head. "This town needs him."

"I think so, too."

Winnie heaved a sigh. "Abigail will be glad. I suppose you heard the news?"

Please, Lord. Let the news be about the jubilee. "I haven't heard anything."

Winnie looked smug. "Frankly, I don't care. My mother wanted me to marry Zeb, but I like someone else."

Nora's stomach turned to acid. "What are you saying?"

"I'm surprised Zeb didn't tell you. He and Abigail are getting married."

Nora's world spun into a gray mist until she steadied herself with sheer discipline. The rumor could still be a lie. It *had* to be a lie. "How do you know?" she asked. "Did Abigail announce it?"

"Mrs. Preston told my mother." Winnie stepped closer, as if they'd become best friends. "Abigail's with child. Can you believe it?"

Nora had overheard the conversation with the Prestons. So far,

Winnie hadn't said anything that proved Abigail's claim. Needing information, Nora turned professional. "Is Abigail sure?"

A smug smile crossed Winnie's face. "At the meeting last night, she excused herself twice to be sick. My mother says she has 'the look.'"

Nora knew that look well. Expecting women often had a glow. "I see."

With Nora struggling to stay calm, Winnie described the conversation with the Prestons, then related Abigail's visit to Zeb's sickbed. "At first he yelled at her to leave. He tried to deny it, but then he spoke with Reverend Preston and made arrangements."

Yesterday Zeb had been close to death. Had he been planning a wedding or his funeral? Nora refused to give up hope. Until she spoke with him, she wouldn't believe a word of gossip.

Winnie sighed. "A wedding makes sense. Before you came to High Plains, everyone expected Zeb to marry her."

"I see."

"Frankly," Winnie replied, "the Johnsons deserve the embarrassment of a shotgun wedding. The way they treated Rebecca was shameful. Now the shoe's on the other foot."

"We'll see," Nora said diplomatically. Until Zeb told her to pack her bags, she wouldn't trust a word anyone said. Surely he'd tell her the truth. But he was a man of integrity. If he had to marry Abigail, he'd do it.

After saying farewell to Winnie, Nora looked down the road to Zeb's house. Before she spoke to anyone else, she wanted to hear the truth from Zeb. Rather than visiting Cassandra as she'd intended, she turned to the river where she could walk alone. She also needed to pray. Somehow it seemed fitting to do it at the foot of the waterfall.

Chapter Twenty-Two

Zeb woke up with a smile on his face and Cassandra at his bedside. He wanted to speak with Nora, but she'd left the house for a breath of air. He knew how fast rumors could fly through High Plains, and he wanted to speak with her before Abigail launched her next attack. He still felt weak, but the fever had broken. His leg hurt, but the pain no longer felt like a beast in his flesh. Gratitude flooded his soul and he silently thanked God for His mercy. In a few days, he'd walk out of Nora's house with crutches or a cane. In a week or two, they'd take that buggy ride and he'd propose to her.

Now, though, his sister needed his attention. Zeb hadn't paid much attention to her romantic quandary in the past week, and he wondered if she'd come to her senses. "So how's Clint?" he asked.

Cassandra's eyes lit up with pleasure, then dimmed to an everyday brown. "He's fine. Dr. Nora gave him cough medicine, and he rested like she said."

"He's a good man." Zeb thought back to the conversation in the mill just before the accident. "I don't suppose he's asked you any important questions?"

She gaped at him. "Of course not. He's a cowboy."

"So?"

Cassandra looked at him as if he were stupid. "I like Clint a lot, but I miss Boston. If Percy—"

"Percy's a dolt."

"I don't think so." She absently handed him a glass of water. "There's a lot to be said for going back East. Even Dr. Nora's considering it."

"What?" Zeb couldn't believe his ears.

"Do you remember how she wrote that doctor about Bess? He wrote back with an offer to work with him. I asked her if she was going to take it, and she said she didn't know."

Zeb felt the sting of a poisoned arrow. He'd expected to wake up and see Nora at his bedside. No wonder she'd been stand-offish yesterday. She hadn't been worried about his leg or his life. She'd been wondering how she'd tell him she'd decided to go back to New York. Rage pulsed through Zeb's body. She'd tricked him into trusting her. He'd given her his heart and she was about to hand it back with polite regrets. He couldn't stay under her roof another minute. "I'm going home," he said to Cassandra. "Do you have the buggy?"

"Yes, but—"

"Tell Carolina I need those crutches she mentioned."

Cassandra didn't budge. "What's gotten into you?"

Zeb swung his good leg over the side of the bed. "Hand me my pants," he ordered. "Now!"

"No!"

"Yes!" They were bickering like brats, but he managed to shove into his trousers. He was tangling with a shirt when Nora walked into the room.

"What's wrong?" she asked.

No way would Zeb let her see his pain. A man had his pride. Right now, that was all he had. He'd leave today, but he'd do it with dignity. He looked at Cassandra. "I need a minute with Dr. Mitchell."

Nora's brow furrowed at the use of her title. Cassandra stood. "I'll wait in the parlor."

As she left, Zeb sat as straight as he could with the leg stretched in front of him. It hurt, but not as much as his heart. Unless he controlled himself, Nora would see right through him. She'd win like Frannie had won. He licked his dry lips, then spoke with all the control he could muster. "Sit down, Nora. We have to talk."

Her faced paled. Zeb knew why. She knew she'd been discovered.

"About what?" she asked in a hush.

"We've had some memorable times," he said. "I won't deny it. But it seems we're destined to go our separate ways."

"Are you sure?" Her voice quavered.

"I'm positive." He put iron in his voice. "A man has to do what's right. So does a woman. Cassandra told me about that letter you received. It's the job of your dreams, isn't it?"

She gave a small nod, then bit her lip. "Are you *telling* me to take it?"

Zeb wiped his hand through his hair. For all his arrogant pride, he loved this woman. He wanted her to stay, but he also wanted her to be happy. "It seems to me you belong in New York."

"I see." Tears spilled down her cheeks.

Zeb didn't know what to think. Women cried when they were happy. They cried when they were sad. Which was this? He wasn't sure. He only knew he'd done the right thing by setting her free. He just wished it didn't hurt so much. The pain took him back to the front of the church where Frannie had left him. Anger had comforted him then, and it strengthened him now.

"Go on," he said roughly. "Get out of here so I can finish getting my things together."

She looked as if she'd been kicked to the side of the road. "Your leg—"

"I'm going home."

"It's too soon." She reached for his hand.

He jerked it back. How much pity could a man stand? He couldn't take the look in her eyes, and he sure didn't want a kiss goodbye. "We're through, Nora. You know it and I know it."

With a tearful nod, she headed for the doorway. With her back to him, she paused. "Your leg still needs attention. I'll have Carolina visit later today."

"Fine."

"One other thing." She faced him with an expression that matched the stones at the bottom of the waterfall, the ones worn smooth by the endless pounding.

"What is it?" he asked.

"I'd like to adopt Alex." Her voice quavered. "I'll be able to take good care of him. He can go to school."

Zeb cared about the boy, too. He'd imagined the three of them making a family. That wouldn't happen, but he still wanted a son. He wanted to tell her no, that he loved Alex and the boy was all he had left, but he couldn't do it. Even more than Alex and a legacy, Zeb wanted Nora to be happy. "Sure," he said. "That'll be good for him."

With a final lift of her shoulders, Nora walked out of the room, taking with her the shattered pieces of his heart.

Alone at her bedroom window, Nora watched Zeb leave with Cassandra. She couldn't imagine anything worse for him than being forced to marry Abigail. Back in his room, she'd wanted to cry with him, but she'd held in her feelings out of respect. By telling her to leave, Zeb had protected her dignity. Now she had to protect his. Fighting tears, she sat at the secretary in her room, selected a sheet of stationery and penned a letter to Dr. Zeiss accepting the job as his assistant. She thanked him for his kindness, then wrote, "I'll leave High Plains at the end of the week."

Nora looked at the words and felt sick. Eventually Zeb would find another doctor for the town. Until then, Carolina could handle whatever needs arose. The women and children would especially be in good hands. Carolina had delivered more babies than Nora. As for paying her way to New York, she'd ask Percy to sell her house. Immediately after the summer jubilee, Nora would leave High Plains the way she'd come, seated next to Mr. Crandall on a freight wagon.

The sooner she left, the better off Zeb would be. He'd doubtlessly marry Abigail as soon as he could stand. The thought of seeing them together crushed Nora's soul to dust. She wrote a second paragraph updating Dr. Zeiss on Bess, then signed the letter "Nora Mitchell, M.D." She'd come a long way from being "Dr. N. Mitchell." She'd earned the respect of the town and of a man who'd accidentally broken her heart.

Nora sealed the envelope and left it on her desk. She'd post it herself when she reached Kansas City. She couldn't bear the thought of seeing the Johnsons, and she didn't want to cope with questions from friends. She'd say goodbye to everyone at the jubilee, including Zeb. Sometimes a woman needed to cry alone. This was one of those times.

Zeb couldn't climb the stairs to his bedroom, so he slept on the sofa in the parlor. Carolina came every day to check his leg. He resisted the urge to ask her about Nora, but his curiosity grew every hour. By now, he'd expected to hear talk about Nora's news. He'd considered asking Cassandra what she'd heard, but he didn't want to stoke his sister's interest in going back East. With his sister tending to him, Will and Emmeline had returned to the Circle-L. Pete came to visit once, but they'd talked about saw blades and nothing else.

The person who *hadn't* visited was Abigail. Zeb saw no reason to send for her. By now, she'd know he was alive and kicking, and that her lies wouldn't hold water. Next time their paths crossed, he'd settle things with a word or two. Until then, he wanted to lick his wounds in private.

He was closing his eyes for a nap when the parlor door flew open. Cassandra marched across the room. "I can't believe it. Zeb, how *could* you?"

He pulled himself upright. "How could I what?"

"You *know* what!" She started to pace. "Abigail! Of all people… She's awful. I do *not* want her for a sister, but if what I'm hearing is true—"

Zeb stifled an oath. He didn't know how the rumor had spread, but Abigail was at the root of it. "Whatever you're hearing, it's a lie."

Cassandra launched into a litany of names, gossip and innuendo. Zeb could barely follow, but he gleaned from her ranting that Mrs. Preston had been present when Abigail spoke with Reverend Preston. She'd said something to Mrs. Morrow, who'd blabbed to Winnie and every woman who'd come for a dress fitting. By the time the story had reached Cassandra, the rumors had him guilty as charged and engaged to Abigail.

"Tell me again," he said to his sister. "Half the town thinks Abigail's carrying my baby, and we're getting married at the jubilee?"

She nodded furiously.

"And," he continued, "because neither Abigail nor I have said a word, people think it's going to be a surprise wedding."

"Exactly." Cassandra dropped down on a chair.

With his heart pounding, Zeb recalled his conversation with Nora. He'd assumed she *wanted* the job in New York. *He'd* told her to leave. Now he wondered if she'd heard the rumors and was leaving out of a sense of honor. It would be just like her to sacrifice her happiness for the benefit of another woman's child, *his* child…a child that had never been conceived.

He had to get to her. He had to tell her the truth before she did something foolish like a hire a wagon to take her away from High Plains…away from him. He tried to stand, but Cassandra nudged him back down.

"So it's not true?" she asked

"Not a word of it." Furious and disgusted, he told Cassandra about Abigail's visit. "I thought Nora was leaving because she wanted the job in New York. Now I think she's leaving because of the talk."

Cassandra bit her lip. "I don't know, but she's going with the Crandalls after the jubilee."

He had three days before Nora would be gone forever. He considered hobbling to her house now, but an idea took hold and wouldn't let go. The people of High Plains were expecting a surprise announcement at the jubilee. Zeb rather liked the idea of making a declaration they'd never forget. He wanted to tell the world he loved Dr. Nora Mitchell, and he wanted to claim her as his wife in front of the entire town.

A second thought nagged at him. What if she really *did* want to return to New York? If he spoke his mind at the jubilee, the whole town would witness his humiliation. He'd be reliving the horrible jilting by Frannie. Zeb thought for less than three seconds. He'd take that chance and he'd do it gladly.

He looked at his sister and thought about Clint, Percy and the tug-of-war for her heart. "What about you, Cassie? What's happening with Clint and Percy?"

When she didn't object to the childhood name, Zeb knew she felt burdened. Suddenly bleak, she bit her lip. "Percy asked me to marry him."

Zeb's blood chilled. "I see."

"I wish I did." She twisted the hankie in her lap. "I don't know what to do. Percy's so…perfect. But Clint—" She bit her lip. "He has a certain way about him. I told Percy I had to think about it."

"That's good."

"I just don't know," she repeated.

Zeb thought of his own situation. He'd fought his feelings for Nora, but they'd bested him. He'd tried to fight God, and the Almighty had wrestled him to the ground with a brush with death. In the end, Zeb had no decision to make. He just had to act with courage. He tugged on a curl of his sister's hair. "You'll know what's right, Cassandra. Just promise me one thing."

"What's that?"

"You won't decide anything until after the jubilee." He didn't tell her about Clint and the arm wrestling and the prize money. The cowboy had to make the declaration on his own.

"All right," she answered. "But I want a promise from you."

"What is it?"

Her eyes glistened with love. "I want you to marry Nora. I already love her like a sister. I think you love her, too."

"I do." Zeb smiled. "This jubilee's going to be memorable for both us."

When his sister hugged him, Zeb hugged her back. He had three days to wait and plan. He'd use the time to practice walking on crutches. Flooded with gratitude, he thanked God for the miracle of healing. He wanted the world to know he'd become a different man, one who wasn't afraid to love and trust a lady doctor. Someday he wanted a little girl with red hair and a medical degree just like her mother.

When Cassandra pulled back, Zeb smiled. "Would you ask Reverend Preston to pay a call?"

"Sure," she said. "Why?"

Zeb wanted to make sure the reverend knew what he intended. "You'll find out at the jubilee."

Cassandra groaned. "I hate secrets!"

Zeb laughed out loud. Not only would Cassandra be surprised by what *he* had to say to Nora, she'd be shocked to her toes when Clint won the arm-wrestling contest and asked her to marry him.

Joy welled in Zeb's chest, but he managed to look smug. "You'll like this surprise," he said. "You might even get more than one. Now go fetch Reverend Preston. I have plans to make."

Chapter Twenty-Three

In the days before the jubilee, Nora packed her things and spoke to Percy about selling her house. As she'd hoped, he advanced her the money and promised to keep the matter confidential. She considered visiting Rebecca and Emmeline to say goodbye, but the thought of leaving put tears in her eyes. Instead, she penned letters telling each woman she'd treasure their kindness forever. She wrote another letter to Bess, encouraging the girl and promising to always keep in touch, and a fourth letter to Cassandra, asking her to take good care of Zeb.

Knowing Alex couldn't keep a secret, Nora didn't tell him they'd be leaving with the Crandalls. She'd speak to him after the jubilee. Carolina helped her pack and promised to look out for her patients. She also spoke with Cassandra, who'd asked her directly about the job in New York.

The day of the jubilee dawned sunny and bright. The festivities started in the late morning, but Nora stayed home until midafternoon. She couldn't stand the thought of hearing talk about Zeb's engagement to Abigail. She had avoided speaking with anyone for the past week, but Carolina had heard talk of a surprise announcement at the Jubilee. No one knew who'd give it or what would be said, but Reverend Preston had announced that something would happen at two o'clock.

Nora looked at the clock on the mantel. She didn't want to go to the celebration, but Carolina and Alex had already left and they'd be looking for her. Earlier she'd put on the brown dress, the one she'd been wearing when Zeb kissed her, and a simple felt hat. She'd considered the stylish bottle-green gown, but the pretty frock spoke of lost dreams. The woman who'd come to High Plains with her chin in the air felt broken and bruised. The brown dress suited her mood.

Thoughts of Zeb had filled her mind all week, and he haunted her now as she approached the crowd near the town hall. The new building stood tall and proud. So did the church with its high roof and white bell tower. Even Dr. Dempsey's office looked dignified. Someone had replaced the windows. Curious, Nora peeked inside. The glass had been swept and the shelves wiped clean. She couldn't see the roof, but the water stain on the ceiling had been painted. Someone had bought the building and started repairs.

Loneliness cut through her with scalpel-like precision. She'd found love and respect in High Plains, but those blessings weren't hers to keep. Except for Alex, she reminded herself. Eager to find the boy, she crossed the street where folks were milling about through a maze of tables.

In spite of Abigail's influence, the jubilee committee had done a wonderful job. Thick ribbons decorated the town hall, and laughter floated in the air like birdsong. Nora spotted Emmeline at the beanbag toss, encouraging Mikey and Missy to aim for a donkey's wide mouth. Next to them, children were playing jackstraws, quoits and marbles. Someone had donated string and metal disks to make whirligigs, and a group of girls were spinning them in the bright sun. Longing for a daughter made her throat ache.

Emmeline flashed a smile. "Dr. Nora! How are you?"

"Just fine."

"Alex is looking for you," she said. "If you hurry, you can catch the three-legged race."

"Where is it?"

"In the meadow just past the baking contests." Emmeline tousled Missy's hair. "Follow your nose and you'll find it."

Nora left with a wave. The aroma of baked goods led her to tables covered with pies, loaves of braided breads and jars of jams, each numbered so the judges wouldn't know who'd prepared the entry. Nora glanced around for Rebecca and Bess. She didn't see them, so she ambled past the goodies to the crowd by the meadow.

She still hadn't spotted Zeb and Abigail, and she wondered if he'd come at all. She knew from Carolina that his leg was healing nicely and he'd become proficient with crutches. Even so, navigating rough ground could be difficult. She almost hoped he hadn't come today, but she knew he'd be here. Everywhere she looked, she saw Zeb's influence. He'd made this day happen and wouldn't miss it. She'd also heard talk about an announcement and figured he and Abigail would be declaring their engagement, maybe even exchanging vows.

Telling herself to stay strong, she joined the crowd lining up to watch the three-legged race. Lanie Briggs smiled at her and said hello. She smiled back, but her heart felt like stone until she spotted Alex. The boy was paired with Jonah. Will Logan was crouched in front of them tying their legs together. When Alex saw her, he waved. Will partnered up for the race with Johnny, Emmeline's younger brother, and someone called for the runners to get in line.

"On your mark!" called the official. "Get set… Go!"

Along with everyone else, Nora clapped and cheered. Boys

tumbled and men went down with them. Alex and Jonah were in the lead, but they lost their balance and went sprawling. Will and Johnny, moving in perfect time, came up from the rear and won.

"Hey, Garrison!" someone called. "With those crutches, you could have run the race by yourself!"

Nora refused to turn around. She'd see him with Abigail and she'd cry or lose her temper. Biting her lip, Nora began counting down from a hundred. Surely Zeb would give her a wide berth.

He didn't.

She felt him standing behind her and saw his shadow mixing with hers at her feet. She wanted to love this man for better or for worse. She wanted to be his wife and raise their children in this town that had become her home.

His voice came from over her shoulder. "Nora?"

She swallowed hard, then turned. Before she could speak, Alex galloped up to her side. "Did you see us? We almost won!"

She tousled his hair. "You did great."

When the boy looked at Zeb, so did Nora. He'd shaved this morning and was wearing a crisp shirt and his usual paisley vest. The crutches took nothing from his height. Hatless, he looked her full in the face.

Alex interrupted. "Zeb, did you see us?"

"I sure did." He smiled at the boy, then dug in his pocket for a handful of pennies. "I need to speak to Dr. Nora. Why don't you get yourself and Jonah some lemonade."

"Sure." The boy took the coins, then looked at Nora. "Can I enter the pie-eating contest?"

"You bet." When he got a bellyache, she'd dose him with peppermint. That's what doctors did. It's what a mother did. As Alex scampered off with his friend, Nora followed him with her eyes, wishing she could run away so easily.

Zeb waited in silence until she dared to look at him, then he aimed his chin down a path that led to the river. "Walk with me."

"That's not a good idea."

"Why not?"

"You know why." If they were spotted walking off alone, people would gossip.

"I can handle it," he said. "I think you can, too."

Her insides fluttered. What did he intend? A goodbye kiss? She couldn't allow it, but neither could she leave without clearing the air between them. She nodded her agreement, then stepped past him, giving him her back so he couldn't see her eyes. She walked twenty paces down the trail, leaving him in the dust as she'd do when she left with the Crandalls.

She stopped and stared at the river. She couldn't see the waterfall, but she felt the force of gravity. She wanted to throw herself into Zeb's arms. She wanted to kiss him one last time and tell him she loved him. For once, though, she stifled her impulses. She could only do harm to them both.

As she took a breath, she heard the thump of his crutches and turned. Zeb touched her arm. "Why are you leaving High Plains?"

"You know why." Her voice came out in a whisper.

"Do I?"

"Yes!" She couldn't stand the heartache, the loss…the *wrongness* of Zeb marrying a woman he didn't love. Even more painful, she couldn't bear the thought of Abigail having his child. Her feelings exploded, and she shouted at Zeb. "I love you! You know that!" She knotted her fists over her heart and pressed, but it still hurt.

His gaze didn't waver. Neither did he speak.

Nora surrendered to the fury she'd been holding inside for a solid week. "I can't do it, Zeb! *I* can't watch you marry Abigail and have children with her. *I* should be the mother of your children! We should be adopting Alex together. You love me, I know it! We *belong* together. But we can't undo—"

He cupped her chin and tilted her face to his. One crutch wobbled and fell, but he didn't bother to catch it. "Nora, listen."

"I can't, Zeb." Tears flooded her eyes. "*We* can't—"

"I'm not marrying Abigail."

Air whooshed from her lungs. "You're not?"

"No, I'm not." His voice rang with truth. "I never touched her. When I think of what she tried to do—" He clamped his lips tight, then steadied himself with a breath. "She thought I was going to die. She tried to blackmail me into marrying her by threatening to harm you."

"That's appalling!"

His irises flashed like fine crystal. "I told her to get out of your house. If there's one thing I know about *you,* Dr. Mitchell, you're capable of fighting your own battles."

"I am," she said. "And you're worth fighting for."

He stroked her cheek with his index finger. "This isn't the buggy ride I promised you, and I can't get down on one knee, but I don't want to waste another minute. I love you, Nora. Will you marry me?"

"Yes!" She threw her arms around him, holding them both steady as the crutches fell from his sides.

He kissed her then. Gentle yet commanding, it left her with the worst case of poison ivy of her entire life. Pulling back, she laughed out loud. She'd have danced him in a circle, except he needed the crutches. She settled for holding him close as together they found a balance they'd share for the rest of their lives.

* * *

Zeb could have held Nora in his arms all day. As strong as oak and as bold as her red hair, she nestled her head in the crook of his neck. It tickled. It teased, and it tempted…a temptation he welcomed with the woman God intended for his wife.

Hugging her tight, he thought of the declaration he'd be making to the crowd. Just as he'd hoped, he'd be announcing wedding plans with Nora. His hunt for a wife was over.

He smiled at her. "If you want a big wedding with your folks, I'm willing to wait. But I'd prefer something sooner."

"Me, too." She blushed prettily. "How about next Saturday?"

Zeb liked the idea, but he also enjoyed teasing her. "Six whole days? I don't know if I can stand the wait."

"We'll manage." She planted a peck on his lips. "Now tell me something. What's that big announcement I'm hearing about?"

"Us," he said.

Humming softly, she nestled against him. "You were sure I'd say yes?"

"I was sure I wanted to ask." He kissed her temple. "I'd have done it in front of everyone if that's what it took."

"I'm glad we were alone. I was so scared …" Safe in his arms, she told him about overhearing Abigail's talk with the Prestons and Winnie's comments. "When you told me to take the job in New York, I thought you were protecting me from embarrassment."

"No," he said. "I wanted you to be happy, and I thought you wanted the job." He paused, then added, "I was protecting myself, too. If you'd left, I couldn't have stood it."

"I'm not leaving," she said. "Not ever."

He kissed her again, sweetly. The wonder of it carried him to the future, but shouts and laughter brought him back to the moment. "Let's go," he said to his wife-to-be. "I don't want to miss the arm-wrestling contest."

She looked puzzled. "Are you in it?"

"No, but Clint is. If he wins, he's going to ask Cassandra to marry him."

Nora wiggled out of his arms. "I don't want to miss *that!*"

He didn't want to miss it, either. If Clint proposed and Cassandra came to her senses, he'd give her the biggest wedding Kansas had ever seen. First, though, Clint had to win.

Chapter Twenty-Four

As he balanced on one leg, Nora bent and fetched his crutches. Together they headed back to the crowd. A few people gave them questioning looks, but most smiled and waved. Zeb had an eye out for Abigail. He didn't know what he'd say when their paths crossed, but he didn't plan on being polite.

"There you are!" Will called from several feet away. He had a blue ribbon pinned to his shirt and his arm around Emmeline's waist. The brunette had a ribbon, too. She'd taken first place for arranging wildflowers. Next to her stood Rebecca with three blue ribbons pinned to her bodice. Zeb had to grin. Just about every woman in High Plains had entered one of the baking contests, including Mrs. Johnson. He heard them bragging about it. Rebecca had swept all three categories—pie, jam and bread—and she'd done it handily.

His friends were standing at the edge of the crowd waiting for the arm-wrestling contest to begin. When the women noticed Nora at his side, their mouths gaped with curiosity and Will's brows shot up.

Zeb grinned at Nora. "This is going to be fun."

"What is?" she asked.

He hooked one arm around her waist, kissed her sweetly on the lips, then looked at his friends. "If that doesn't answer your question, I'll do it again. We're getting married."

Emmeline ran to Nora and hugged her. So did Rebecca. As the women chattered, Zeb maneuvered closer to Will. "Remember that idiot who wouldn't hire a lady doctor?"

"I sure do."

"He's dead and gone," Zeb replied.

"That's good news," Will answered. "Considering the rumor I heard, I was worried about you."

"Abigail's a liar." Zeb looked at Nora with the same calf-eyed expression he'd seen on Will's face when he talked about Emmeline, and on Pete's face when he bragged about Rebecca. He'd come a long away from doing battle with "Dr. N. Mitchell." In a few days, she'd be Dr. Garrison and he liked the sound of it.

He wanted to tell Cassandra, so he skimmed the crowd. In her candy-pink dress and white bonnet, she'd stand out among folks wearing denim and muslin. Instead of spotting his sister, he saw the Johnsons. As the owners of the mercantile, they were usually surrounded by folks wanting to impress them. Today Zeb could see a ring of grass around them, as if an invisible wall had been built. Mrs. Johnson looked as smug as ever, but Abigail seemed to be hiding her shame under a floppy bonnet.

The irony struck Zeb full force. Abigail had been the victim of her own gossip. It seemed a fitting judgment for how she and her mother had treated others, especially Rebecca.

To Zeb's surprise, Abigail broke from her parents and walked in his direction. Smelling trouble, he wedged the crutches tight, hooked his arm around Nora's waist and pulled her close. No way would he let Abigail harass Nora. If she wanted to tell more lies, she could deal with him.

Abigail diverted her gaze to Nora, but she kept approaching. Nora was congratulating Rebecca and didn't see her, so Zeb murmured into her ear, "Don't look now, but here comes trouble."

Nora turned and saw Abigail. "I see."

"If she starts anything, she'll get an earful," he muttered.

"Let her talk," Nora advised.

Abigail reached them in ten steps. She greeted Will, Emmeline and Rebecca, then faced Zeb. "May I speak with you in private?"

"Right here's fine," he said in full voice. "*And* you can say your piece in front of my *fiancée.*"

"Of course." Abigail spoke in a hush. "Whatever you want."

Not once had Zeb heard this woman sound contrite, but she had that tone now. She could barely look at him. "I don't deserve your forgiveness, Zeb. But I want you to know, I'm truly sorry."

Was she sorry she'd lied, or sorry she'd been caught? He said nothing.

Abigail focused on Nora. "I lied about everything. Zeb never even kissed me. I saw him falling in love with you. I was jealous."

"There's more," he said through gritted teeth. "You wanted my money *and* my good name."

"That's true." She looked him in the eye. "You were my only chance for a decent husband. Just how decent, I didn't realize until I told that lie. No one's speaking to me now, not even Winnie. When people come into the store, they look at my mother like she's poison. The lie was all my idea. She's furious with me for shaming her."

Considering how Mrs. Johnson had carped about Rebecca, the rumors about Abigail had to sting.

The blonde squared her shoulders. "I'm leaving. I have a cousin in Charleston. She'll—"

"Hold on," Zeb said. "If you run off now, folks might believe what you said. They'll think the worst of both of us."

"No, they won't." Her eyes shimmered with regret. "I asked Reverend Preston to make things right. Ever since I told that lie, I've been sick to my stomach. I didn't mean to hurt you, Zeb. As things turned out, I hurt myself."

"When are you going?" he asked.

"I leave tomorrow with the Crandalls." Her voice had no life, no spunk. "My mother says it's for the best."

Zeb had no desire to hold a grudge. He'd made mistakes, too. "It's over, Abigail. Go start a new life."

"Do you mean it?" she asked

"I do." He traded a look with Nora. It seemed fitting for Abigail to take Nora's spot with the Crandalls.

The blonde took a deep breath. "I better go. I just wanted to tell you I'm sorry."

Nora offered a kind smile. "Stay safe, Abigail."

"Thank you, Dr. Mitchell." Looking weary, Abigail melted into the crowd.

Zeb blew out a breath. "That was a surprise."

"A good one," Nora added.

Will, Emmeline and Rebecca crowded around them. Will looked at Zeb. "We heard every word."

"Glory!" Rebecca shot a look to the heavens. "I can't believe it! Mrs. Johnson calls me names and her own daughter—"

"—acts disgracefully!" Emmeline finished.

"I forgive her," Nora added, "But I'm glad she's gone."

Zeb felt the same way.

The women were still chattering when a handbell clanged. They all turned to the roped-off section of grass where a long table had been set up for the arm-wrestling contest.

Pete bellowed over the noise of the crowd. "Attention ladies and gentlemen! The first annual High Plains Arm-Wrestling Championship is about to begin. Contestants, take your places."

Zeb took a deep breath to clear his thoughts of Abigail. He had other priorities today, including Cassandra. He skimmed the crowd and found her in the front row, directly across from the table. They hadn't spoken again about Clint and Percy, but yesterday she'd broken a *luncheon* date with the attorney. Today she looked as nervous as Clint. Zeb took it as a good sign.

Nora touched his elbow. "It's a big purse. I'm surprised Pete's not entered."

He laughed. "He'd win for sure. Back in Bellville, we declared him lifetime champ."

Rebecca leaned close to them both. "Besides that, we're rooting for Clint."

After trading smiles, Zeb and Nora turned to the competition. Eight men had signed up. In addition to Clint, Zeb saw Edward Gunderson, Tom Briggs, three ranch hands, a millworker and Percival Walker. Edward would be a tough match, but he felt certain Clint would easily beat the others.

Pete held up a black bowler, then shouted to the crowd, "There are four pairs of buttons in this hat. To determine the first-round matches, each man will draw a button and pair off accordingly."

As Pete passed the bowler, the men made their picks and took their seats at the table. Clint was matched with a local ranch hand. When Percy sat across from Edward, Zeb almost smirked. He felt certain the banker would lose to the Norwegian. The rest of the men paired off, and the contestants rolled up their sleeves.

"Gentlemen, square off!" Pete called.

The competitors matched palms and tightened their grips. Pete raised his hand in the air. "Ready! Set! Go!"

Clint won his match in two seconds flat. So did Tom Briggs, who'd been paired with one of the ranch hands. The third ranch hand and the millworker were more evenly matched, but the millworker eventually won. Zeb looked at the fourth table where Percy and Edward were eye to eye, each turning red, their neck muscles popping. Zeb had expected the attorney to go down in a blink, but the man hadn't broken a sweat. To Zeb's surprise, Percy slammed Edward's hand to the table.

Will crossed his arms. "Looks like Clint's got some competition."

Rebecca spoke from behind them. "He was champion at his club in Boston. He bragged about it at the boardinghouse."

The thought of handing Percival Walker the prize money turned Zeb's stomach. Nora hooked her hand in his elbow and squeezed with reassurance.

Pete put four buttons in the hat. Clint and Tom Briggs drew a matching pair. Percy squared off with the millworker, a man Zeb knew to be strong. Pete counted down and the match began. Percy beat the millworker easily. Clint battled with Briggs but still won.

Sweat rose on the cowboy's brow. He wiped it with a bandanna and took a deep breath. Percy played to the crowd by flexing his biceps. When he struck a pose with both arms out to his sides, the crowd hooted. Clint's expression shifted from glum to snarling.

Briggs and a ranch hand pulled back the long table and replaced it with a square one for the final round.

Zeb's gaze went to Cassandra. She looked as pale as the moon. He'd have gone with Nora to his sister's side, but Pete raised both arms into the air. "Gentlemen, shake hands and take your seats."

Clint didn't budge. Neither did Percy. They stood like two bulls about to butt heads. Neither wanted to shake hands and

Zeb didn't blame them. When it came to winning Cassandra's heart, they were mortal enemies.

Pete cleared his throat. "It's the rule, gentlemen. Now shake hands."

Clint's jaw twitched, but he extended his arm. Percy shook Clint's hand like it was a dead fish, then indicated that Clint should sit first. It was an arrogant gesture, one meant to take control. Zeb found himself praying for Clint under his breath. That kind of treatment usually made the cowboy clam up. Today he had to stay good and mad.

To Zeb's relief, fury burned in the cowboy's eyes. Holding Percy's gaze, he indicated the other chair, then spoke like a perfect gentlemen. "After you, Mr. Walker."

Behind Zeb, Rebecca clapped her hands. "He knows his manners, all right!"

Staring hard at Clint, Percy made a show of stretching his arm. Zeb couldn't see his face, but he could see Cassandra. When her mouth gaped, he wondered what the attorney had done. Clint must have seen the gesture, because his eyes narrowed and his jaws clenched.

Percy, with deliberate slowness, lowered his body onto the chair, planted his elbow on the table and wiggled his fingers. "Ready when you are, *Clint.*"

Judging by the cowboy's snarl, he wanted to knock Percy right into next week. Instead, he sat, planted his elbow and locked hands with the attorney. "I'm ready."

Pete raised his arm high. "Ready… Set… Go!"

As the men did battle, the crowd went still. Clint stifled a grunt. Percy whistled through his teeth as he sucked in air. Seconds turned into a full minute. Someone cried out Clint's name. More voices followed, including a cheer from Nora. A chant began…"Clint! Clint! Clint!"

Zeb felt the force in his own chest. Balanced on the crutches, he shouted and cheered for the cowboy. At his side, Nora bounced on her toes. Clint had fire in his eyes. With each second it burned brighter. He gained an inch on Percy, then another. With a final cry, he slammed the attorney's hand to the tabletop.

Pete grabbed Clint's arm and raised it high. With the crowd stomping and shouting, Clint broke from Pete's grasp and went straight to Cassandra. In front of all of High Plains, he clasped her fingers and dropped to one knee. No one but Cassandra could hear what he said, but Zeb saw his sister mouthing "Yes! Yes! Yes!" With tears streaming down her face, she gripped Clint's hand in both of hers. The cowboy pushed to his full height, then drew her into his arms and kissed her. It was bold enough to give Zeb pause.

Nora leaned close and whispered in his ear. "I thought Clint was shy!"

"So did I," Zeb replied, half grumbling.

They'd both been wrong. When it came to Cassandra, the cowboy knew his mind. He didn't talk a lot, but he was showing the world exactly how he felt.

Zeb reached for Nora's hand. "Let's go. I want to talk to them."

Together they pushed through the crowd. Clint saw them first and shook Zeb's hand. Cassandra hugged Nora with tears in her eyes. "I'm getting married!"

"Me, too," Nora cried.

As the women hugged, Zeb wiped his sister's tears with his knuckle. "You made a good choice, Cassie."

She beamed a smile at Clint. "I did."

The cowboy smiled back. "What made you decide?"

"You," she said sweetly. "The way you looked when Percy winked at me. I thought you were going to murder him!"

"I thought about it," Clint said in a drawl.

"I know." Percy's voice came from over Zeb's shoulder.

As Zeb stepped to the side, the attorney offered his hand to Clint. The men shook, then Percy tipped his hat to Cassandra. "It's been a pleasure, Miss Garrison. I wish you and Mr. Fuller all the best."

Zeb watched his sister for signs of regret. Instead, he saw a genuine contentment in her eyes. "Thank you, Percy."

As the lawyer slipped into the crowd, Reverend Preston rang the handbell. As the cheers increased, he waved for Zeb to come forward. Zeb looked at his wife-to-be with a grin a mile wide. "Come with me."

Nora smiled. "I'd be honored."

Together they joined Reverend Preston in the center of the grassy circle. To command attention, Zeb raised one crutch in the air. As the crowd settled, someone started to clap. The noise turned into a pulsing rhythm, then died to silence in anticipation of what he'd say.

Zeb cleared his throat. "You all know I'm about to make an announcement. Here it is… Next Saturday at two o'clock, you're all invited to a wedding. Dr. Nora and I are getting married."

Grinning, he took Nora's hand and raised it to his lips.

Whoops and hollers filled the air. When Alex broke from the crowd and hugged Nora with all his might, Zeb's heart turned into pudding. On a dark day in June, in the middle of a tornado, he'd faced death and discovered a yearning for life. He'd risked love and found the greatest of blessings…a wife, a son and a legacy that would last for generations.

A week from today, he and Nora would take their vows in the High Plains Christian Church. Surrounded by friends and family, they'd be joined as man and wife for the rest of their days. When Nora smiled, Zeb smiled back. Joy hung between them, along with an awareness of the promises they'd soon make. Bold as always, his red-haired wife-to-be winked at him. Grinning, Zeb winked back. This time they meant it.

Epilogue

"Are you two sure?" Reverend Preston asked. "That's quite a gift."

"We're positive." Nora squeezed her husband's hand. They'd been married for exactly twenty minutes, but they'd decided yesterday to mark their wedding day with a gift to High Plains.

Zeb stood at her side. Dressed in a black suit, a brocade vest, white shirt and shiny boots, he looked as polished as silver. She particularly liked the vest. He'd picked one with swirls of dark green and copper. The green matched the fancy dress she'd thought she'd never wear again. Zeb thought the copper matched her hair.

He'd retired his crutches, but Nora had insisted he use a cane. Even the walking stick couldn't detract from his presence. Looking strong, he tapped the cane on the floor of the town hall. "We'd like to make the announcement now."

"Of course." The reverend indicated the room overflowing with friends. "It's your wedding."

Zeb smiled at Nora, then kissed her on the cheek. Together they faced the crowd. Two months ago, Nora had arrived on a freight wagon. She'd been alone and challenged at every turn. Today she knew every person in the room and a few who'd stayed home or moved on. The Johnsons hadn't come to the celebration to avoid being shunned, and both Percy and Abigail had left High Plains, at least for now.

Nora couldn't imagine living anywhere else. She belonged in this town. Even more important, she belonged with Zeb.

Reverend Preston raised his voice. "Ladies and gentlemen, it's my pleasure to present Mr. and Dr. Zebulun Garrison."

Nora's mouth gaped. She hadn't expected to be called "Dr. Garrison" at her wedding. Later, yes, but not today. The title was a gift from Zeb, and she accepted it by kissing his cheek.

Reverend Preston waited for the applause to stop, then indicated Zeb and Nora should step forward. Hands entwined, they took in the smiling faces. Zeb looked around until he spotted the Logan family, all of them. Nora saw Emmeline looking lovely in a lilac gown. Bess stood next to her. Instead of the lost child Nora had met in Dr. Dempsey's office—her office now, a wedding gift from Zeb—she saw a young woman chattering with a friend. Emmeline's mother, Joanna, and her new husband, Hank, were keeping an eye on the brood of children. Johnny, Glory, Mikey and Missy all had on clean shirts or dresses, but Nora knew that would change as soon as Rebecca and Mrs. Jennings served the cake.

Zeb motioned to the Logan clan. "Will, come up here."

Will shared a look with his wife, then came to stand at Zeb's side.

Zeb scanned the crowd again, then motioned at the blacksmith. "Pete, you, too."

Nora wouldn't have guessed Pete to be debonair, but he looked like a European prince in a dark suit. Rebecca had stuck a flower in his lapel and he'd slicked back his hair.

Nora smiled at the first friend she'd made in High Plains. Dressed in pale blue calico, the blonde looked both happy and proud. Her brother Edward stood at her side. He hadn't spoken for Winnie Morrow yet, but Nora thought that day would come soon.

As Pete made his way to the front, Nora searched the crowd for Alex. During the wedding ceremony, she and Zeb had broken tradition. They'd taken their vows, then asked the boy to come forward. The three of them had held hands and promised to be a family forever.

It had been a special moment, but afterward Alex had been glad to race out of the church. She spotted him poking at Jonah while Mrs. Jennings kept an eye on them.

Next to the boys, Nora saw Clint with Cassandra. Zeb had promised his sister a wedding to rival the biggest event in Boston, including a white gown made by Mrs. Morrow. They'd set a date for October and had plans to move into Nora's little house, another gift from Zeb. Instead of holding down two jobs, Clint has decided to work full-time at the mill so Cassandra could teach through the winter.

Knowing what Zeb intended, Nora slipped into the front row as Pete took his place next to Will. This moment belonged to the men of High Plains.

Zeb looked at her with a proud smile, surveyed the people in the town hall, then raised his voice. "Almost two years ago on Christmas Day, Will and I founded this town. When we saw the land, we knew we'd come home. On that day, Will thanked the Lord for bringing us to this place. He prayed that God would keep us mindful of His plan and guide our paths." Zeb looked at his friend. "It seems fitting to recall that prayer."

"Yes, it does," Will acknowledged. "It took faith to build this town the first time, and more faith to rebuild after the storm. This is a day of celebration, but I think Zeb and Nora would agree. It's also a day to remember loved ones, both present and gone."

Silence settled and Nora bowed her head. Emmeline had lost her father in the tornado. The twins had come close to death, and others like Alex's brother had been lost to eternity. Nora had a bit of loneliness of her own. She missed her mother and father terribly, but Carolina had helped her dress. Someday her parents would visit. She felt blessed indeed.

Will looked at his wife. "It takes faith to survive in this world. It takes faith to work and raise children. It's hardest to believe when things are the darkest, but that's what we do in High Plains. This very building—a town hall that will stand for years to come—is evidence of who we are and what we do. No matter the cost, we support each other. No matter the risk, we *believe*."

The crowd broke into applause.

At Zeb's urging Pete stepped forward. "There's a verse in the Bible we live every day. It's this—'Perfect love casteth out fear.' It's no secret, friends, that I had a fearful time even before the tornado. After the storm, we all did. But I learned something in a dark cellar on that fateful day. Love is stronger than fear. When I look at my lovely wife—" he stared straight at Rebecca "—I thank God for bringing us together. I thank God for the love in this entire town."

Nora saw tears of happiness in Rebecca's eyes. When Pete grinned, the room exploded with whistles and clapping.

The applause faded and Zeb cleared his throat. "This town was built on three principles. Faith, love and fortitude. Faith got us started. Love gives us a purpose. Fortitude is what keeps us going. When a tornado destroyed this town, we rebuilt it. We accepted the challenge—every one of us. I'm proud to be a part of that effort, and even prouder to count you all as friends."

People clapped their approval, but Zeb asked for quiet. "Rebuilding High Plains was a community effort. To commemorate the sacrifices we all made, my wife and I—" He gave a lopsided grin. "I like the sound of that."

The crowd laughed with him.

"My wife and I would like to make a gift to the town. I've already written to a master craftsman in New York. By this time next year, High Plains Christian Church will have the prettiest stained-glass windows in all of Kansas."

A hush settled over the room. Not only had the Lord restored the fortunes of High Plains, He'd done more than anyone could have asked or imagined.

Reverend Preston spoke from the sidelines. "Let us pray."

And so they bowed their heads, everyone from young to old, and the reverend offered a prayer of thanks. As Nora closed her eyes, she imagined the church with two rows of tall windows, a glorious mix of blue, red, yellow and even purple. The windows would be a tribute to this moment for generations to come. Blessed and full of joy, she thanked God for His wondrous gifts.

* * * * *

Dear Reader,

Research, romance and real life touched in a big way in this story. Shortly after learning I'd be writing the third book in "After the Storm," I fussed to my husband that I didn't know a thing about sawmills. He frequently hears me ramble and he sometimes offers ideas, but being married to a writer can be a strange experience. What can he say about imaginary people with imaginary problems?

But this time was different. We'd just left church when I heaved a big sigh and said, "I *really* need to find a mill."

The next thing I knew, we were doing a U-turn. This wasn't your garden-variety U-turn. We burned rubber. I was in mild shock. "Where in the world—"

"A mill. We're going to a mill." He sounded like James Bond.

"Where?"

"Up the road."

You can imagine my excitement when we arrived at the Colvin Run Historic Mill in Great Falls, Virginia. For the next two hours, my husband waited patiently while I looked at every detail and asked the miller a hundred questions. We saw a demonstration of wheat being turned into flour, all powered by a waterwheel. I'll never forget the sound of water spilling as the wheel turned and the millworks went into motion.

Colvin Mill was constructed in northern Virginia in the 1830s as a gristmill. In my book, the town needed a sawmill. More research provided the answer. In the nineteenth century, sawmills were frequently converted to gristmills as the number of trees diminished. This change was common in eastern Kansas where this story is set.

I had a great day at Colvin Mill, but the best part was my husband's thoughtfulness. I am blessed, indeed!

All the best,

Victoria Byb

QUESTIONS FOR DISCUSSION

1. As a female physician, Dr. Nora Mitchell encounters prejudice because of her gender. Do you think prejudice against women doctors is still a problem? Do you think a female pediatrician is more easily accepted than a female neurosurgeon?

2. Zeb Garrison feels deceived when "Dr. N. Mitchell" turns out to be Dr. Nora Mitchell. Is his anger justified? Was Nora deceptive when she used only her initial? How did she justify her action to Zeb?

3. Bess Carter is suffering from hysterical muteness as a result of the tornado. What kind of treatment does Dr. Nora recommend? How does treating Bess as if everything is normal encourage her recovery? Do you see a connection to living a life of faith?

4. The town hall is very important to the people of High Plains. What does it represent?

5. Cassandra is torn between Boston and Kansas. What are the best things about living in a big city like Boston? What are the best things about a town like High Plains? Which would you pick?

6. Nora has a strong faith and believes in taking calculated risks. What risks have you taken in your life? Have you moved far from home? Or maybe taken on a new career? Which challenges were the hardest?

7. Being jilted by a former fiancée has left Zeb bitter. What steps lead to his eventual ability to forgive and love again? How does Nora react to his initial judgment of her?

8. Clint Fuller and Percival Walker are both vying for Cassandra Garrison's attention. What does Cassandra see in Percy? What does she see in Clint? What tips the scale in Clint's favor?

9. What happens to finally make Zeb accept Nora as a physician? Do you see a connection between being in need and crying out to God?

10. If you knew a tornado was headed your way, and you had ten minutes to gather your most precious possessions, what would you take?

11. What does the waterfall represent to Nora? What does it mean to Zeb? Have you ever looked down the road of your life and seen a big change? How did you cope with it?

12. When the jubilee committee meets, Abigail insults Nora. Does Nora turn the other cheek or fight back? Would you describe her reaction as prideful or wise in the ways of the world?

13. Zeb and Nora share similar traits. How are they alike? How are they different? If you could write another epilogue, what would you imagine for them in ten years?

14. The women in High Plains all have worthwhile occupations. Emmeline is a rancher's wife and is raising a family.

Rebecca is a cook and has plans to open her own inn. Cassandra teaches school, and Nora is a physician. If you lived in High Plains in 1860, which career would you pick? One of the above or something different?

15. All of High Plains comes together at the jubilee. For those readers who have read all three books, which heroine would you most like to meet? How do they each show faith, love and fortitude?

*When his niece unexpectedly arrives at his
Montana ranch, Jules Parrish has no idea
what to do with her—or with Olivia Rose,
the pretty teacher who brought her.
Will they be able to build a life—
and family—together?*

*Here's a sneak peek of "Montana Rose"
by Cheryl St.John, one of the
touching stories in the new collection,
TO BE A MOTHER,
available April 2010
from Love Inspired Historical.*

Jules Parrish squinted from beneath his hat brim, certain the
waves of heat were playing with his eyes. Two females—one
a woman, the other a child—stood as he approached.

The woman walked toward him. Jules dismounted and approached her. "What are you doing here?"

The woman stopped several feet away. "Mr. Parrish?"

"Yeah, who are you?"

"I'm Olivia Rose. I was an instructor at the Hedward Girls
Academy." She glanced back over her shoulder at the girl who
watched them. "My young charge is Emily Sadler, the daughter
of Meriel Sadler."

She had his attention now. He hadn't heard his sister's name
in years. *Meriel.*

"The academy was forced to close. I thought Emily should

be with family. You're the only family she has, so I brought her to you."

He took off his hat and raked his fingers through dark, wavy hair. "Lady, I spend every waking hour working horses and cows. I sleep in a one-room cabin. I don't know anything about kids—and especially not girls."

"What do you suggest?"

"I don't know. All I know is, she can't stay here."

Will Olivia be able to change Jules's mind
and find a home for Emily—and herself?

Find out in
TO BE A MOTHER,
the heartwarming anthology from
Cheryl St.John and Ruth Axtell Morren,
available April 2010
only from Love Inspired Historical.

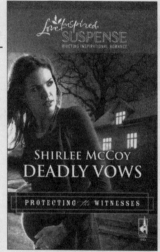

REQUEST YOUR FREE BOOKS!

2 FREE INSPIRATIONAL NOVELS
PLUS 2
FREE
MYSTERY GIFTS

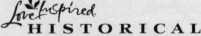

Love Inspired.
HISTORICAL
INSPIRATIONAL HISTORICAL ROMANCE

YES! Please send me 2 FREE Love Inspired® Historical novels and my 2 FREE mystery gifts (gifts are worth about $10). After receiving them, if I don't wish to receive any more books, I can return the shipping statement marked "cancel". If I don't cancel, I will receive 4 brand-new novels every other month and be billed just $4.24 per book in the U.S. or $4.74 per book in Canada. That's a saving of over 20% off the cover price. It's quite a bargain! Shipping and handling is just 50¢ per book in the U.S. and 75¢ per book in Canada.* I understand that accepting the 2 free books and gifts places me under no obligation to buy anything. I can always return a shipment and cancel at any time. Even if I never buy another book, the two free books and gifts are mine to keep forever.

102 IDN E4LC   302 IDN E4LN

Name	(PLEASE PRINT)	
Address		Apt. #
City	State/Prov.	Zip/Postal Code

Signature (if under 18, a parent or guardian must sign)

Mail to Steeple Hill Reader Service:
IN U.S.A.: P.O. Box 1867, Buffalo, NY 14240-1867
IN CANADA: P.O. Box 609, Fort Erie, Ontario L2A 5X3
Not valid for current subscribers to Love Inspired Historical books.

Want to try two free books from another series?
Call 1-800-873-8635 or visit www.morefreebooks.com.

* Terms and prices subject to change without notice. Prices do not include applicable taxes. Sales tax applicable in N.Y. Canadian residents will be charged applicable provincial taxes and GST. Offer not valid in Quebec. This offer is limited to one order per household. All orders subject to approval. Credit or debit balances in a customer's account(s) may be offset by any other outstanding balance owed by or to the customer. Please allow 4 to 6 weeks for delivery. Offer available while quantities last.

Your Privacy: Steeple Hill Books is committed to protecting your privacy. Our Privacy Policy is available online at www.SteepleHill.com or upon request from the Reader Service. From time to time we make our lists of customers available to reputable third parties who may have a product or service of interest to you. If you would prefer we not share your name and address, please check here. ☐

Help us get it right—We strive for accurate, respectful and relevant communications. To clarify or modify your communication preferences, visit us at www.ReaderService.com/consumerschoice.

LIH10